DARK SPACE

LISA HENRY

CONTENTS

CHAPTER ONE

I WAS TRYING hard to get drunk.

I took a swig of Hooper's moonshine and made a face at the taste, and then the burn. It was so rough I almost spat it over the recruiting poster tacked onto the wall of the storeroom. *Join the Military and Save the Earth*. Bullshit.

They probably just couldn't fit *Join the Military and Become Fucking Cannon Fodder for Aliens* on the posters. Or *Join the Military and Get Abducted and Fucked-Up by Faceless Nightmares in Ways You Can't Even Imagine*. I mean, look at Cameron Rushton.

We were just talking about Cameron Rushton. We usually were. He was one of the standard topics of conversation on nights like these. He came in at number three on what was a pretty short fucking list.

First we talked about girls. Not girls like any of us had seen in the flesh, but those girls in magazines with huge tits and puffed-up lips and sleepy eyes, like they'd been fucked hard all night and they were mostly pouting now because the guy finally pulled out.

We talked about those girls a lot. And it was all talk. Every single one of us was conscripted at sixteen. Some of us might have copped a feel of some girl from home, but we sure as hell hadn't been plowing busty centerfolds until they went cross-eyed. Any guy who reckoned he'd been with a girl like that was full of shit.

After girls we talked about the officers, and which ones hated us most that week, and how we never did anything to deserve it, and they were just assholes, and if they didn't have those stripes on their shoulders, they wouldn't be so tough. Man-to-man, we could take them. That was all talk too, I guess.

Then there was Cameron Rushton and the Faceless. Couldn't have one without the other.

"The Faceless will take you apart cell by cell," Hooper said, taking the bottle off me. "Cell by cell, and you'll feel every cut."

Hooper was crazy, though.

He worked on the Outer Ring, in the Tubes.

I hated the Tubes. I didn't like knowing there was only one little air lock between me and asphyxiation. The Tubes were sleek tunnels that led from the hangars on the Outer Ring straight out into the black. The Hawks were launched from the Tubes.

I wouldn't go to the Outer Ring if I could avoid it. I liked to stick to the Inner Ring and the Core. It was just as precarious in the Core, probably, but it felt more solid somehow. I felt like I could never get enough air in the Tubes.

"That's impossible," Cesari scoffed.

"It's not! It's nanotechnology!" Hooper was in engineering, so maybe he knew what he was talking about. But he was also crazy. Some of that was probably down to the fact he spent half his life breathing in solvents and fumes from fuel hoses, and the other half making moonshine in the scrubbers, but Hooper was more stir-crazy than all of us. He'd been on the station longer. Hooper was eight years into his ten-year service, and eight years was a long time stuck in a tin can in space with no women.

The government said that women were too valuable to risk, so they couldn't serve on the stations anymore. Fucking government. Fucking Faceless.

"It's nanotechnology!" Hooper said. "Right, Garrett?"

Why the fuck was he asking me?

"Dude, like what they're developing for med techs!"

I didn't want to get drawn into this shit. I was just here for the booze and the cards, but apparently Hooper had decided I was his expert witness. I shrugged. "I read in a med journal they're making nanobots that you can inject right into the heart. Doesn't mean the Faceless have them, though."

I hated even saying that word. What if I choked on it and all the guys laughed at how afraid I was? Or maybe what I believed when I was a kid was true: say their name aloud and it would summon them. Like demons, like every horror story I ever heard and every nightmare I ever had.

"I'll bet they do! I'll bet they used them to cut Cameron Rushton up!"

Cesari rolled his eyes. "They didn't take Cameron Rushton to cut him up into pieces, Hooper. They took him to make biological weapons they could use on us!"

It was more logical than Hooper's theory, but not exactly comforting.

"Yeah," Hooper said. "And *after* that they cut him up!"

The worst part was, he was probably right.

"That's right, hey, Garrett? Hey, Garrett?" he asked me. When I didn't answer quickly enough, he switched to my given name. "Hey, Brady?"

I scowled. "How the fuck would I know, cocksucker?"

I'd been on Defender Three for three years. My dad would be appalled at my language. Like Hooper I was just counting down my ten years so I could get back planetside. I'd been here since I was sixteen as well, and I still had seven years to go.

Sometimes it felt more like seventy. Sometimes it felt like forever.

Hooper just laughed at the insult and handed me the bottle.

"To Cameron Rushton," I said and took a swig. It burned all the way down, but you couldn't expect too much from Hooper's gut rot. It got you buzzed, which is all that counted. "Are we here to play cards or what?"

"Yeah," Cesari said. "Let's play some cards and shut the fuck up about the Faceless for once."

Hooper grumbled and began to deal.

My gaze slid back to the recruiting poster and Cameron Rushton's face. It was a good-looking face, with all the right angles for a poster like the one he'd ended up on. He had an easy smile, green eyes, and an officer's haircut: a short back and sides with something left on top instead of the extreme buzz cut they gave us enlisted guys.

I looked away from the poster, from that smile. Whatever had happened to Cameron Rushton, I'll bet his smile was the first thing they took.

Four years ago Cameron Rushton was taken by the Faceless. I'd seen the footage; everyone had. They even showed it on Earth. Cameron Rushton had just got his commission as a junior lieutenant. He was a Hawk pilot, which was what everyone supposedly aspired to be. Not me, though. I preferred to keep my head down. But the pilots were the heroes of the fleet. Just ask them; they'd tell you. Assholes.

The day that it happened Cameron Rushton wasn't piloting a Hawk. He was piloting a Shitbox between Defender Eight and Nine. The transport shuttles weren't really called Shitboxes. Could you imagine some engineer showing off the prototype?

Gentlemen, the Shitbox! But they were squarish and ugly, so that's what everyone called them. There were five people on board that Shitbox: Cameron Rushton, his copilot, a gunner—not that he did them any good—and two officers transferring to Nine. Then, out of nowhere, for the first time in years, the Faceless came.

They found the Shitbox later, turning slowly in the black.

The gunner hardly got a shot off before the Faceless took out the weapons array. And there was no way a Shitbox could outrun a Faceless ship. So they were boarded.

The Faceless were like nothing else I'd ever seen. Tall and terrifying. They were more or less like people—the shape of them, I mean—but nobody knew what they looked like underneath their black battle armor. It stuck to them like thin latex, but nothing got through, not bullets, not blades, and not blasters.

You could see on the footage that everyone in the Shitbox knew what was coming. Cameron Rushton and his copilot abandoned the controls and started handing out weapons. Then the five of them stood and waited, and that must have been the worst.

On the footage the time ticked away in the bottom right corner. It took three minutes and forty-six seconds for the Faceless to cut their way into the Shitbox. Then they were inside: three tall Faceless in head-to-toe black, looking like the things that come at you in your nightmares. Unstoppable.

And they killed everyone real quick—except Cameron Rushton.

In tactical orientation they showed us the unedited footage. Fucking wish they hadn't. There was no noise on the footage. I don't know if that was because there was a fault with it, or because our trainers didn't want to scare the living shit out of us by making us listen to Cameron Rushton scream. Because he did. A silent openmouthed moment of horror.

"*Fucking pussy,*" someone in my tactical orientation class had said when we saw it, but his voice shook.

I'd just looked at Cameron Rushton's face and tried not to imagine that happening to me.

He kept fighting them even after they killed everyone else, even though it was pointless. The Faceless pushed him down onto the bodies of the others and twisted his arms behind his back. Then they did something. The view was obscured. They used a syringe, probably, or maybe the Faceless had venomous claws under their black gloves, but suddenly Cameron Rushton stopped resisting. They pulled him to his feet again.

He was stumbling. And with his arms still twisted behind his back, they pushed him out of the view of the camera, and he was gone.

Minutes passed.

You could tell the moment when the Faceless ship disengaged with the Shitbox, because all the corpses on the floor got sucked out into space, like puppets suddenly wrenched up on their strings.

They showed that footage on Earth a lot, at least the edited version, because Cameron Rushton was a good-looking guy, and because they said he was a hero. And they showed it because some people said that the Faceless would never come back, and the stations were a waste of money. They used the footage in ads mostly, just that part when he was still fighting: *The Faceless threat is real. Support the defense of Earth. Buy bonds.*

I always felt sorry for Cameron Rushton's family whenever I saw those ads. Who the hell would want to see that over and over again?

I took another swig of moonshine and pretended the bad taste in my mouth was all down to that. We played some cards, and the conversation moved back to the girls with big tits we'd like to fuck and which asshole officers had it in for us.

Then, right in the middle of Hooper telling us just what he'd do to Captain Kerslake if he ever got the chance, the door to the storeroom was wrenched open, and Branski was standing there.

"Holy fuck, you guys!" Branski was a skinny streak of a guy with a crooked nose and dimples in his cheeks when he smiled. He wasn't smiling. "Did you guys *hear?*"

"Hear what?" Hooper asked.

"Fuck! You guys!" Branski's eyes were wide. "Rushton! Cameron Rushton's back!"

"You're shitting me," I said.

"Saw him with my own eyes," Branski told me. "I was outside the docking bay when they unloaded him. He's in stasis."

My heart thumped louder. "Stasis?"

Branski's face fell. "Or something. Shit, I never saw anything like it!"

Coming from anyone else I wouldn't have believed it, but Branski knew more about what was happening on Defender Three than most of the officers. He worked in the Q-Store, and he was the go-to guy if you needed cigarettes, alcohol, meds, or other contraband. Branski ran the station black market almost single-handedly.

Beside me, Hooper shifted restlessly. "Anything like what?"

"He's in water or something," Branski said. "But he's alive, they reckon. Dunno how, because he looks like he's drowned. And. Jesus, his skin!"

"What about it?" Cesari's voice was hardly louder than a whisper.

Every Faceless horror story I'd ever heard came back to me, despite the fact that nobody knew what the Faceless did. It didn't stop anyone from trying to guess, like campfire stories in the big black. It was always night out here.

"They wrote all over it," Branski said. "Like tattoos or something. And it fucking *glows.*"

"Bullshit," I said, even though I didn't know whether to believe it. Better to be cynical than gullible, right?

"It's true," Branski told me. He shook his head slowly. "I never saw anything like it."

The look in his eyes scared the hell out of me.

CHAPTER TWO

I MISSED PHYSICAL TRAINING, but nobody even noticed because by the time the last bell went the whole station knew that Cameron Rushton was back. It was all anyone could talk about back in my barracks.

"He's not what people remember," Moore said, coming out of the head with a towel wrapped around his waist. "That's why Commander Leonski won't announce it."

"What do you mean he's not what people remember?" Micallef asked. Micallef was new, a skinny sixteen-year-old with buckteeth and a homesick pallor.

Normally Moore would have ignored a newbie like Micallef, but he was just itching to tell the story. And maybe itching to scare the shit out of Micallef. "The Faceless ruined him," he said, leaning close to Micallef and lowering his voice. "They wrote in his skin, newbie! They carved him up all over!"

Moore worked in the docking bay, so maybe he'd seen it.

Micallef went pale, and he wasn't the only one who suddenly felt how very, very far from home we all were, spinning alone in the big black like a silver lure on a line.

"Leave him alone, Moore," Cesari said, and he wasn't just looking out for the newbie. Everyone was thinking the same thing: the Faceless were back.

When I got the message to go to the medical bay, the guys in the barracks all looked at me, half-afraid and half-envious, and my heart thumped.

I headed up to the med bay, hurrying along one of the station's arms that led from the barracks in the Inner Ring to the Core. The Inner Ring was living quarters, barracks, rec rooms, refectory, and training rooms. The Core was main operations for Defender Three. It had the Dome, operations, the medical bay, administration, and underneath all that, engineering and the reactor core. Almost everyone you ran into in the Core was an officer. My arm was sore from saluting by the time I finally arrived at the medical bay.

I wondered the whole time why Doc had asked for me.

Doc had always liked me. His name was Major Layton, really, but I called him Doc. He only let a few of his students do that, and I was probably the youngest. He'd told me after my first introductory class that he'd make a decent medic out of me, and for three years he'd been making good on that threat. He said I was smart enough to be a doctor like him, but he didn't push it. He knew I didn't want to stay in the military any longer than I had to, and if I graduated as an officer, that would mean another five-year commitment at least. I'd rather stay on the lowest pay grade and get the hell out at the first opportunity, thanks.

When he called me to the med bay, I figured it was probably to check out some idiot who'd fallen off the climbing wall and busted his ankle. That happened at least once a month. It couldn't be anything to do with Cameron Rushton, because Doc had at least another five doctors working under him, plus a bunch of officer cadets he was training up as doctors. I wasn't important enough for anything big.

The doors to the med bay opened. For a moment I thought the place was deserted; then Doc appeared from one of the quarantine rooms. He was a big man. His belly pushed at the buttons of his uniform tunic. Doc was also grumpy as shit, and he frowned a lot. You wouldn't think he'd have much of a bedside manner, and most of the military doctors didn't, but Doc was a good guy underneath all his bluster. He'd joined late in life, after his wife died, and he didn't hold much with all that rank bullshit. It was why I liked him so much.

He was smoking as well, even though he always threatened to kick my ass for the same thing.

"Garrett," he said, and I knew without looking around that there were other officers nearby. Otherwise Doc just called me Brady.

"Major," I said and gave him my best salute. Which was shit.

His eyes crinkled with a smile, but his voice was gruff. "Garrett, follow me."

He turned and headed back into the first quarantine room.

I hated those places, and not because of the quarantine rules. In three years on Defender Three I'd only ever seen them used for one thing, and it wasn't for disease: they were where Doc put the patients he couldn't leave in the open ward, the ones who needed somewhere quiet to die. They were burn victims, mostly, like after the fire in the reactor. Two engineers and one recruit had died that day, or had begun to die that day. The recruit was called Smith. He'd been in some of my classes. It took him three days to die even after all his skin burned off. I sat with him for a lot of it, because his friends had been too freaked out to do it. It was after Smith died that Doc had told my career supervisor to put me into the medical stream.

I followed Doc inside, and the doors slid closed behind me with a hiss. Another air lock. I stood there with Doc while the air lock cycled through, and then we were inside the quarantine room.

There were six officers inside, including Commander Leonski who was in charge of the station. I was fairly sure he wouldn't have known my name if it hadn't been stitched on my uniform. There were over six hundred guys on the station, after all. I wondered what the hell I was doing in this company.

That was when I saw it. Branski had said Cameron Rushton was in stasis, and I guess I'd thought of some sort of plastic pod, all sleek and smooth and rounded, like a throwback to those old sci-fi movies. But this was nothing like that.

This was black, the same oily black as the Faceless battle armor, and it wasn't sleek. It was bulky and misshapen. It reminded me of a beetle's carapace. Back home in Kopa we used to get those big hissing rhinoceros beetles, with sharp mandibles and articulated legs. The stasis unit could have passed for one of those, except it was about ten feet long, lying on its back with its legs clamped around an opaque sac of fluid with veins through it. It was fucking terrifying.

Just looking at it, I could feel the blood draining from my face.

There was a body floating inside the milky fluid, and I didn't have to ask: Cameron Rushton. It looked like he was being consumed by a giant insect, or hatched by one.

I couldn't take my eyes off it. It was grotesque. Why the hell had Doc asked me to be here for this? Whatever this was. I fought the urge to shove my shaking hands inside my pockets. I tried to remember to breathe. If I hadn't been surrounded by a bunch of officers, I would have cut and run. No fucking question.

"Is this Garrett?" one of the officers asked. He had the stripes of a lieutenant commander on his sleeve, but his arms were crossed over the chest of his plain gray fatigues, and I couldn't read his name.

In my experience it was never a good thing when a ranking officer asked someone to confirm your name. That was normally the first step to spending a while in the brig. I'd got there twice before in three years, both times for fighting. Six hundred guys, no girls, locked in a tin can in space: everyone spent time in the brig.

"In the flesh," Doc drawled and clapped me on the shoulder.

"You're a medic?" the lieutenant commander asked me, drawing his brows together keenly.

I don't know where I found my voice, or how I tore my gaze away from the Faceless unit.

"Not yet, sir," I told the lieutenant commander, straightening my shoulders. "I still have three months before I complete my training."

He waved it away like it didn't matter, and I wondered again why the hell I was there. Why did they want a medic anyway? I could strap an ankle, I could treat blisters and cuts, and I could, in theory, plug a sucking chest wound well enough to evac a guy back to a medical bay, but what the hell was I doing in a quarantine room looking at some sorry bastard in a Faceless stasis unit? It was way above my level of training. Hell, it was probably way above Doc's as well.

But nobody told me.

"Take a look, Garrett," Doc said and pushed me forward.

Shit no.

My stomach clenched and churned.

My skin crawled. I didn't want to be in the same room with the unit, let alone close enough to touch. I didn't want to get closer. I wanted to be outside. I wanted to be in my barracks. I wanted to be a million miles away, with the sun at my back and my feet in the dirt. Not here. Not in the black, in the cold, with a nightmare right in front of me.

The unit hummed like a living thing, and I couldn't shake the idea that if I got too close, it would suddenly attack. One of those mandibles would detach from the sac in a split second and stab me right through the guts. It would be like every horror movie I'd ever seen. Maybe that's why all those officers wanted me there. I was their test bunny.

I looked back at Doc.

Please. Please don't make me.

He waved me forward.

I moved closer to the unit, the soles of my boots squeaking on the floor. The unit was inky black. I could see my reflection in it, more or less: a pale face with big, scared eyes and a bad haircut.

Keep it together, Garrett.

I reached out and touched the bug. It was warm underneath my trembling fingers. It was smooth. It even felt like a carapace. I couldn't see a power source, but I could feel power humming through it, below the seamless outer casing. I ran my palms over it, just to be sure it wouldn't move. Then I raised myself up onto the toes of my boots and took a look inside at Cameron Rushton.

A pallid face lay close to the surface of the opaque fluid.

It was the most famous face of my generation's war, a face I'd seen a hundred times on posters and TV. Immersed in that milky fluid, Cameron Rushton's face was pale, paler than mine, and thin and angular as though the skin was stretched too tight across the bones of his skull. His eyes were closed; dark lashes lay against his cheeks. There was a tiny bubble caught between the lashes of his left eye. I found myself reaching out to wipe it away. I stopped myself before I touched the sac. Shit. My heart raced. What the hell was I thinking?

Cameron Rushton was naked. He looked like a corpse. Were they sure he was alive? How could they be sure?

I turned around, and all the officers were staring at me.

"What do you think, Garrett?" Doc asked me.

"Is he dead, Major?" I asked, my voice wavering. I thought I could see his body moving slightly, rippling almost, but maybe that was the power thrumming through the unit. What the fuck did I know about Faceless technology?

Doc came and stood beside me. "Touch it."

You fucking touch it.

Doc winked at me. The gesture was so out of place, so fucking absurd when we were standing beside a piece of humming Faceless technology that could be *anything*, that could mean we were already dead, that I almost laughed. I caught the laugh before it broke free, smothered it into a cough, and then remembered that this was terrifying.

"Go on," Doc murmured. "It's okay, Brady."

How the hell could he know that? I made a face at him that the other officers couldn't see and reached out to touch the sac. It was warm. It bowed under my fingertips like a bladder of water, and I pulled back like I'd been stung.

"What is it?" I asked, keeping my voice low. "Is it like, um, amniotic fluid?"

Doc breathed smoke in my face and shrugged. "I've got no fucking idea, Brady. Never seen anything like this before."

I pretended to look at the carapace again and squeezed my eyes shut instead. "Why am I here, Doc?"

"Touch it again," Doc said. "Put your palm on it."

Three years in the military had taught me you never get a straight answer.

I pressed my palm against the sac. It pulsed slightly, like it really was amniotic fluid, like there really was a heartbeat echoing through it. And then Cameron Rushton moved.

His hand came up, palm upward, and pressed against mine. Right against it, like he knew it was there even though he hadn't opened his eyes. The weird rubbery skin of the sac slid between our palms.

"Jesus!" I jumped back again, my heart racing and my throat

dry. My guts felt like a pan of water. I wanted to vomit. That was it: that was my horror movie moment.

Doc grabbed my arm. "Watch."

And holy crap, Moore hadn't been lying. He glowed. Cameron Rushton *glowed*. Writing appeared on his torso, a line of alien characters that went from his ribs down to his hip like they'd been carved deep into his flesh. They glowed silver against his pale skin. Like starlight.

"What is it?" I asked as the characters faded away into nothing.

Doc shrugged. "No idea."

"Shit, Doc," I whispered, "why am I here?"

Doc smiled at me grimly. "Because it's time to wake Sleeping Beauty."

You never get a straight answer.

CHAPTER THREE

I GOT AS FAR OUT of the way as I could while Doc worked. He'd called in two other doctors to assist: Captain Loh and Lieutenant Wagner. I'd once seen those guys do microsurgery to reattach a severed finger. They were good. They were the best surgeons on Defender Three.

That still didn't explain what the hell I was doing there.

I retreated to a corner of the room and tried not to get in the way of the officers.

Lieutenant Commander Chanter, who'd finally uncrossed his arms and let me figure out who he was, ran his gaze over the oily black surface of the Faceless stasis unit like it was a thing of beauty, like he'd crawl right in with Cameron Rushton if he had half the chance. Chanter was OIC of engineering. He was a small guy, but he looked sharp. He was probably a genius. How else do you keep a rust bucket like Defender Three hanging in space?

Commander Leonski narrowed his eyes. "Talk me through it, gentlemen."

"Could be a biohazard," Loh suggested, peering at the unit.

"Could be a bio*weapon*," one of the other officers said.

"Could be any sort of weapon," Chanter growled.

I tried not to shrink back any farther. Was this why we were in a quarantine room? Would they open the unit and it would be smallpox city? Or maybe the Faceless weren't that old-fashioned, and the whole thing would just explode.

"It's not a bomb," Commander Leonski said. Commander Leonski was solid. He was all muscle. He had large, square hands that he kept at his sides in the way that career military men do. His hairline was receding underneath his short back and sides. He had a lantern jaw and a hooked nose that looked like it had been broken in the past. He wasn't a handsome man, exactly, but he had clever eyes with wrinkles in the corners from laughing. He was a long way from laughing now. "As for biological, we can't tell. Layton?"

Doc only shrugged. "And we won't tell until we get it open."

That led into a whole other problem: none of them knew how.

Some guys on the station were all about getting in with the officers and playing eager little kiss-ass, but not me. So I pretty much zoned out while the brass talked in circles around shit I wasn't qualified to have an opinion about. I slunk around the wall until I was near the unit again and stared at it for a while. It didn't seem any less frightening, but Cameron Rushton did. Shit, wasn't his fault he was in there.

I touched the sac again, because nobody said I shouldn't, and Cameron Rushton raised his hand to meet mine again. Our palms touched. I held the contact this time and watched as the silver characters appeared on his pale flesh.

Weird.

It reminded me a little of those battery testers, where you lined up the points and it glowed green if there was any power left. It was like that, I thought, when my hand touched his. It even seemed a little less creepy this time.

"Hey," I told him, even though he was suspended in milky fluid and his eyes were closed. "Welcome back."

The characters on his body glowed silver. I wondered what it meant. Maybe the electric signals passing through the sac between our palms activated the glowing characters. Maybe it was instructions for the stasis unit. Maybe it was a warning to other Faceless that it was a bioweapon. Or maybe it was like a dog tag: *If lost, please return to the Faceless.*

Poor bastard. Cameron Rushton looked at peace, but so did the dead. I wondered if there were any thoughts running through his head. Did the stasis unit let him dream? His hand was pressed against mine, but did he even know I was there?

I lifted my hand and watched his sink slowly back down. I touched the sac again: curling characters lit up like neon against his flesh. His hand touched mine through the sac. I splayed my fingers, and he splayed his. I shifted my hand lower, and his followed. The skin of the sac slid between our palms.

Are you even in there?

I shivered. My hand shook against the sac and broke and remade contact a hundred times in the space of a few breaths. His palm jerked against mine, his fingers twitched, and the writing flashed on and off.

I was doing that to him, whatever it was.

I held my hand against the sac until it stopped trembling. So did his.

Behind me, the officers were still figuring out what to do.

"We could send it planetside," Lieutenant Commander Chanter said, and I bet it hurt him even to suggest it. His engineer's brain must have been dying to get to grips with the pod.

"That's not an option," Commander Leonski said. "If we open it, we open it here. That's from the war room."

He watched me pressing my hand against the sac, but he didn't say anything. Maybe he was wondering the same thing as me: was Cameron Rushton really there? Maybe he was just an empty shell.

The edges of Chanter's mouth tugged up in a tight smile. "Can't have a war hero coming home in this sort of box. It wouldn't play well for the cameras."

I couldn't tell if he was mocking Cameron Rushton or the government or the media or everyone. I didn't dare look at him again in case he was mocking me as well.

"They want him to walk off a transport back on Earth," Commander Leonski said, "or not at all. So we either open it or destroy it."

Holy hell. That was harsh, and it wasn't the way I was used to hearing officers talk about the government. Had they forgotten they were in the presence of a lowly recruit with scuffed boots and bad grades? No, they couldn't have forgotten, because I was making Cameron Rushton light up like a fucking Christmas tree.

More silver writing appeared, this time on his throat. The stasis unit thrummed where I leaned against it. It was like a battery tester, I thought again, and I was the battery. I removed my hand from the sac almost unwillingly, like I was leaving him all alone, and watched as his hand sank back down toward his body.

Did he know I was gone? I could feel the loss of contact like a sudden itch. My palm tingled, and I wiped it on my fatigues.

"There are no releases on it," Chanter said, all business now. "At least none that we can see. There's a seam along the bottom, but it doesn't appear to yield. The most obvious point would be where the sac meets the casing, but it seems almost..." His voice faltered for a moment before he recovered himself. "Almost organic."

I looked down at it. The black shiny carapace didn't stop

when the sac began. It sort of melted into the opaque sac instead. Creepy.

"So?" Commander Leonski asked. He ran a hand over his short, graying hair.

"So we cut the sac," Chanter said.

Doc raised his eyebrows. "Cut it?"

"Why not?" Chanter asked.

Doc counted the reasons off on his fingers. "Because we don't know how that will affect him. We don't know how it's keeping him alive. We don't know if ripping him out of there will send him straight into shock, or maybe just electrocute him. We don't fucking know anything!"

"That's why we're doing it here," Chanter said, "instead of engineering."

"It could kill him," Doc said.

Chanter shrugged his narrow shoulders.

"We might as well know sooner rather than later," Commander Leonski said, and just like that it was decided.

It might have been funny, if it wasn't someone's life.

Commander Leonski and the other officers left, and Doc locked the door behind them. The four of us waited around until the separate air cycle kicked in.

"Doc," I said, watching Captain Loh and Lieutenant Wagner climb into their orange hazmat suits, "what the hell am I doing here?"

Doc opened a cupboard and pulled out a suit. "You're here in case he survives this, Brady."

"What?"

Doc showed me his nicotine-stained teeth in a smile. "You, Garrett, have a half-decent bedside manner, and you're from Fourteen Beta, just like him."

"It's a big region, Doc," I said, scowling as he shoved the hazmat suit at me.

Six million people in Fourteen Beta, and we sure as shit were not all created equal. But Doc just wanted Cameron Rushton to hear a familiar accent if he lived, and my bedside manner didn't totally suck.

I hauled the hazmat suit over my fatigues and checked all the seals. Doc double-checked them for me.

I wasn't sure what I was supposed to be doing while I waited to see if Cameron Rushton survived—I wasn't sure why I couldn't wait outside like everyone else, if I was honest, but I'd always liked to make myself useful in the med bay where I could.

So I hung back behind the three doctors and laid out everything on the trolley.

"Do we have a heartbeat?" Doc asked, his voice muffled by his suit.

Lieutenant Wagner pressed a stethoscope against the sac. "The hell if I know."

I didn't hear what Captain Loh said, but he reached back for a scalpel and positioned the blade against the sac. We all froze for a moment in anticipation. Then Loh sliced into the sac, and everything went to shit.

Suddenly the floor was awash in fluid, and it was slippery as hell underfoot. Captain Loh, who'd borne the brunt of the wave, ended up on his ass against the wall, holding his scalpel up like Excalibur. Lieutenant Wagner was struggling to stay upright himself; he'd half fallen into the stasis unit. And Doc was shouting: "Get me a defib! Get me a fucking defib!"

I hit the edge of the trolley as I tried to move, and knocked the tray of instruments to the floor. It hurt.

I don't know how Cameron Rushton, so thin and pale, hadn't just washed over the edge of the carapace with the tide and ended up on the floor like Captain Loh, but he hadn't. When I skidded across the floor with the defibrillator, hauling it out of the case as I went, I saw that he was lying in a shallow pool of glistening fluid, and he wasn't moving.

Doc wrenched the defibrillator out of my hands and slapped the pads down onto Cameron Rushton's chest. They wouldn't stick in the goo.

I wrapped my gloved fingers around his wrist and held it for a while, concentrating. "No pulse."

I wondered if he'd ever been alive at all. Maybe the way his hand had moved had just been a Faceless trick to get us to open the unit.

I looked at his pallid, narrow face and those long, dark lashes that rested on his cheeks. He looked thinner than he had in the footage from the Shitbox, but not really any older. It was hard to tell through the weird slime that stuck to him like ectoplasm.

"Fuck it," Doc said at last and dropped the defibrillator.

Fluid dripped onto the floor. I looked down, and that was when I saw the jagged gash in the thigh of my hazmat suit. There was blood as well. I must have collected a scalpel when I ran into the trolley.

My blood ran cold. I heard a buzzing in my ears.

"Doc," I said, and something in my flat tone of voice caught his attention right away.

He twisted his head to look at me and followed my gaze. His eyes widened behind his mask. "Oh Jesus, Brady."

My heart thumped loudly, and I tried to ignore it. If the Faceless had turned Cameron Rushton's corpse into a bioweapon, I'd be the first one to know it, but it was too late to do anything about it now. Then I looked at that pale body lying in the remains of the stasis unit and remembered that I was the battery.

In for a penny, in for a pound.

I stripped my glove off. My hand felt cold as I reached out to touch his chest. His skin was smooth and still warm from the unit, but there was no heartbeat. I pressed my palm between his ribs, right where Doc had taught me for CPR. The heel of my hand slipped in the fluid, but I held it there and splayed my fingers out over his heart.

I don't know what I expected. Silver letters maybe, curling their way down his ribs toward his hip. Electricity maybe, but there was nothing. I was annoyed, I think, annoyed that I'd cut my suit, annoyed that I was bleeding, and annoyed that I'd put my naked hand right in the middle of that Faceless goo and got nothing. I sure as hell wasn't going to give up then. He was still warm. Maybe he hadn't been a corpse at all, at least not until Captain Loh had ripped the sac open. If he was still warm, there was still a chance CPR might work.

I positioned my other hand, and that's when I felt it: the thumping of his heartbeat. My breath caught in my dry throat. I wanted to tell Doc I had a heartbeat, but I couldn't make a sound. A fraction of a second later Cameron Rushton's eyes flickered open, widened in panic, and he started to choke.

"Get him out! Get him out!" Doc yelled.

It was like he weighed nothing. Between the three of us—Loh was still struggling to get up—we hauled Cameron Rushton out of the unit. It was hard to hold on to him, but we got him to the floor. He thrashed weakly against us as we pushed him onto his side into the recovery position, then Doc held his head while he vomited.

There must have been liters of the disgusting milky fluid. I thought Cameron Rushton would drown before he cleared his lungs. I thought that'd be just our luck.

I slipped in the goo and ended up on the floor, knocking the trolley again. I saw Cameron Rushton's eyes roll back in his face and heard his first gasping, choking breath. It ripped wetly through his lungs. The sound was awful.

He was terrified. I guess because he couldn't breathe, and I guess because he'd woken up with a bunch of guys in orange suits looming over him. He opened his dripping mouth and tried to scream, and it was as silent as the one I'd seen on that footage from four years ago.

"Hey," I said, my voice echoing in my suit. Shit, my suit. I ripped off the helmet. "It's okay. You're okay."

He fixed on the sound of my voice and twisted his head toward me. His terrified gaze caught on my very human face. He had green eyes, and they were so wide that they seemed to take up most of his pale face.

I unzipped my suit and shrugged it down and pulled off my remaining glove. "You're okay," I said, even though my own heart was racing.

A part of me had thought he was dead. A part of me still couldn't believe he wasn't.

Doc released him gently, and Cameron Rushton drew his knees up. He could move. That was good. He was breathing. That was better. Whether he could understand where he was or what I was saying, that was debatable.

I slid closer to him through the goo. It stuck to my skin like mucus, and it stank as well. It turned my stomach. "You're okay," I repeated.

He was trembling.

"Get a blanket," Doc said to Wagner, and Wagner climbed gingerly to his feet.

Cameron Rushton was like a frightened animal. I reached out my hand to him slowly, and he shrank back.

"It's okay," I murmured and wished Wagner wasn't making so much noise rattling around behind me.

He let me touch his shoulder, even though he flinched. His skin was still warm, but it was rapidly cooling outside the artificial warmth of the stasis unit. It was sticky and slippery as well.

Wagner shuffled back, passing the blanket to Doc. Doc draped it around Cameron Rushton's shoulders, and he shuddered like he couldn't bear the weight of it. His green eyes filled with tears, and I wondered how long he'd been suspended in fluid.

"It's okay," I said again, shifting closer.

The blanket probably wasn't enough. Not if he was cold, and not if he was going into shock. I put an arm around his shoulders —he was thin but not wasted away—and slowly drew him against me. He tensed for a moment and then gradually relaxed. He was still shaking, but he didn't resist.

I sat there on the flooded floor of the isolation room, with my arms wrapped around a slimy war hero wearing nothing but a blanket, wondering if I was a dead man or not.

THERE WERE four isolation rooms in the medical bay, each with independent air and water supplies. There was also a double air lock, like a hyperbaric chamber, on every entrance so that isolation was maintained. The isolation rooms could be opened up to one another and the shower room, in case there was a major outbreak of disease and they needed to be transformed into one ward. Lucky for me, because I wasn't going anywhere for a long time.

Doc and I eventually coaxed Cameron Rushton to his unsteady feet and walked him into the shower. I sat with him on the tiles, my uniform soaking through, until we were both clean and gunk-free. The cut on my thigh stung.

One thing about being exposed—I didn't have to help with the cleanup in the first room. It was Captain Loh and Lieutenant Wagner who had that messy job.

Cameron Rushton didn't say a word under the gentle warm spray of the shower, so I did the talking for him. Mostly I just told him that he was okay, that he was on Defender Three, and that my name was Garrett. I said we had to get cleaned up, and I helped him with that as well. He shivered every time I made a pass over his skin with the sponge.

I'd thought his skin was pale when he was in the pod, but it wasn't. Mine was paler. Now that he was warmed up, Cameron Rushton's skin had lost its pallor. It was slightly tanned. He was in better shape than I'd thought as well, once I wiped the goo off him. He was taller than me, and slender without being scrawny. There was no muscle wastage. I could see his muscles moving under his skin every time I drew the sponge over the planes of his back and he trembled. He was frightened, so I put my hand on his shoulder while I worked, just to let him know it was okay.

Living on the station for three years, I'd pretty much gotten over any ideas of modesty I'd ever had. I showered with guys every day, but not like this. It was one thing to stand in a line with a dozen other guys arguing about who had the fastest time on the wall and wondering when the hot water was going to run out; it was a whole other thing to be sitting on the tiles in your uniform with a naked guy while you gently scrubbed his trembling back. And tried not to notice his erection.

It was nothing, probably. Who the hell knew what getting out of stasis had done to his body? There were probably all sorts of chemicals and endorphins and hormones running mad in his system. So when he tried to twist away in embarrassment, I made a face.

"It happens," I said. "Don't worry about it."

Color flooded his face for the first time: a blush.

I continued to wash him and wondered what the hell had happened to him in those four years. Where had he been? How did he get back? What did the Faceless do to him? What did the Faceless *look* like? But that wasn't why Doc had called me in. He'd called me in for my familiar accent and my bedside manner, and it wasn't my place to ask those questions.

And I didn't want to know. Fuck no. Because whatever I could imagine, whatever any of us could, what if it was worse than that?

The water didn't run cold in the med bay. It was still nice and warm when I turned the tap off and found Cameron Rushton some towels. I wrapped one around his hips and slung one around his shoulders and then gently ushered him toward the cot that was waiting for him.

I helped him dry off. It reminded me a little of when I'd done the same for my sister. I think it was probably his hair. It came down to his shoulders in little wet twists like Lucy's hair. I used to dry it and brush it for her when Dad was working. A twinge of homesickness caught me then.

Cameron Rushton trembled, and a shudder ran through his body like an electric current. I helped him into bed and piled a few blankets over him, and then Doc came in, squelching along in his hazmat suit, to attach the heart monitor and take his blood pressure.

"There's a dry uniform next door, Brady," he said. "You'll have to stay here. You understand?"

"Yeah," I said, trying not to think about what viruses or nanos might be coursing through my bloodstream.

I went and changed and then headed back to Cameron Rushton's cot to discover that he was still trembling, still cold, and practically shitting himself because Doc was trying to take blood.

"It's okay," I told him, and he turned his plaintive face in my direction. I said to Doc, "The suits freak him out, I think."

Doc handed me the syringe. "Can you do it?"

I could use a syringe if I had to, but I was only supposed to do it in the field if there wasn't a doctor available. And that was really only to pump a wounded man so full of morphine that he wouldn't feel the pain as he died. When you're overdosing a guy, you don't have to be that accurate.

Narrowing my eyes, I found a vein in the crook of Cameron Rushton's elbow, and he let me do it. Only the stuttering beep of the heart monitor told me how nervous he was as the needle slid into his flesh.

"Good lad," Doc said, and I didn't know if he was talking to me or to Cameron Rushton.

I stuck a plaster on the tiny wound and felt for a second like a real doctor. I'd done a good job, and I was proud of that. A warm glow of satisfaction settled in my belly.

Doc patted me on the arm. "Stay with him, Brady. Yell if you need anything."

"Okay."

I leaned on the wall and watched as Cameron Rushton slowly slipped into sleep. It took a while. Every time I thought he was almost there, his eyes would flash open, and he would gasp.

"It's okay," I murmured every time, just like I would with Lucy when she couldn't settle after a nightmare. "You're okay."

In the end I got tired of his panicked face and the rapid beep of the heart monitor, so I pulled a chair close and held his hand. Even under all those blankets he felt cold. I worried that he might be going into shock, but eventually his heartbeat dropped back into a healthy range.

He relaxed finally, and so did I. The slow, steady rhythm of his heart monitor lulled me into sleep as well.

CHAPTER FOUR

I WAS STUCK in isolation for the next twenty-four hours, so I never got to see the skin of the sac stretched out on a frame in a secure room in engineering. It dried like, well, *real skin*, Doc told me. Maybe it was. We'd never know for sure. It dried and fell to pieces apparently, and Lieutenant Commander Chanter was pretty pissed about that. He still had the shell of the unit to study, but that wasn't enough to figure out how it all worked.

I was bored in isolation as well, but I didn't let it show. I knew better than to look that gift horse in the mouth. I read the medical journals Doc loaned me, and sat next to Cameron Rushton's cot and watched him sleep. You wouldn't think someone who'd been in stasis needed that much sleep, but what the hell did I know? He slept a lot.

Still, I didn't mind watching over a sleeping guy for a day. It was better than classes, and better than PT. And I might have slept in a chair, but at least I didn't have O'Shea in a bunk above me, snoring like a bastard.

Doc took my blood every four hours. He watched it keenly for changes, but I felt fine the whole time. I had my own room, I didn't have to go to class, and the next day I showered alone for the first time in three years. Quarantine was like a fucking holiday.

Cameron Rushton had been twenty-two when the Faceless took him four years ago. He still looked twenty-two. I guess four years doesn't always have to show on a guy, but when he's been a captive of the Faceless, you sort of expect some sign of it. At first I wondered if maybe he'd been in stasis the whole time, but that was stupid, because his hair had grown. It was wavy and mostly light brown with a few golden streaks in it like the sort made by the sun. He wasn't as pale as everyone on Defender Three either. He had a faint uniform tan all over his body.

I wondered if he'd had seen any suns in the past four years.

The glowing writing that had freaked everyone out was gone. I wondered about that for a while, and it turned out I reached the same conclusion as Lieutenant Commander Chanter: the writing was never on his flesh. It had been projected there from the skin of the sac. Maybe it really was the Faceless equivalent of *If lost, please return to...*

That was supposed to be funny when I thought it up, but it wasn't. What if the Faceless really were looking for him? Shit, Defender Three had never been attacked by Faceless, but there was a reason the numbering system of the stations jumped from Three to Six. Four and Five had been lost years ago. Thirteen hundred men in total, and they hadn't stood a chance. Sure, we'd upped our weapons technology since then, but so had the Faceless, probably.

So I looked at Cameron Rushton, and I watched him sleep, and I wondered why the Faceless had kept him alive at all and if they wanted him back. Maybe his return wasn't a miracle after all. Maybe it was a harbinger.

All he did was sleep. Sometimes he opened his green eyes, and they would widen with fear like he didn't know where he was. Then his gaze would find my face, and the beeping heart monitor would find its rhythm, and he'd drift off again. And while he did I'd read aloud from the medical journals, sometimes skipping over the big words I couldn't pronounce, just so Cameron Rushton could hear the voice of someone from Fourteen Beta.

I was never any good at school. Linda, my stepmother, reckoned it was because I was dumb as a post, but she wasn't exactly in any position to judge, you know. And my dad was probably the dumbest of the lot of us, because he had this crazy fucking idea that a boy needed a mother, and this even crazier fucking idea that Linda fit the bill.

She walked out on him two years later, leaving us holding a bunch of her debts and the baby. I wasn't dumb enough to miss her. I missed Dad and Lucy, though. Missed them more than sunlight.

I was born and raised in Fourteen Beta, in Kopa township, which used to be just one more refugee camp along the line until people got tired of walking and put some roots down in the dirt there. That was almost sixty years ago, when the Faceless first attacked the Earth. Millions died, and millions more were displaced. Refugee camps like Kopa appeared all over the planet overnight. People still called them camps, even though they were permanent. None of the remaining cities wanted to be overrun by reffos.

Cameron Rushton was famous enough that I knew he didn't come from anywhere like Kopa. He came from the southeast of Fourteen Beta, where there were wide bitumen roads and universities and cities and beaches and thousands of shops to spend the money that it seemed everyone down there had to spare. I'd seen pictures.

I had nothing at all in common with the guy, not really. I was from a piss-poor factory town that stank of smoke, where

the dirt was red with bauxite. He was from the city. He'd probably never had to get out of bed at five a.m. so he could cook his
dad some breakfast before work. He'd probably never had to
scrounge for money. He'd probably never listened to the wail of
the emergency siren spreading out through the town and
wondered if it meant his dad wasn't coming home from his
shift.

It's not like I envied him, though. Shit no. Whatever the fuck
had happened to Cameron Rushton out in the black, he could
keep it.

I was learning about surgical debridement when he woke up.
He'd been restless in the last few hours, and my voice was hoarse
from reading. I'd just got to the part where the journal talked
about how maggots could be used to get rid of necrotic flesh.

"Millions of years of evolution, and we're back to fucking
maggots," I said. "That's a fucking kicker!"

Cameron Rushton stretched and sighed. His eyes flickered
open. "Chris?"

I dropped the journal and jumped out of my chair so fast that
I felt my spine crack. I leaned over the cot. Cameron Rushton
was awake, properly awake, and his eyes were fixed on mine like
they were seeing me for the first time. And he looked so fucking
disappointed in what he saw that if it hadn't been for my breath
catching in my throat, I would have stammered out an apology.

"Hey," I managed at last. "It's Garrett, remember?"

Apparently not. His eyebrows drew together, and his green
eyes darkened. He swiped his tongue over his dry lips. "Where
am I?"

"Defender Three," I told him.

If he'd been a guy who was dying or a guy who was thrashing
in pain, I would have held his hand again. But he was just a guy
lying there trying to figure out where he was in the big black, and
I didn't know him. I knew his face, and I knew his history, but I

didn't know him. And he sure as shit didn't know me, familiar accent or not.

"Something's wrong." A shadow passed over his face. He pressed his lips together, and they whitened.

"You're okay now," I said. It occurred to me for the first time that I had no idea what to call him. Lieutenant? It was strange to remember that he was still an officer, and he still outranked me.

He blinked at me and sighed. "Okay."

"Okay." I stooped down to pick up the journal.

Rushton closed his eyes again. "The Faceless are coming."

A chill went through me.

Well, that was a fucking kicker as well.

———

A BUNCH of officers in bright orange hazmat suits crowded into the quarantine room. I hung back, expecting to be thrown out at any moment. Well, thrown into one of the other quarantine rooms at least. They would hardly put me out into the general population when there was still a chance I was a walking contagion. But nobody even noticed me once Cameron Rushton began to speak.

He talked in a low voice, without inflection, like this was something that had been rote-learned. He couldn't even look Commander Leonski in the eye.

"The Battle Regent Kai-Ren has a message for the commander of this station. He is coming here."

A Faceless. He was talking about a Faceless like it had a name—a name and a title. And a fucking mission. I could feel the blood flooding from my face as the implications of that hit me: the Faceless were coming. We were all dead men.

The reason I wasn't officer material was immediately apparent. Commander Leonski didn't even flinch when Cameron

Rushton delivered his speech. He only folded his arms over his chest and looked down at him.

"And how does this *battle regent* know where to find us?" he asked.

I thought it was Lieutenant Commander Chanter who spoke, but it was hard to tell them all apart in their orange suits: "We should have destroyed that pod."

"Too late now!" one of the others snapped.

"He's not tracking the pod," Cameron Rushton said. "He knows where I am. He sent me."

That shut them up for a minute.

Cameron Rushton plucked at the blankets with his long, slender fingers. His heart rate rose, and the monitor beeped faster. "Battle Regent Kai-Ren has sent me as his envoy."

Commander Leonski's voice was even. "And how is it that you can speak for the Faceless, Lieutenant Rushton?"

Cameron Rushton flushed, and the monitor spiked for a second. "I know their language," he said at last. His voice wavered. "He taught me."

I felt sorry for him. Everyone in the room was looking at him like he was a traitor. Shit, maybe he was. What the hell did I know?

Commander Leonski didn't say anything. Maybe there was nothing to say. His gloved hand clenched into a fist, unclenched, clenched again like he didn't know what to do with it.

Fear settled like water in my guts. I remembered those black-armored figures, tall and forbidding. And I wondered what it must have been like for Cameron Rushton. The terrible things in your nightmares, what sort of faces do they wear? Claws and teeth, I thought with certainty. Claws and teeth and pain and horror.

The officers turned on Cameron Rushton then, and Commander Leonski didn't stop them. They fired questions at him from all around—fast, sharp, stinging—and he had nowhere to go. I couldn't even tell which of the orange hazmat suits was spitting out the questions. With their backs to me they all looked the same, and their voices, strained with anger, maybe with fear, all hit the same pitch.

"What did you tell the Faceless? About our defenses?"

"No," he said over the rapid beep of the monitor. "I didn't—"

"What about our stations?"

"What about our weapons?"

"What about *Earth*?"

The officer's voice snagged on that word, and for a second I thought it might break. Mine would have, if I'd had to speak.

"He didn't ask." Rushton's face was pale, and his voice trembled.

"What did they do to you?"

"How did they turn you?"

"I didn't. I wasn't." His gaze slide from masked face to masked face to face, but they were all closed to him.

"Did they torture you?"

His mouth opened and closed, but they didn't give him time to answer.

Then Commander Leonski leaned in. "How much did you tell them?"

"Please, please..." Rushton struggled for breath. His chest rose and fell too quickly.

Leonski lifted his clenched hand and repeated the question. "How much did you tell them?"

"Sir," Rushton said. "Please..."

The alarms sounded on the monitor.

"Garrett!" Doc's voice cut through all the noise. "Get over here!"

The orange suits parted, and I made my way to the cot.

Doc didn't seem too worried. He wheeled over an oxygen

tank and placed a mask over Rushton's mouth and nose. It misted over as he breathed. I reached out to adjust it.

I thought I imagined the jolt of electricity when my fingers brushed his cheek, but Rushton recoiled like he'd felt it too, and his eyes widened.

"The pod," he managed in a ragged voice. He squeezed his eyes shut. "You didn't shut it down, did you? You cut me out!"

"We cut you out," Doc confirmed.

Rushton bit his lower lip. "Yeah," he said. His voice wavered. "Should have guessed."

Then he flatlined.

One second he was talking, and then he was gone, and Doc was shouting for a defibrillator.

It should have been me running for the defib, because none of the officers knew where one was, but I didn't. I reached out and put my palm against Rushton's bare chest, the same way I'd done when we'd cut him out of the Faceless pod. I don't know how I knew to do that, but I did. Behind the buzzing in my ears, behind my thumping heartbeat, I knew exactly what to do: *Touch him, Brady. Touch him. You're the battery, remember?*

I could feel the smooth skin of Rushton's pectorals and the dip between them. He felt warm. My palm tickled as a faint current of electricity traveled between us.

"Garrett?" Doc asked me, his bushy brows drawn together behind his mask.

That was when I felt it: Rushton's heartbeat. It was faint at first but grew steadier, *stronger*. And then his chest expanded as he drew a deep breath, and his eyes fluttered open.

He caught my wrist in his hand, wrapping his long fingers around it. "Don't move. I need you."

My head swam. Holy fuck, I *was* a battery! I knew it, and he knew it, but nobody else did.

"What the *hell* is going on?" Commander Leonski growled.

The heart monitor beeped out its rhythm: a little fast, a little scared, but strong. And it wasn't reading him, I realized. That was *me*. That was my fucking heartbeat.

"You cut me out," Cameron Rushton said, the color slowly coming back into his face. His voice was weak, and his breathing was labored, but he kept going. "You didn't let it cycle through. It's a backup system if the pod fails. Another person's electrical impulses can be used to stabilize mine." He looked at me and flushed. "It's only temporary, I think."

"How temporary?" Doc asked.

Good question.

"I don't know," Rushton said. He forehead creased in a frown. "Kai-Ren will know."

Back to him. Back to the fucking Faceless nightmare. I would have ripped my hand away right then and let Rushton die if he hadn't still been holding my wrist.

"And when is he coming?" Commander Leonski asked in a stony voice.

"Soon," Rushton said. "He's coming soon."

Better and better.

My heart beat a little faster, and so did Rushton's. Okay, that was creepy.

Lieutenant Commander Chanter said, "We're almost on the outside."

All the stations had orbits, like planets. Most of the time we wove together through the solar system like connected threads, a cat's cradle. Sometimes we were close enough to see the other stations. Sometimes we could even see Earth. But in a week we would be at our most vulnerable: on the outer curve of our ellipse, alone.

My hand trembled against Rushton's chest, and he tightened his fingers around my wrist.

"Kai-Ren isn't coming to kill us," he said. "I believe that, Commander."

Leonski shook his head. "They could wipe us out of the fucking black in a second!"

I tried not to fucking hear that. It was true. Everyone knew it was true, but officers weren't supposed to say shit like that. Officers were supposed to spruik all that empty fucking rhetoric about duty and the war effort and how we were here for the people back home. They weren't supposed to be as scared as the rest of us.

"He won't do that," Rushton said with quiet certainty.

I wanted to rip my hand away again. Who the hell was he to tell us the word of a Faceless was worth anything? Jesus, the officers had been right. He'd been well and truly compromised. We couldn't trust the Faceless, and we couldn't trust this asshole either.

"He wants to talk," Rushton said. "It could mean peace, Commander."

It could also mean the total annihilation of Defender Three, of every other station in the network, and of Earth. But it wasn't like we could stop the Faceless from coming, was it? It's not like we had a choice.

"And you're his envoy," Commander Leonski said. His lip curled. "Which side does that put you on, Rushton?"

His heart beat faster, or mine did. *Ours* did.

"I don't know," Rushton said. He dropped his gaze, and didn't that just say it all?

Fuck you. Fuck you, Cameron Rushton. Fucking traitor.

I felt his homesickness wash over me, and it felt almost the same as mine. This wasn't just about his body reading mine. This wasn't just about a heartbeat. I could feel what he felt as well. His homesickness, his fear, his sadness, and hiding underneath it all and skittering away when I tried to pin it down was a sickening sense of shame.

I swayed on my feet for a moment, dizzy. Shit. Where the hell had that come from? I tried to open my mouth to tell Doc maybe I was sick after all, but I couldn't even manage that.

Doc put a hand on my shoulder and maneuvered me to the cot. "Scoot up there, Garrett."

I was too tired and too dizzy to argue. I climbed onto the cot. Rushton linked his fingers through mine, and I felt it again: shame, and a twinge of something new. My brain didn't recognize it, but my balls did. Holy shit. It was lust.

The heart monitor beeped faster.

We lay there, shoulder to shoulder, hip to hip, with only my uniform and his blankets separating us. We held hands, and I told myself that it was just like the shower. It was some weird cocktail of hormones and chemicals coursing through his blood. It was a purely physical reaction. It didn't mean anything.

But why was I feeling it?

I closed my eyes and tried not to imagine how fucking humiliating it would be to get a hard-on in a room full of officers.

"You're okay," Rushton whispered, but it wasn't a whisper. I heard it in my head.

My eyes snapped open, and I twisted my neck to look at him. *"You're okay."*

He wasn't even looking at me. He was talking to Commander Leonski. And I was so tired I couldn't make out the words over the quiet, steady sound of his voice. I couldn't even focus my eyes anymore.

"You're okay, Garrett. I just need to borrow your strength for a bit."

Holy hell, I thought as I drifted off to sleep, he's a fucking vampire.

CHAPTER FIVE

"TALK ME THROUGH IT," Doc growled.

I kept my eyes closed and tried not to listen.

"I don't really know, sir." Rushton's voice was strained. "It's the backup system. It wasn't supposed to happen like that."

"Why Garrett?"

"Because he touched me skin to skin."

Fuck him. I was still touching him, still pressed up against him, and I wished I was still asleep. Not lying here pretending, when Rushton damn well knew I wasn't asleep, and Doc must have suspected it.

If I hadn't held his hand when he'd been in the cot, maybe he'd be dead right now. Maybe I wished he was. It wouldn't stop the Faceless from coming, but it would stop me from knowing about it.

Fucking Faceless. If they'd taken the time to make Rushton learn their language, you'd think they could have got him to do up a sign in English for the pod: DO NOT CUT. Or BEGIN RELEASE CYCLE BY PRESSING HERE. We'd cut into the thing instead, like a kid ripping open a birthday present, destroying the pod and almost destroying Rushton in the process.

"Is this harming him?" Doc asked.

"I don't know." Rushton's voice was low. "I don't think so."

I'd fallen asleep for real after the officers left. I'd had weird dreams where I saw flashing lights and heard strange hisses like steam escaping. A few times I'd tried to struggle out of sleep, but I lost that fight most of the time. The more I slept, the more he was awake. I remember being worried that the stronger he got, the weaker I got—would this process suck all the life out of me?—but it seemed to even out by the end of the day. Now I just felt a little more tired than usual, maybe a little hungover as well, but Rushton sounded a lot stronger.

Thinking about hangovers made me want a drink. I wondered how Hooper was going on the new still he'd set up in the maintenance locker near Tube Seven. None of us were meant to drink, but shit, there was not much else to do on Defender Three. We weren't supposed to gamble either, but we did. Hooper still owed me cigarettes for a hero call on aces high.

We didn't just gamble on cards; we gambled on everything. We gambled on what order the Shitboxes would arrive in. We gambled on who could climb the wall fastest. We gambled on whether or not that newbie would cry on his first night. We gambled on whether or not he'd get rolled in the showers, and whether or not he'd tell.

I was lucky. That only happened to me once, and instinct had told me to shut my mouth. You don't get much respect for crying to your career officer about what happened, but that one day when you unhook a guy's rig when he's on the climbing wall and he falls, well, he knows what he did to deserve it, and he knows better than to tell as well. I can still remember the look on Wade's face when he saw I was on top of the wall, at the anchor point for his rope. I'd let him get all the way to the top, so it was a thirty-foot drop back to the mats when he lost his footing and the ropes didn't catch him.

"*Little fucker!*" Wade screamed at me when they were carrying him to the med bay. A few of his friends beat the hell out of me for it, but it was still worth it. I wasn't the one with the permanent limp.

I thought about that, and Rushton curled his fingers through mine.

"*You're okay,*" I heard in my head.

My eyes flashed open.

Hell. Did Rushton *hear* that? Did this shit go both ways? Was it an echo of what he'd thought before I drifted off to sleep earlier, or was Rushton in my head right now, a sick voyeur, learning all about what that asshole Wade did to me that time in the showers? Because I wasn't a sniveling fucking kid anymore, and I didn't want him to think I was. That was three years ago, and I'd manned up since then. I'd got my payback.

I shifted away from him as far as I could, until I hit the rails of the cot. It was narrow enough that we were still touching anyway.

"I'll get you your dinner," Doc said, his face ghostly behind the mask of his hazmat suit.

"Hell, yes, Doc! Med bay rations!" I tried to say it with my usual enthusiasm, but it fell flat.

So did Doc's laugh.

Food on Defender Three wasn't that good, but it was slightly better in the med bay. The vegetables were steamed instead of canned, and the meat didn't come apart like a wet sponge when you poked it with a fork. The food was one of the reasons I hung around the med bay so much. Sometimes I got to finish off what the patients didn't.

Rushton looked at me sideways. Had I just outed myself as a bin scab? That's what we called the ibis that foraged through the rubbish tip back home: bin scabs. Sometimes thinking of that would make me smile. Not today. Today home wasn't a comfort. Today it was a fucking black hole pulling me in.

Doc came back a few minutes later with our trays of food. He drew up a chair and watched us eat. "Your blood's still clear, Brady," he told me. "If there's no change by morning, you're a free man. Well, as free as you can be in these circumstances."

Relief spread through me. Through *us*. Jesus, it was almost enough to put me off my dinner. "Doc, I dunno what's happening here. It's weird shit."

I was half-afraid he'd think I was crazy. I was hearing Rushton's voice in my head, for Christ's sake. What else would he think?

Doc laid his gloved hand on my shoulder. "Tell me."

I looked at Rushton. He was tired again. I could see it in the shadows under his green eyes, but more than that I could *feel* it.

I picked at a bean. It was kind of slimy. "Doc, I feel what he feels. I can hear his voice in my head." I tried not to let my voice waver, but I couldn't help it.

Doc's eyes widened behind his plastic mask.

Don't freak out, Doc, please. If you go, I'll go too, and then where the hell will we be?

Rushton shifted, and I felt the electricity tickle when the back of his hand brushed against my wrist. "It's temporary," he said. "It's a shared connection. My system is piggybacking on his. The downside is it creates a sort of feedback of electrical impulses and biochemistry."

I raised my eyebrows. *That* was the downside? The electrical impulses and biochemistry I could deal with. It was the frigging telepathy I didn't need.

Rushton glanced at me. A wry smile tugged quickly at the corners of his lips.

I scowled at him. *Not. Fucking. Helping.*

"You need Garrett to live," Doc said. "Is that right?"

Rushton nodded. "Yes, sir."

"And this is only temporary?" Doc asked. He narrowed his eyes.

"I think so, sir."

"Good," said Doc. He squeezed my shoulder like I was the patient. "Because this kid's going to be my best medic, aren't you, Garrett?"

"Yes, Doc," I said.

No, Doc. The Faceless are gonna kill us all.

"Good," Doc said again. "Now shut your mouths and eat your dinner, and I'll see about releasing you in the morning. I don't want to hear another peep out of you. Got it, Garrett?"

"Yes, Doc."

"Good lad," said Doc. If I'd had hair, he would have ruffled it. As it was he scrubbed his gloved hand across my buzz cut a few times. Doc's kids were all grown up, but that didn't stop him trying to treat me like one. And it didn't stop me from secretly liking it.

But not today.

Rushton looked at me. "I can't eat all this. Do you want it?"

Maybe that half smile was meant to be comforting.

Maybe he wasn't just another asshole officer after all.

Shame he was a fucking traitor.

His smile faltered, faded, and then it was like it had never happened at all.

I couldn't tell if the guilt that burrowed into my guts was his or mine.

———

THEY WAITED until the middle of the night to move us. Night was arbitrary. It was always night in the black, but the clocks were all twenty-four hour, and we still had a seven-day week. So it was technically a Tuesday morning, at 0300 hours when they moved us, even though it looked no different from any other moment in time on Defender Three.

Cameron Rushton was wearing a borrowed uniform with the name *Coleman* stitched on the pocket. It didn't suit him. Maybe it was just the way his hair curled around the collar. He looked too different from anyone else on Defender Three, with his long hair and his faint tan. Not that there was much chance of running into anyone else.

Most guys were snoring in their barracks. The lights had automatically dimmed at last bell and wouldn't come on again until 0600, when the flickering tubes would try to fool our bodies into thinking it was a natural morning, that we were still diurnal creatures, and that all this time in the black wasn't slowly draining the life out of every one of us. We'd spent millions of years evolving on a planet with the sun and the moon and the changing seasons, and our biology didn't cope well with the sterile, lifeless stations we'd made. *"The yellow sun makes things grow strong and tall,"* Lucy used to sing, but I guess the military never heard the song. Once a month we were ordered to strip off to our underwear, put on goggles, and walk through the lights in one of the UV chambers, but it was never the same as feeling real sunlight on your skin.

In the middle of the arbitrary night the arching gray hallways of Defender Three were almost empty. There were still crews working, but they were either in the Core or on the Outer Ring, where the work needed to be done. The Inner Ring was a ghost town.

Doc, Rushton, our two armed escorts, and I only passed a couple of guys on our way to my barracks. I had to collect my gear, so Rushton had to be with me. Doc wanted to make sure we were okay, and the armed escorts were Commander Leonski's idea.

"Make it quick, Garrett," Doc said when we reached my barracks.

"Yes, Major."

I slipped inside, wondering if I'd feel it if Rushton's heart stopped beating. How long would our weird biochemical elastic stretch before it snapped? Now wasn't the time to test it.

My bunk was three across and two down. I could find it with my eyes closed. I could always just follow the sound of O'Shea's snoring. The barracks was dark. It smelled of sweat and dirty socks, the same as always. I slipped down to my bunk and opened my footlocker as quietly as I could. I hauled my pack out and shoved some clothes into it. It was too dark to see what I was doing, but it's not like I had much stuff anyway. I just had what they'd issued me the day I'd arrived, and a book my dad had given me. I'd read it a thousand times already, but I put it in. I didn't want any bastard to steal it while I was gone.

I thought everyone was sleeping, but as I moved back toward the doors a hand knocked against my leg.

"Garrett?" Moore sat up in the gloom. "Thought you must've got sucked out an air lock. What happened in the med bay?"

"That's classified."

Moore was too tired at the moment to react, but he'd be pissed off in the morning about that. "Where you goin'?"

"Classified," I told him again and slipped away.

"Asshole," I heard him mutter.

It felt good to annoy Moore like that. It felt good because underneath everything I was shit scared, and I needed the distraction. Not only was Rushton going to be stuck to me like a wet tissue for the foreseeable future, but the foreseeable future was pretty goddamn short. The Faceless were coming. And I didn't believe that they wanted a treaty. Nobody believed that. They wanted what they'd always wanted: to wipe us out.

That's why women weren't allowed on the stations. What's

the best way to annihilate your enemies? You break the breeding cycle. Your enemies can't breed without their women. Well, humans can't. Who the hell knows about anything else out there in the big black? So now the Earth had a web of stations tracking in its night sky, protecting our most precious resource: our women.

It was stupid, my girlfriend Kaylee said. Well, she'd been my girlfriend when I was sixteen before I got conscripted. *"Why shouldn't girls have the right to work on the stations? Give me a gun, and I'll learn how to use it!"* But she was born in the same shit-hole town I was. I didn't know if the girls from nicer places were that fierce. Shit, fighting Faceless might have felt like a better option for most of the girls in Kopa. Better than the factories, anyway.

"It's not just that they'll kill you," I'd told her, trying to sound more knowledgeable than I was. *"It's that they'll come out of their way to do it. Everyone knows that."*

And you don't put targets on your defenses.

Last I heard Kaylee was getting married to Mark Dimetto, whose parents owned the general store. I wondered if Kaylee would ever tell him she was one of the kids who'd outrun him that night we broke in and he chased us. I could still remember the way my lungs hurt from running. I'd thought my heart would burst out of my ribs. And all we got was a lousy bottle of vodka. That was my farewell present from Kaylee. That, and a handjob under the railway bridge.

I slipped outside the barracks into the hallway, and I felt it. It was like I'd stepped into a fog. Weariness washed over me. I was tired, but I wasn't. *He* was tired, I realized; I was just feeling an echo. The walk from the med bay had worn him out, and our brief separation had taken its toll. His heart wasn't in sync with mine anymore. It was tachy. It had an echo as well, an echo I could sense without touching.

Weird. And maybe creepy as well, but now wasn't the time to dwell on that. Now he needed me.

He was leaning against the wall, looking at the floor. His hair had fallen forward, hiding the angles of his face.

"Hey," I said and reached out my hand.

Rushton didn't even look up. He just raised his palm to where he knew my hand would be, and we touched. I spread my fingers, and his curled through them.

A faint look of disgust passed between our armed escorts. I didn't need telepathy to read it: faggots.

Fuck, I wish.

"You wish?" Rushton murmured. He looked up and raised his eyebrows. His lips curled into a faint, teasing smile.

I made a face. "Less weird, I meant."

Electricity crackled between our palms.

His smile grew. "Yeah."

Doc knotted his bushy eyebrows together and looked at us keenly. "Okay?"

I nodded. "We're good."

Jesus, what we must have looked like walking down those hallways hand in hand. Doc offered to carry my pack, but I didn't let him. I'd really feel like a girl then. There weren't many guys in the hallways at that hour, but the few we passed couldn't stop staring. Was that because Rushton was famous, or because we were holding hands?

We crammed into the lift at the end of the hallway. When the doors opened, we were on level three of the Inner Ring: officers' quarters. It was quieter. The hallways were narrower, and I knew what that meant even before the doors to our room opened: the space had been sacrificed in the hallways so that the rooms were bigger.

Holy hell. I'd spent three years living in a cramped barracks with forty-one other guys. And it was one barracks room in a whole hallway of them. This was a wide, open room, with a *window*. We were high enough up on the Inner Ring that the window overlooked the curve of the Outer Ring, straight out past it into the black. A rush of dizziness overtook me.

Rushton tightened his grip. *"You're okay, Garrett."*

The window wasn't the only luxury I hadn't seen in a long time. There was another one: a private bathroom. Well, not exactly private, but I'd never shared a bathroom with fewer than two other people—Dad and Lucy—so this was like a five-star hotel. And it was better than anything I'd seen since getting to Defender Three, where I showered with any number of those same forty-one guys I bunked with. I wouldn't have to stow everything in a locker here. I wouldn't have to worry about some bastard stealing my razor if I left it on the sink.

I dropped my pack on the floor.

There was only one bed, and I looked at it wonderingly. Not for the reason our armed escorts were trying not to snigger, though. A real bed. A double bed, with a proper mattress. No more fucking burns from canvas that was too new, or putting your foot through canvas that was too old. Or worse, waking up to a weird ripping sound and suddenly having O'Shea crashing down on top of you. *"What the fuck? What the fuck?"* he'd gasped, and I couldn't fucking say a thing because all the wind had been knocked out of me. Everyone had laughed about that for weeks, but they weren't the ones with cracked ribs.

Assholes.

"I'm on call if you need me, Garrett," Doc said. "If you need anything else, get one of the marines to radio for it."

"Yeah, Doc," I said, and he left us.

The doors slid shut, and I heard the mechanism lock.

So this was how I was going to spend the rest of my life: locked in a room with Cameron Rushton. Shit, at least I'd have a real bed, right? At least I wouldn't have to run laps or climb the wall. Could have been worse. I just would have liked to see my dad and Lucy again. The need grew inside me, a real, physical ache that settled in my tight chest.

Rushton frowned. "It's not the end. He wants peace."

"Whatever," I said. I didn't want to talk about the Faceless and Kai-Ren the battle regent or whatever the hell it called itself. I didn't need to know the name of the thing that was coming to kill me. I dropped his hand. "I've got to piss."

A shiver ran up my spine as my body read his fear of abandonment. My guts twisted, and I gasped. How was that fucking fair?

"I'll be quick," I muttered.

When I came out of the bathroom, he was lying on the bed. I swallowed. This would be awkward, probably. I thought back to the teasing smile he'd shown me outside the barracks, and my heart beat a little faster. I was fairly certain he was gay. I just didn't know why I wasn't more panicked by that idea.

"Any preference?" Rushton asked me.

"Excuse me?" It was a nicer way of saying, *What the fuck?*

He snorted, like he knew exactly what I was thinking. He did, right?

"Which side of the bed do you want, Garrett?"

"Oh," I said, the heat rising in my face. "I don't care."

He shifted over. I fetched my book out of my pack and settled down beside him. Our fingers linked together, and after a moment, our heartbeats synchronized. Jesus, if a thirty-second toilet break threw him out of whack, it was going to be awkward when I needed to shit.

"I'm getting stronger all the time," he told me. "Tomorrow I'll be better, I think."

"But you don't know?" I asked.

"No, I don't know." He was silent for a while. Then he said, "You're warm."

"What?"

"Your hand's warm," he said in a low voice. "Not cold. It's nice, you know, after..."

Don't fucking tell me. I don't want to know. Fuck. Please don't.

His gaze faltered. "Sorry."

My heartbeat raced—so did his—as I tried to swallow down my fear. I frowned at my book, and he stared out at the black.

A faint sense of wonderment crept up on me as I read, and it had nothing to do with the book. I'd read it a thousand times. It took me a second to realize it was coming from Rushton.

"I haven't seen these stars in a long time," he said. "It's like being back on Eight."

"Is Eight as shitty as Three?" I muttered, refusing to turn and look out the window.

He smiled. "Yeah, I guess so. Don't you like the view?"

"What I don't like," I said, "is knowing there's only a thin sheet of glass between me and a fucking vacuum."

And feeling the black creep up my fucking spine like it was now.

His smile grew. "It's not glass, Garrett."

"That's not the point," I muttered. "I just don't like it, all right?"

"All right," he said. His gaze was drawn to the window again. I could see the stars reflected in his green eyes. "I was a pilot. I love the black. I always did."

"After everything?" I asked in surprise.

His smile faded.

"Sorry," I said. *Real smart, Garrett.*

He changed the subject. "What are you reading?"

I flushed. "Fairy tales."

"Really?" He shifted closer and reached out to tilt the book so he could see the page.

The book was old and tatty. It had belonged to my mother. She'd read to me when I was a kid. I could remember her voice still, but not her face. I knew all the stories in that book by heart, but I liked to look at the dog-eared pages and the illustrations that had been scrawled over in crayon by my mother and then by me, a generation apart. We'd both had a go at writing our names inside the front cover in awkward childish letters: *This book belongs to: Jessica. Brady.* And there was a new scrawl from Lucy in the bottom corner. It was the one thing I had from home.

Jesus. I didn't want to die on this fucking station. I wanted to go home. I *had* to go home.

Rushton raised himself up onto his elbow and stared at me intently. His green eyes widened. "It's not war, Garrett, I promise. He wants peace."

"Yeah," I said. My heart skipped a beat when he lifted his free hand to touch my face. "Whatever."

"Can't you tell that it's true?" he asked.

His fingers were cool on my cheek, or I was suddenly hot, or something. I swallowed and tried not to think about how good that touch felt. It was just biochemistry and electricity. "I know that you think it's true. But how do I know you're not an idiot?"

He smiled slightly and leaned closer.

He was close, too close. My mouth was dry, and my heart beat faster. I don't know what I thought would happen. No, I do. I thought he'd kiss me. Fuck, I thought he'd lean down and kiss me. And I thought I'd let him.

His breath tickled my ear. "You'll just have to trust me, Garrett."

He leaned away again. I sighed with relief, or maybe disappointment. Shit, I don't know.

"Yeah, whatever," I said again, hating the way my voice, pitched too high, wavered.

He flopped back down onto the mattress and closed his eyes. "Read your book. I'm going to sleep."

Like I could concentrate on my book. I closed it instead and shoved it under the pillow. I squeezed my eyes shut and lay there and wished I didn't have to hold his hand. And wished I didn't like it.

And then I couldn't sleep for ages.

CHAPTER SIX

THE NEXT DAY there was an evacuation drill. Doc came and sat with Rushton and me, and we listened to the sounds of the siren. In theory a station like Defender Three could be evacuated of all personnel in twenty-eight minutes, provided there were enough Shitboxes, which there never were, and provided that the Faceless would give us twenty-eight minutes, which they never would. They'd destroyed Defender Five in under ten minutes, and everyone was probably already asphyxiated by the time the explosion took out the reactor core. And that was a long time ago. I bet the Faceless had improved their weaponry since. We were like insects to them, after all. One slap and we were dead.

"This is a waste of time," I said. The siren was annoying the shit out of me. It was the usual high-pitched Klaxon: *awooga, awooga, awooga.* In the event of the real thing they wouldn't play the accompanying audio: *"This is a drill. Proceed to your evacuation point. This is a drill."*

"It distracts the men from their endless speculation," Doc said mildly, looking out the window.

"How does an evac drill take anyone's mind off what might be coming?" I muttered. "Doesn't it point to the obvious?"

Doc flashed me a smile before turning to gaze out the window again. "It gives them the feeling they're doing something," he said. "So they're not just sitting around waiting."

Like we are, I thought and looked over at Rushton.

He was lying on the bed, reading a magazine that Doc had brought. Some tech magazine, I thought, although I'd only got a glimpse of the cover before he took it. Privileges of rank, I guess. I was stuck with the second magazine: a travel magazine from Six Delta. If I was ever on a driving tour through Old Quebec, there was this quaint little B and B...that would be toast just like the rest of the planet in a fortnight.

Looked too fucking cold anyway.

Rushton smiled then, at something he'd read or at my bad temper, or maybe the thought of me slipping and sliding and landing on my ass in a snowdrift.

It was weird sharing my head with someone else. As near as I could figure it out, we didn't share everything, exactly. We shared that place where things usually went unsaid: the sarcastic comments you bit back before they got you in trouble or the words that you formed as articulate sentences in the front of your brain but you didn't say aloud. Those were as clear as day. The conscious mind—that is, the part of the mind that knows it is thinking—had a voice we both heard. And it was weird.

The subconscious was different. Feelings and vague, unformed ideas—I got a sense of them, but they weren't spelled out. That was even weirder.

The dreams were the weirdest of all. With our conscious minds shut down, we shared our dreams totally. It was crazy. I dreamed of darkness and of flashing lights and of weird hissing noises that tried to talk to me. And in those dreams I was cold and frightened, and my heart beat so fast I could hardly breathe. For some reason, the dreams always made my cock hard. His freakish wet dream was my freakish wet dream. If his body reacted, so did mine. And don't ask me why flashing lights and weird noises and fear turned him on. I knew it was something to do with the Faceless—those dreams had *alien* written all over them—and I didn't want to fucking know anything else.

In his waking hours Rushton seemed normal. I was the only one who knew how fucked-up his dreams were. I didn't want to know. I was just the poor bunny along for the ride. Sucked to be me.

I figured Doc's visits would keep me on the right side of sane.

I shivered as he ran the stethoscope over my bare back.

"Deep breaths," he reminded me.

The slight wheeze when I inhaled reminded me that I'd gone for days without a cigarette, and that Hooper still owed me that packet. Probably not much chance of collecting on that now.

Doc didn't comment on the wheeze. "All right," he said at last. "Your turn, Rushton."

This was our routine from now on. After the marines delivered our breakfast, Doc came and took our blood pressure, listened to our hearts, and drew blood. He also gave us vitamin shots. The inside of my elbow looked like a junkie's already.

I sat down on the floor with my magazine and tried to get interested in pictures of autumnal leaves in Old Quebec. Green to yellow to orange to red to brown to nothing. Such is life. I'd never seen seasons like that. In Kopa we had two seasons: dry and wet. Drought and flood. It was harsh country, but it was all I ever knew, and it was the only place I wanted to be.

Not spinning in a tin can in the big black.

I heard Rushton's sharp intake of breath as Doc pressed the stethoscope against his skin. I felt it too, in the shiver that ran down my back. The examinations made him uncomfortable. He tensed with embarrassment every time he was touched. Doc was a good guy, but after four years with the Faceless Rushton was sick of being studied like a thing.

I shifted up onto the bed and held out my hand. Rushton bowed his head as he breathed nice and deep for Doc. His hair hung over his eyes, but it didn't matter. He knew I was there without looking.

He reached out his hand to mine. Our fingers entwined, electricity prickled our skin, and our heartbeats synchronized. He lifted his head to look at me and smiled.

"Thanks."

Was it weird that I was starting to enjoy the little spikes of lust that thrilled through him when we touched? That thrilled through *us?* I liked the way he looked at me. I liked the way his touch made my heart beat a little faster. I liked the way he needed me. I liked the way I was important to him.

It wouldn't last. Either we'd die like I thought, or Kai-Ren would fix this connection thing like Rushton said. Maybe, either way, it was okay to enjoy it while it lasted.

It had me stuffed how Rushton knew what I was thinking when half the time I didn't. Did I *want* to want him now? I couldn't fucking tell. I only knew I liked the buzz of electricity when we touched.

We'd shared our first shower that morning. It shouldn't have felt so strange. I'd showered with guys before, with heaps of guys, but with just the two of us it had been awkward. I couldn't help but look at him. And trying to avoid his eyes by looking down had been a mistake, because suddenly I'd been looking right at his cock. I could have forgiven him his morning glory if the sight of it hadn't caused my own cock to harden. After that I'd had to turn away and face the wall and hope it didn't look like a fucking invitation. I'd burned with shame under the hot jets, and it was no good pretending nothing had happened because he could read my fucking mind. My heart raced, which was no good for him.

"*Garrett,*" he'd said, and I'd heard the panic in his voice.

I'd turned around to find him swaying on his feet. I'd caught him around the wrists, and we'd stood facing each other until he was stronger. I'd known then that my embarrassment didn't matter, and neither did his courtesy. I hadn't touched him the whole time we'd been in the shower because I wasn't a faggot, and Rushton was too much of a nice guy to force the issue. So it had to be me who manned up and reminded myself of my responsibilities.

And I kind of liked the way the electricity when we touched made us both shiver.

Rushton tightened his fingers around mine and turned his head to look at me as Doc listened to his heartbeat. Our heartbeat.

Rushton's hair curtained his face, and I resisted the urge to reach forward with my free hand and wipe his hair away from his brilliant green eyes. And maybe trace the pads of my fingers along his jawline.

Fuck! Where did that come from?

My first instinct was to pull away from Rushton, but I didn't. And it wasn't just about the fact that I'd almost let him collapse in the shower. It was more about the fact I liked this.

Rushton's lips quirked in a shy smile, and color rose in his cheeks.

The night before I'd expected him to kiss me, and I would have let it happen, passive. Now I wanted to push him down onto the bed and kiss him instead. I wanted to hold his head still by twisting my fingers in his hair. I wanted to lie against him so he could feel my erection pressing into him. Hell, I wanted to feel his pressing back.

If Doc hadn't been there, fuck knows what I would have done.

———

I WOKE UP WITH A START. I was lying next to Rushton. He was nestled into my side, with one arm lying across my chest. I shifted slightly, not wanting to wake him but needing to shake off that dream somehow.

I'd dreamed of a Faceless. It had towered over me. I'd been restrained somehow, hanging from my wrists. I couldn't move, and it was behind me breathing down my neck. Its breath was cool, and it hissed at me like a reptile. And I just hung there, the muscles in my shoulders burning, waiting for the Faceless to strike. Waiting for fucking fangs.

Christ. Where had that come from? From Rushton or from the recesses of my own fucked-up imagination? It was terrifying.

Rushton stretched. "Garrett?" he murmured. "You okay?"

"Yeah," I said in the darkness. "Just had a weird dream."

"Okay," he murmured and rubbed his hand against my sternum. Not as fucking relaxing as he intended. "You want me to sleep on the window side?"

Like I was a little kid. I flushed. "Okay."

We jostled against each other as we shifted position. For a moment I was lying underneath him, and I was afraid my body would respond, but then we'd rolled away from each other.

"You really hate space?" he asked, turning his head to look at me in the gloom.

"I really hate it," I said.

"Why?" He reached out and linked his fingers through mine.

Our heartbeats synchronized.

"Because it's cold and black, and it'll fucking suck the air out of you until your lungs burst and your eyeballs pop out," I said. "Isn't that enough?"

He smiled. "I guess."

We lay there for a little while longer. I still couldn't properly shake that dream. It was still lurking there in the back of my mind. I was afraid that if I went to sleep, I'd fall straight back into it.

"I like the vastness," Rushton said at last. "I always found it liberating to feel that insignificant. So small, and so privileged to be a part of the wonder of the universe. Time and space and eternity."

I raised my eyebrows. That's what my dad would call a five-dollar education. It dressed up any sort of bullshit to sound pretty.

"The universe is vast," he said.

I made a face. "Mine isn't."

Rushton sighed. "When you were a kid, didn't you ever look up at the stars and let them take your breath away? Didn't you ever wonder what it would be like to be up there?"

"Now I know," I said. "And it sucks."

Rushton didn't answer, so I relented a bit.

"I like the stars fine from Earth," I said. "But it's bad enough being up here on the station, where a single machine breaks down, and you can't breathe. Or an air lock blows, and you're all fucked. It stuffs me why you'd want to jump in a Hawk and put even less protection between yourself and a vacuum that will rip your body apart from the inside out."

All Hawk pilots were crazy, Hooper said. And he knew crazy.

"It's beautiful out there," Rushton said and turned his face to the window. "Chasing starlight."

His sense of wonder settled over me like a soft breath, and I pushed it away.

"Bad shit comes from space. Shit that will kill us all." I stared at the ceiling and drew a shaky breath. And there was the dream again, at the back of my mind: hanging in the darkness and cold, waiting for that thing to strike. "I like dirt on my feet and sunlight on my back and all the air in the world."

He squeezed my hand. "Sunlight is just starlight. You're chasing it as well."

"I'm not chasing anything," I said. "I just want to do my time and go home."

We lay silently for a while, and then Rushton turned toward me and slid his hand up under my T-shirt.

"What the hell!" I tried to wrench away.

He pressed his palm against my sternum. "Just close your eyes for a second, Garrett. Don't freak out."

Don't freak out? Was he serious?

"Just close your eyes," he said, and I heard the smile in his voice. I didn't know if I trusted it. "I'm not going to jump you."

"Whatever," I muttered, wishing my heart wasn't thumping so fast against his palm.

"Close your eyes," he repeated.

I squeezed my eyes shut unwillingly and told myself I could throw him off if I really had to. If I really wanted to. *Shit.*

He spread his fingers out, and my skin prickled. My breath hitched in my throat, and my cock stirred. *Shit. Shit, shit, shit.* A thousand times *shit.*

"Don't freak out," Rushton said again, his breath hot against my ear. "Just *feel.*"

I swallowed. He wasn't holding me down with any real force, so why wasn't I moving? What the hell was wrong with me? I swiped my tongue against my dry lips and wished I hadn't. What if he took it as an invitation? Would he kiss me? Did I want him to kiss me?

"Just feel." His voice was low.

I drew a deep breath and held it for a moment. When I let it out, I felt all my resistance go with it.

I was in a dark place, but this time I wasn't scared. I turned and blinked, and light caught in my lashes. Starlight.

I pressed against the window, my fingers splayed.

It was beautiful. I stared into the big black, and it revealed itself to me. Layers upon layers peeled away. Midnight blue and purple and orange and white. It was a kaleidoscope, except I was the one turning inside it. Slowly spinning in the middle of eternity. So much color. So much beauty. It was a revelation.

I pressed forward, and the window yielded under my touch. Like skin.

I was in the pod. I was floating in space in the Faceless pod. Surrounded by that weird milky fluid, filling my lungs with it. And I wasn't afraid. Why wasn't I afraid?

"Do you feel it?" It seemed as though his voice came from far away.

"Yeah." I sighed, turning my head to see the colors. I was so small, less than a speck of dust in the vast writhing cauldron of space. And I wasn't afraid, because I was a part of it. Whatever happened, I wouldn't be afraid.

I drifted, listening to my heartbeat, with eyes wide open.

"Okay, Garrett," Rushton murmured in my ear. "It's okay. You can come back now."

Okay.

It was like waking very slowly from a dream.

I blinked a few times. I was looking at the ceiling. I turned my head, and Rushton's face was very close to mine. I could feel his breath on my lips. "What was that?"

He smiled slightly. "That was a memory."

"I thought you were unconscious in that pod," I whispered. I couldn't stop looking at his lips.

They curled again. "It's hard to explain. Sometimes I opened my eyes. I wasn't awake exactly, but I saw."

"Didn't it scare you?" I asked.

He shook his head and lifted a hand to brush his hair out of his eyes. "No. I knew where I was going. I knew Kai-Ren would make sure I got here."

The mention of the Faceless made me anxious. I shifted to put some distance between us. "Sorry we cut you out. We didn't know."

He shrugged. "Doesn't matter."

"I thought you were dead," I said, shivering suddenly.

"Just dreaming," he answered. He reached for my hand again.

Electricity sparked between us, and I shivered again and wondered what it would feel like if we were pressed together, flesh to flesh.

And maybe he heard the thought, because his eyes widened in the gloom.

"Sorry," I muttered and turned away.

"It's okay," he said, settling back down beside me.

I'm probably not even his type.

Before I could even wonder where the hell that thought had come from, I had his answer: *"You could be."*

Fuck. I wrenched myself upright, pulling my hand away from his and heading for the safety of the bathroom. I slammed the door shut, shoved the seat down on the toilet, and sat there shaking.

Fuck, fuck, fuck. What the hell was the matter with me? *I'm not gay. I'm not gay. I'm not gay.* So how come I had a hard-on?

"Garrett?"

I jerked my head up. "I need a minute."

"I'm coming in." He gave it a moment and then opened the door. He hit the switch, and I squinted as fluorescent light flooded the bathroom. Great. What was that line from Shakespeare? *Must I hold a candle to my shames?*

He raised his eyebrows.

"Yeah, I know some Shakespeare," I muttered. "Fucking surprised?"

"A little," he admitted.

I might have left school at twelve, but we had books. The Shakespeare belonged to my mother. Every time Dad had to sell some books, we kept the Shakespeare. You have to read Shakespeare, my dad reckoned. I liked the tragedies, even if I didn't understand every word. Dad liked the histories. My mother, he told me, had liked the sonnets. Her favorite was the one about love being an ever-fixéd mark. *It is the star to every wandering bark, whose worth's unknown, although his height be taken.* Turns out Shakespeare was chasing starlight as well.

"Well, we're not all ignorant reffos in the north," I told Rushton.

He showed me a faint smile. "And we're not all latte-drinking faggots in the south."

Fucking touché.

He sighed and crouched down on the floor in front of me. "I know what this is about."

"That's the fucking problem," I muttered.

He wrinkled his nose. "I was the same with Kai-Ren at the beginning. Because he knew everything, *everything* I was thinking. And it was awful. So I guess I'm trying to say that you don't have to be afraid of whatever random crap you think. I've been there. I won't think any less of you."

I glared at him.

La la la la la. What am I thinking of now, asshole? Not sex. Aw, shit.

Rushton laughed. He threw his head back, and the light gleamed on his throat. "Garrett, you're killing me!"

"Not yet," I said, "but I'm keeping my options open."

He held out his hand. I took it almost unwillingly.

"I'm sorry about all this," he said. "I am. I know how uncomfortable it makes you, and I wish we didn't have to do it."

"Not your fault," I muttered. I relaxed slightly. Maybe there was nothing to freak out about. I could trust him not to blurt out all my secrets, couldn't I? And we'd all be dead soon enough. Not that I should have found that comforting at all. Just grasping at straws, I guess.

Rushton stood up, still holding my hand. "So let's try and get some sleep, okay?"

"Okay," I said, standing up.

We headed back into the bedroom. He lay down on the window side of the bed again.

I shoved a pillow under my head. "Look, thanks for before."

I didn't have to tell him I was talking about him showing me his memories.

"That's okay."

"Space has always freaked me out a bit," I said, forcing a smile. "Maybe I won't have nightmares this time."

Rushton was silent for a long while. When he spoke at last, his voice was soft. "Sorry."

I twisted my neck to look at him. "What for?"

His face was grave in the gloom. "Those aren't your nightmares. Those are mine."

CHAPTER SEVEN

ANOTHER DAY into our joint detention and I was ready to climb the walls. Sharing a room with Rushton was bad enough. Sharing a bed was a whole other level of torture.

"I've had enough of this!" I said, twisting away.

But Rushton was right there, as always. Right fucking beside me, his fingers around my wrist.

I'd never wanted to be back in the barracks so much in my life. Screw this big room with its big bed and its bathroom and its dizzying view of the silver stars glinting in the black. I didn't fucking care. Give me my narrow canvas cot and O'Shea's snoring any day. This was beyond claustrophobic.

The problem was sharing the bed, and sharing his head. Rushton's dreams had gotten more focused, and most of them—I hoped to hell they weren't mine—seemed to involve cock. Not that I was a homophobe. I mean, Jesus, I'd been on Defender Three for three years, and there were no girls, so sometimes some shit happened that you didn't exactly write home about, but you weren't supposed to dream about it either. You weren't supposed to want it. You settled for it; that was all. Or if you were an asshole like Wade, you took it even if the other guy wasn't into it.

But suddenly I was dreaming of cock. Fisting it, sucking it, riding it, in glorious fucking Technicolor. And the worst part was both nights it had happened I'd woken up with a raging hard-on and had to race into the shower and beat off quickly. I had it down to about a minute and a half, because any longer than that apart and Rushton would start to flag.

He was slowly getting stronger; that was true. He looked a million times better than when we'd got him out of the Faceless pod, but it wasn't fast enough for me. I needed my own space. I needed him out of my fucking head.

"I've had enough!"

"I'm sorry!" His fingers caught around my wrist. His face was red, all the way to the roots of his light brown hair. He knew exactly what this was about. "I'm sorry."

"Yeah, whatever, LT," I said, turning away from him. I sat up and put my feet on the floor, but I didn't pull my wrist away. I couldn't, could I? Turning my back was the only way I could get any distance between us at all, but it wasn't enough.

I'd started calling him LT because I couldn't bring myself to call him *sir*. It's hard to call a guy sir when every night you see him in your dreams, on his fucking knees like that. When every night you *are* him in your dreams. I knew exactly how his mouth watered when he tasted cock. I knew exactly how he moaned *Chris, Chris, Chris,* when he wanted to make that other guy come.

"Hawk pilots are all faggots," Hooper used to say. Turns out he was right in Rushton's case.

I looked out the window at the black and tried not to remember the taste of cum. Because it hadn't really happened. "Look, how long is it going to take until you don't need me, LT?"

"I don't know." His voice was low. "The more contact we have, the stronger I get. Maybe we can speed it up."

I tensed. It was hard not to jump to conclusions when I'd been inside his dreams. And they were vivid dreams. Jesus, even the rasp of my zipper when I took a piss meant something different to me now: it caused a frisson of excitement I couldn't ignore. Eyes closed, waiting for Chris to walk up behind me. Waiting to feel his warm hands slide around my hips. Waiting for him to pull me back and... And who the hell was Chris anyway? I didn't even know the guy, so I sure as shit didn't deserve to be haunted by him.

"How do you mean?" I asked, trying to keep my voice level.

"Lie down," he said.

Aw, Jesus. This could not be a good idea. I'd spent most of the night dreaming of some guy I'd never even met, dreaming of sucking him off and then riding him, and now Rushton wanted me to lie down? My heart raced, and so did his probably, and that was the worst. Not because I was nervous, but because he knew I was. There were no fucking secrets between us. That was what decided me in the end. If I refused, he'd know it was because I was embarrassed. So I didn't refuse.

He was lying on his side, facing away from me, and he drew my arm over him.

I put my head on the pillow and closed my eyes.

I was spooning a superior officer. Never thought that would happen. I snorted with amusement.

"It's not exactly how I imagined the service either, Garrett," he murmured, and I could hear the smile in his voice.

"It creeps me out when you do that, LT," I told the back of his head. His hair smelled nice. Shit, what if he'd heard me think that?

"Sorry," he said.

We lay like that for a while.

"Do you feel stronger?" I asked.

He shifted, and I realized he was pulling off his T-shirt. He shrugged it off, and my gaze fell onto his shoulders and the line of his spine and the way it twisted when he pulled his shirt over his head. I could see the play of his muscles under his skin. And that skin, slightly golden—so different from mine, so different from anyone's on Defender Three.

"Two," he said.

"Two what?" I asked.

"There were two suns." He settled back onto the mattress, settled back toward me. "A twin solar system. Take off your shirt, Garrett."

I sighed and obeyed. Hell, it might work, right? Skin-on-skin contact, and it didn't have to mean anything. It just would have been a hell of a lot easier to do if I didn't know what he dreamed about. What we both did.

I dropped my shirt on the floor and put my arm back over him. My forearm grazed against his hip, and then I shifted closer. My chest met his back, and we both gasped as we felt it: the tickle of electricity where we touched.

"Fuck," he murmured. "That's it."

I felt dizzy and blinked it away. "Yeah."

"Tell me about Lucy," he said.

A slow smile spread across my face. His weren't the only dreams we shared, apparently.

"My baby Lucy," I said. I was tired. I thought I could hear the air crackling around us. "I miss my Lucy."

I thought of the sound of her laugh and how she squealed when I tickled her. I remembered the mornings when I was getting our breakfast ready and how Lucy would sleep in her cot until I had to wake her. I'd brush my hand against her downy hair and watch as her eyes flickered open, and she would smile and reach her fat little starfish hands up toward me.

"She's seven now," I said. Could he see her face as clearly as I could? Could he feel how much I loved her? After Linda left, I was stuck with Lucy. Twelve years old, I'd quit school to look after her. I wore her in a sling. Her heartbeat against mine all day; when I put her in her cot at night, I'd feel like a part of me was missing.

God. Would I feel like that when Rushton didn't need me anymore?

He linked his fingers in mine and sighed.

I thought of Lucy, my heartbeat. Missed her. Missed Dad.

"You got family, LT?" I murmured.

"Yeah."

"How come I don't know that?"

"I keep it on lockdown."

"You can do that?" I'd never been good at hiding my thoughts, and that was before some guy was living in my head. Every insubordinate thought I'd ever had got written plain across my face, which is why I was usually in the shit for something. "I don't know how to do that."

"I don't want you to," Rushton whispered.

He nestled closer. His hair tickled my lips. His flesh was so warm where we touched. He shifted his hips, and then his ass was pressed against me. My cock hardened in my pants, but I was too tired to pull away.

"Feels good," he murmured, and thought: *Chris.*

I sighed, and I wasn't sure why. It was natural he'd think of his...his—boyfriend? lover?—of Chris when he was lying in someone's embrace. It was totally natural. So what was the strange sting I felt? Jealousy? How could it be? It had to be the chemical process that connected us, and nothing else. I wasn't gay, and I didn't even know Cameron Rushton.

"It's Cam," he murmured.

"What?" I breathed in the scent of his hair.

"Cam," he said. "I always hated Cameron."

"Oh," I managed, closing my eyes. "Okay. Cam."

MOST TERRIFYING DREAM EVER.

"Cam-ren. Cam-ren. Cam-ren." It was like a sibilant hiss. The sound of it made my chest tighten and my throat constrict. My breath came in shallow gasps. Every nerve in my body was on edge. It was close. It was so close.

"Cam-ren." I could feel breath on my skin, leaving a trail of gooseflesh.

Oh God.

I couldn't see. Why couldn't I see?

Oh fuck. Something scraped up my bare ribs, exerting just enough pressure to sting. Something sharp and thin and pointed. A claw? Jesus, was it a claw? I twisted my head from side to side, but I couldn't see. I was blindfolded. I was naked. I tried to twist away, and I couldn't move either. I was chained, wrists and ankles, and I couldn't move.

My arms were pulled above my head. My shoulders hurt when I tried to move. Pain flashed down my spine. My bare feet scrabbled on the floor but couldn't get purchase. I couldn't get away. There was nothing to do but take it.

I felt a sudden stinging pain in my neck, and I whimpered. Not a claw, then—a syringe. I could feel the drug—the *poison?*—coursing through my blood as though it was as thick and heavy as molasses. I felt my heart pump and squeeze. Drowsiness followed, and then I didn't feel anything at all. It stole my fear.

"Cam-ren."

No, not all my fear. There was still some of it when I heard that voice. There was enough to make my breath hitch in my dry throat.

Another whimper escaped me as a hand brushed over my hip. It was cold. My body jerked, but there was nowhere to go. A second hand on my other hip. *oh God, oh God*, but I only sighed.

The touch of those hands started off featherlight, ghosting over my skin. Long fingers slid over my ribs, explored the shivering planes of my body, and moved up to settle on the racing pulse point in my throat.

There was a Faceless touching me and—*Oh shit*. Every touch of those cool fingers brought me out in gooseflesh. Pain would have been better. Pain I would have understood. This, fuck, this was almost nice. This sent tiny shivers of pleasure to my balls. This made my cock twitch. Why couldn't he just kill me?

"*Cam-ren.*" I could feel its breath on the back of my neck. Not warm, like a man's. It was as cool as its touch. It was a cold-blooded thing.

Those cool fingers counted the knots in my spine, moving lower and lower down my trembling back. I tried to speak—couldn't. My head hung forward. *Please, please no.* My numb lips couldn't form the words.

And then my cock hardened, and the thing behind me hissed again: a low, amused sound of approval. Fingers traced down the crease of my ass, and my whole body shook.

No, no, no. Oh God, no.

A single long finger probed around the entrance to my body. It pressed, and the muscles suddenly yielded. I made a noise then: a drawn-out whine like an animal.

No, please! But my cock was still hard. I shook my head from side to side. My face was wet with tears and snot, and I still couldn't form an articulate word. And that cool finger pushed inside me, stinging at first before the pain transformed into a familiar ache. The finger curled, and a thin nail scraped against the bundle of nerve endings inside. Pleasure sparked. My balls tightened, and my cock jutted up. *No, not like this. Not like this.*

I whimpered again.

"*Cam-ren. Cam-ren.*"

It removed the finger, and I slumped in the chains. *Just fucking kill me. Please, just kill me. Not this.*

It growled, and then its cool hands were parting my buttocks.

"*Cam-ren,*" it hissed again, and I felt the large head of the Faceless's cock nudging against my asshole. It pushed forward.

White pain flared in front of my eyes.

I screamed.

———

MY EYES FLASHED OPEN. I could feel Cameron Rushton —*Cam*—trembling. I was too, I think. I was cold. I was as cold as if that thing had just touched me for real.

"*Your hand's warm,*" he'd told me that first night. "*It's nice, you know, after...*"

Don't fucking tell me, I'd thought. *Please don't.*

His dreams had done it for him.

It was late. The lights had dimmed. It must have been past last bell, but I couldn't look at my watch without shifting. And at that moment I didn't want to move. I wasn't sure if I could. Jesus, I thought I could still feel breath on my back. My skin crawled.

"Did that really happen to you?" I asked in the darkness.

I knew he was awake. I could feel it.

He released a shaking sigh, and his answer slipped off the end of it, a slow breath of regret: "Yeah."

His back was slick with sweat.

I'd felt his fear. It was still in me now, twisting in my unsettled guts like ice. It pressed down on my chest. It tasted like bile in the back of my throat.

"Oh Jesus." I wanted to be sick. My hand shook where it rested on the curve of his hip, on the place where his skin met the fabric of his waistband.

He reached back and curled his fingers through mine. "It's okay."

"It's *not* fucking okay, LT." My voice caught in my throat. I wanted to pull away, to break our contact, to let him slip away. I wanted him out of my head, but it was too late for that. I couldn't unfeel it, couldn't unsee it.

He squeezed my hand. "It's just a memory."

I exhaled, and his hair feathered. The skin on the back of his neck looked soft. "Scared me."

He sighed. "It was a long time ago." He was silent for a while. "I'm sorry for the things I dream, Garrett."

"You can't help it," I said. "Jesus, I know that. I'm just sorry that shit happened to you."

His voice was quiet. "It wasn't like that every time. One memory isn't the whole picture."

A strange sort of quietness stole over us, calming my rapid heartbeat, calming Cam's. It was the quietness of the afterglow, I think. A soothing touch after a frightening one, a whispered endearment after a throaty cry. I felt the truth then, and it scared me more than the dream: Cam didn't hate the Faceless. He didn't hate Kai-Ren. After that first time he'd liked it.

Fear and shame shivered down his spine. He was afraid he'd disgust me.

"Shit," I whispered to the dark. "For real, LT?"

He turned his face into the pillow. "Yeah."

"I don't hate you," I told him. "Maybe I don't understand you, but I don't hate you."

"Thanks," he murmured, his voice heavy with sleep. He was beginning to drift again, and I drifted with him. And caught in that place just before sleep, his memories shifted from the Faceless and back to Chris. It was Cam's wet dream, and I was just along for the ride. There was no fear this time; there was just desire. Hard bodies touching. Lips meeting. Hands everywhere.

If I fought sleep, maybe I wouldn't have to share his dream. I knew from experience that I'd share his physical reaction, but maybe I wouldn't have to see the accompanying pictures.

He can't help what he dreams.

I knew that; I did. I was just tired of being in his head. I was tired of feeling desire that wasn't mine. I was tired of responding to it.

My cock hardened. *Shit.* Was that a filthy idea skittering through his skull or mine?

I eased away from him gently, intending to head straight for the toilet and jerk off.

"Don't," he whispered in the darkness. "Please, Chris."

"It's not Chris," I muttered. "It's Garrett, LT."

"Stay." He sighed. "Please stay, Brady."

"I gotta, um..." I said, swallowing. "I gotta take care of this."

I should have been beyond embarrassment, the things we'd shared in those dreams, but Jesus, I could feel myself flushing just thinking about how we were lying, about how I was hard and how it felt so good with my cock pressed up against his ass. It was in my head now. All his memories, all his desires. But I wasn't Chris. I was Brady Garrett, lowly fucking recruit, and he was a lieutenant. I saluted guys like him. I didn't fucking spoon them, and I sure as hell didn't do anything else.

"Just stay," he whispered. "Let me be close to you. Let me hear you."

If he'd said *watch*, I would have shit myself. But it was dark, and the bed was warm and comfortable, and he'd hear me in the bathroom anyway, wouldn't he? He was already inside my head. Whatever I did, he'd know.

And weren't we already dead? It didn't matter; nothing mattered if we were already dead.

I rolled onto my back, squeezing my eyes shut. I unzipped my fly, pushed my briefs down, and grabbed my cock.

I didn't have a great technique. Until sharing Cam's dreams, I didn't know there was such a thing. Every time I'd ever jerked off I'd done it quickly, quietly, just trying to get it over with. Needing to come was like needing to piss; no point making a fucking production out of it. So what was it about the fact that Cam was lying beside me, listening, that made me want it to last longer?

My cock was hard, jutting up against my stomach, and my balls were tight. Shit, this wouldn't take long at all. I wrapped my fingers around the head and stroked quickly toward the base.

Cam shifted, and I opened my eyes to find him lying on his side looking at me. His face was pale in the darkness.

"Shit, LT!" I gasped. "Don't look at me!"

I tried to roll away, and he caught my shoulder.

"Don't, Brady," he said. "Stay."

Maybe it was because I was tired, maybe it was because it was dark, or maybe it was the sudden intensity in his voice, a note of quiet command that secretly thrilled me, but I stayed. It felt strange to feel someone else's touch while I stroked myself, and my heart beat faster. He splayed his hand across my chest, and the electricity made me tremble.

He kept his eyes on mine. That was good. I think I would have freaked out if he'd tried to look at my cock. Jesus, not that it mattered. I knew he could feel every tiny shudder of pleasure as I worked my cock, each one building on the last and tightening in my balls.

He moved his hand up to my throat, and then my jaw, and gently turned my head toward his. I could feel his breath on my face, and I shivered as I stroked myself faster. I didn't know it could be like this. I didn't know it could feel so intense. It was more than any biochemical connection, I think. It was the fact that he was staring into my eyes in the darkness. I'd never been this close to anyone in my life.

"Gonna come," I gasped, my muscles tensing.

"Do it," he whispered and leaned forward to kiss me.

Oh God. I came, jerking and shuddering, as Cam pressed his lips against mine. Warm semen splashed onto my stomach and chest, dripped from my fingers. I sank back into the mattress, my head still twisted toward Cam's, and lost myself in that kiss.

It was gentle and soft, and it made me shiver. His lips opened slightly, and mine did the same, and then his tongue swiped against my lower lip. I sighed. Felt so nice.

"So good, Brady," he murmured, drawing away. "That was so good."

"Yeah," I said, flushing as the realization hit me. I'd just jerked off for a guy. Not with a guy, when we were both racing the clock and laughing about it, but for a guy. And not just any guy either, but the one who could read my mind. I couldn't pretend it didn't mean anything.

And I'd let him kiss me.

Cam reached down and drew the blankets up over us. I squirmed and made a face in the darkness as he sought out my hand. He had to go for the sticky one, right? I thought he'd realize and let it go, but he didn't. He drew it up to his face and then pressed his lips against it. I felt his tongue against my fingers, tasting my cum, and it was all I could do not to pull away.

"Jesus, LT," I managed shakily.

I could see the starlight from the window reflected in his eyes. "You taste good." He smiled.

Then he lay back, closed his eyes, and drifted off to sleep.

Bastard.

CHAPTER EIGHT

I DON'T KNOW if it was that weird moment we shared in the middle of the night, but Cam was stronger the next day. He only had to press his palm against mine a few times when Commander Leonski came to question him. I stood by silently with my eyes fixed on my boots and pretended I wasn't actively listening.

"Are you a threat to this station and the men on it?" Commander Leonski barked.

"No, sir."

The two armed marines in the doorway told us that the commander wasn't taking any chances.

"Why did the Faceless take you?"

"I don't know, sir," Cam said, but our heart rate rose: lust, shame, and the memory of being touched. "I believe Battle Regent Kai-Ren wanted a translator. I believe it had been an intention of his for some time. But I don't know why they picked me out of everyone on that Sh—that transport."

Commander Leonski rubbed his forehead. "Did they torture you?"

Cam hesitated.

I reached out my hand, and our palms touched. It wasn't for strength this time, at least not physical strength.

Cam squeezed my hand quickly. "I don't believe anything that was done to me was intended as torture. In order to create a chemical bond between us, so that I would learn, I was, *ah—*" He faltered.

I looked up in time to see Commander Leonski narrow his eyes.

"You were what?" he asked.

I hated him for that question, but of course he had to know. It couldn't go unsaid. I just wondered how Cam was going to say it. At the same time understanding spread through me as Cam thought back to what had happened. It hadn't been rape, at least not from the Faceless' point of view. It was intended as a means to facilitate communication. It had been about making a connection.

The Faceless couldn't speak English. They didn't have the same palates or tongues we did. They couldn't form the sounds that made human languages. Kai-Ren couldn't explain what he was doing. But Cam had understood that once the connection had been made. He'd excused Kai-Ren for that first painful violation, because after that it had been good. So fucking good, once they could communicate.

Harder. Faster. More.

And he'd learned so much.

I saw twin suns wheeling in an unfamiliar sky. I saw a city, strange and terrible, with towers that reached up toward the purple heavens. And I saw a glimpse of long white hair, pale skin, and a thin, smiling mouth as a Faceless touched my face: *Kai-Ren.* Holy crap. The face of the thing in my nightmares looked almost human. Almost.

I sucked in a shallow breath, and Cam released my hand.

Commander Leonski stared at us both, and for the first time

it occurred to me that if they shoved Cam out the nearest air lock, I'd be going with him. Because if they didn't trust Cam, they wouldn't trust me either.

"Speak up, Lieutenant," Leonski growled.

Wasn't fair that he was going to make Cam say it in front of those marines. Wasn't fair he was going to make Cam say it at all.

Cam folded his arms across his chest and hunched over slightly. "I was taken by force by Kai-Ren." He cleared his throat. "As I said, it was done to create a bond between us."

Commander Leonski frowned. "You're defending the thing that *raped* you?"

Don't say that word. That word tasted like fucking bile. It was like a fist in my guts.

"It's okay, Brady."

Except how the fuck was it okay? How the fuck was it anything even like okay?

"Take a breath, recruit."

Whatever. He couldn't pull rank on me, could he? After what we'd done?

I took a breath.

"They're aliens," Cam said to the commander. "They're not like us. It wasn't his intention to hurt me."

Leonski cocked an eyebrow. "It was his intention to kill every other man in your Shitbox."

"Yes, sir," Cam said and looked away.

"They were unnecessary. They were not required." The faint sibilant hiss told me Cam was remembering the words of Kai-Ren, and that they still stung. *"What is the matter, Cam-ren?"*

Kai-Ren really hadn't understood. That was the most frightening thing. The Faceless had killed those guys like we swatted flies. No muss, no fuss. They were cold-blooded things.

And we were supposed to believe that the Faceless wanted peace? Shit, I couldn't believe it, and I was inside Cam's head. I just wanted to go home and keep my eyes on the red earth and never have to look up at the night sky again. I didn't want to look at the place my nightmares came from.

I closed my eyes. I just wanted to go home.

"What's a battle regent?" Commander Leonski asked. He turned and stared out the window into the black, his hands clasped behind his ramrod-straight back. Branski always joked that the first thing they did to a guy in officer training was shove a stick up his ass. And the second thing they did was surgically remove his personality.

"There's no direct translation," Cam said. His voice was wary. He was looking for the pointed attack that had to be lurking just behind the question. So was I. "He's like a general, I guess, but I never saw any chain of command like we have. I got the impression he was born to the rank. I, um, I translated it that way, Commander."

Commander Leonski didn't turn around. "How many of them are there?"

"I don't know," Cam said. "Millions. Maybe billions."

My chest constricted, and my throat ached with sudden tears. They'd kill us all. I'd never see Earth again, or my dad and sister. I'd never feel the sun on my skin again. I'd never hear the wind or see the ocean again. And Lucy would never grow up. Why the fuck was I stuck on this station, when I should have been with them? I couldn't help them, couldn't save them, but at least we could be together at the end.

"He wants peace," Cam said, looking at me intently. "I promise!"

Commander Leonski shook his head and turned around. "Why the hell would the Faceless want peace? They know we're no match for them. Are we?"

They'd killed those guys in the Shitbox like they were nothing. They'd taken out Defender Four and Five like they were nothing. They'd targeted our women to break our fucking breeding cycle, like we were nothing.

"You're right," Cam said. "Kai-Ren doesn't care, but that's the point. We're not a threat. We've got nothing they want. He thinks war with us is wasteful. It costs too much in resources and time for absolutely nothing in return. He wants peace with us because we're just not worth the months it takes them to travel this far. All we are to the Faceless is a cheap victory for the lower generals. Kai-Ren is proud. He'd rather win real victories."

My stomach churned. This was what Cam hinged his faith on? That we were lower than fucking insects to the Faceless? How was that meant to be at all comforting?

"And he sent you all this way in that pod to tell us that?" Commander Leonski asked. He shook his head. "You're a fucking liar, Rushton."

Hell, we were all thinking it.

Cam wasn't intimidated. How could he be, after the things he'd seen? But he was way too calm for a man being accused of treason. It just made him look guilty.

"He sent me to say he was coming," Cam said. "The rest is my understanding, sir."

Commander Leonski smiled tightly. "You'll forgive me, Lieutenant, if I don't want to risk the lives of the six hundred men on this station on your *understanding*."

"Yes, sir," Cam said, and I could feel the determination swelling in him, "but you don't really have a choice."

My jaw dropped. Not fucking smart, LT! Did he want to get thrown out the nearest air lock? Because fuck him. I didn't.

Cam squared his shoulders. "Kai-Ren is coming, sir. His ship is just outside sensor range now. It's been there for some time. He's set the schedule, not you, sir. And if you don't welcome him, he *will* destroy this station, and every other station in the network. And then he'll poison the Earth's atmosphere."

The two marines in the doorway reached for their sidearms.

Holy shit. I'd always been afraid I'd die on Defender Three, but not like this.

Commander Leonski actually laughed. "Now there's an interesting threat from something with peace on its mind."

"He will have peace," Cam said, ignoring the marines. "Either through a treaty or through annihilation. He means to end this pointless conflict one way or another."

"When?" Commander Leonski asked.

"I don't know, sir," Cam said. "Soon."

Commander Leonski looked at the marines and then back to Cam, like he was considering giving them the order then and there. No nasty little tribunal to muddy the waters.

Cam wasn't scared. Didn't matter. I was scared enough for both of us.

Leonski shrugged. "I can't get anyone from the war room up here in under a month. And I can't make a deal on behalf of humanity, Rushton."

"Sir, he's bringing a treaty," Cam said. He flushed. "I wrote it with Kai-Ren. You just have to sign it, and they'll go away. They won't come again. They honor their treaties. Treaties are sacrosanct."

"Lieutenant Rushton," Commander Leonski said, "cultural adviser to the Faceless."

"Not by choice," Cam said from between his teeth.

Leonski raised his eyebrows. "Hmmm."

Cam frowned and regrouped. "This treaty will stop the lesser generals attacking us," he said. "And it will stop Kai-Ren from taking more drastic measures to end the conflict."

Commander Leonski fixed his gaze on Cam. "If you're lying to me," he said in a slow voice, "I will make sure you pay for that before we all die. Do you understand me?"

"Yes, sir," Cam said.

"And I will make sure that the war room tells the people back home exactly what happened," Commander Leonski said, "so that they'll know you were no war hero, and every human being on the planet will know who betrayed them to the Faceless. Millions of people will curse your name at the moment of their destruction."

Cam nodded and pressed his lips together until they whitened.

An echoing twinge of shame and regret settled uneasily in my gut, but what had Cam expected? To be welcomed on Defender Three with open arms? Hell, he was the worst messenger ever, and he was lucky we hadn't disregarded that old saying and shot him on the spot.

Commander Leonski looked at him like he was still considering it, and then turned sharply on his heel and left us alone. The marines left with him, locking the door behind them.

Cam sank down onto the bed and put his head in his hands.

His misery felt a lot like homesickness. He'd found his way back to humanity after four long years with the Faceless, but he wasn't home. And he'd just realized that he'd never really be home again. The more he told them, the more people would look at him like he was as bad as a Faceless.

Or maybe worse. The Faceless were what they were, but Cam was supposed to be on our side. That's not the sort of thing people forgive.

———

SOMETHING WAS UP. As much as I hated the window, there was nothing else to do in that room other than stare out it into the black. And in the past three days there had been a steady stream of traffic arriving at and departing from Defender Three—much more than was usual when we were this close to the outer edge of our ellipse.

Cam rested on his stomach on our bed and read my book.

I sat beside him and counted the Shitboxes.

"Third one today," I said. "That's a record."

I thought of the guys on the Outer Ring. They'd hate all the extra work in what should have been their downtime as we slipped farther from the Earth and farther from the other stations. I wished I was out there with them. I wondered what people were saying. They must have known something was happening, and they must have connected it to the surprising reappearance of Cameron Rushton. I wanted to know what Commander Leonski was bringing in. Reinforcements? Seemed kind of dumb, given the Faceless could blow the station straight out of the black however many guys we had crammed aboard. Weapons, maybe. Maybe our scientists had actually developed something that could punch a hole in a Faceless ship.

If they had, it had taken them fucking long enough.

"He wants peace. I told you," Cam said, turning a page.

I rolled my eyes. "Pardon me if I don't take Kai-Ren's word for it."

"You would," Cam said, "if you ever met him."

My stomach clenched, and I tried not to remember that flash of Cam's memory: the long white hair, the pale skin, and the thin mouth curled into a cruel smile. "What," I snorted, "he's really decent and honorable once you get to know him?"

"You can't judge the Faceless by our standards," Cam said. His green eyes met mine. "He is honorable, in their sense. But he also really does think we're lower than pond scum."

I shifted away from him and remembered the cool, gentle touch of Kai-Ren's fingers on my—*Cam's*—trembling flesh. "Didn't seem like that."

Cam's lips quirked slightly. "Okay, he thinks you're lower

than pond scum. He elevated me to the status of good little puppy."

I swallowed. "You shouldn't talk like that. That's not funny."

He raised his eyebrows. "It's kinda funny."

Unease settled in my gut. It was like that instinct you get when something's wrong but you haven't figured it out yet. Like you're the last one left in the showers, and you hear the door squeak open—a vague shiver of worry that turns quickly to sick anticipation when you turn around.

"What?" His smile faded.

"You need to shut up now, LT." I narrowed my eyes and chased down my unease. The realization took a little while to form. It coalesced slowly, and then it was as plain as day, and I felt like an idiot for not seeing it before. "Because while you've been reading you haven't touched me, and you've gone out of sync. I can hear your echo, and it's fast. Your blood pressure's dropped again, and you've got reflex tachycardia."

His eyes widened.

I lay down on my stomach beside him and slid my hand up underneath his gray T-shirt. I closed my eyes and fought the typical rush of dizziness that always accompanied what I'd begun to think of as a reconnection. I was his battery, after all.

"You should have told me this was happening," I said.

We'd been experimenting over the past few days. Hell, it's not like we had anything else to do. Cam could go for longer and longer without my touch now, sometimes up to an hour. He was stronger every day. I should have been more pleased about that than I was.

"I didn't realize," Cam said. "I thought I was just tired, I suppose. I didn't think anything of it."

I shook my head. "You've got to tell me everything, even if you don't think it's important. Patients don't know shit, Doc says."

I rubbed my hand against his back, my fingers finding the knots in his spine. I liked touching him, and I knew he liked to be touched. We hadn't done anything more than this since I'd jerked off beside him three days before, but shit, we'd both wanted to. Instead we held hands, spooned at night, and knocked awkwardly against each other in the shower.

Cam rested his chin on his crossed arms. "You could be a doctor," he said. "You're smarter than you let on."

I snorted. "Doesn't mean I'm smart enough for that. And I'll be fucked if the military is getting another five years out of me."

"Would that be so bad?" he asked, a teasing smile tugging at the corners of his lips.

My eyebrows shot up, and I flushed. He did not mean the five years. "It's just an expression."

"You could be an officer," he said, his smile slowly fading. "You'd be on better pay."

"Not interested. I've got seven years to go, providing the Faceless don't blow us out of the sky, and then I'm going home." I stared out the window as I rubbed his back.

"You'd make a great doctor, Garrett."

"Don't push it," I muttered.

So he hadn't picked it up from my dreams yet, or from my thoughts. Hadn't, because my mind shied away from it. It was more than homesickness. It was more than missing my family. It was even more than hating the military.

And now I was thinking it.

My dad didn't have seven years. He was sick. A lifetime of working in the factories, breathing in the fumes, had made him that way. Lots of people got sick in the factories. It always went the same way. From the first time they coughed blood, they had about five years at the outside, and my dad had been sick awhile. He probably didn't have twelve months.

He'd made arrangements for Lucy, more or less. His friend

Denise had agreed to take her in. When it happened, every lousy dollar I earned would go to Denise, and I knew it wouldn't be enough. It took more than a shitty wage to stay safe in Kopa. I should have been there. And if there were any way off Defender Three, I would have fucking taken it the second I got Dad's letter.

Cam's forehead was creased with worry. He touched my arm. "Has he seen a doctor?"

As though it were that simple! I scowled. *"No fucking doctors in Kopa, city boy."*

He flushed. "I'm sorry."

"Whatever," I said. He tensed underneath my touch, and that annoyed me most, like he thought I was some feral piece of shit who couldn't even accept an apology. "I left school when I was twelve, LT. Who the fuck do you think you are, telling me I'm smart? Who the fuck do you think you are, asking me if my dad's seen a doctor, like maybe it had just slipped his mind? You don't know the first thing about my life."

I tried to pull away, and he caught me by the wrist and pulled me back down.

"Let me go, asshole!" I got an elbow against his chest, but he managed to dislodge it. And he twisted his hips away protectively before I had a chance to knee him in the balls. Turns out he remembered his basic combat training a hell of a lot better than I did, but of course Cameron Rushton had been the perfect golden-boy soldier, hadn't he? That's what all the ads said. I wondered what they'd say if they knew he'd liked being fucked by a Faceless.

He pinned me down and straddled my hips. His eyes blazed. "Is that it? You're going to throw that back in my face?"

"You can't help what you dream," I muttered, struggling under his weight. "I can't help what I think!"

He was holding my wrists against the mattress, his fingers digging in painfully. "I'm sorry you're stuck in my head, Garrett, and I'm sorry I didn't grow up dirt poor in some shit-hole town no one's ever heard of."

I struggled. I wanted to punch the arrogant asshole.

He tightened his grip on my wrists. "And I'm sorry I never had a bitch of a stepmother who liked to slap me around and call me stupid. I'm sorry I never went hungry. I'm sorry you had to drop out of school to look after your sister, and I'm sorry that your dad is sick."

I pushed my hips up to try and unseat him, but it was useless.

"I'm sorry you got drafted," he said, "and I'm sorry you got rolled in the showers. I'm sorry you can't go home."

The fight drained out of me as I listened to the miserable fucking litany of my life. I squeezed my eyes shut. I didn't want him to see me cry. Hadn't he humiliated me enough? "Just get off me, please."

"No," he said.

My eyes flashed open.

He leaned down until his face was close to mine. "And I'm so sorry that you never got a fucking break."

I hated him at that moment, and it didn't matter. I tilted my head back to meet his kiss. I felt his hot breath first, and then his lips met mine. It wasn't gentle like the other time. This time it was a hungry openmouthed kiss that met my anger and matched it. His tongue pushed into my mouth, and I let it. I more than let it. I pressed my tongue against his, raising my head off the mattress, and tasted him.

Felt good. Felt good to be held down like this, his hands gripping my wrists, his weight pinning me to the bed. My cock hardened underneath him, and he groaned. The sound vibrated in our mouths. I gasped for breath, sharing his.

"Brady," he murmured, his mouth leaving mine to explore my throat with lips and the gentle pressure of his teeth. "Don't hate me."

I moaned and arched my back. Should have thought it was pretty damn obvious this wasn't hate anymore.

He traced the line of my jaw with his mouth. He ground himself against my erection, and I moaned again.

"Need to come, LT," I managed. "Gonna come if you keep doing that!"

"Take a breath," he murmured. "Slow it down."

I squeezed my eyes shut for a moment, trying really hard to think of something else apart from my cock. And his. I looked up into his eyes and struggled to control my breathing.

God, he was beautiful. I'd never looked at another guy and thought that, but I'd never had one do anything like this to me. His eyes were beautiful, and his lips were beautiful, and his skin, just a hint tanned, was beautiful as well. What'd he see in someone like me? Just biochemistry, I guess. Just an aftereffect from the stasis pod.

He frowned at me slightly, and I pushed the thought away before he could find it.

"Keep going," I said. "Keep doing whatever you're going to do."

Anything. I'd let him do anything as long as it felt as good as this moment.

His voice was low. "I'm going to let your wrists go now, but I want you to keep them there. Can you do that for me?"

"Yeah." I sighed, rolling my hips to try and find some friction. "What for?"

He sat back and unwrapped his fingers from my wrists. His green eyes were wide. "So I can do this, and you can't stop me."

He plucked at my T-shirt, sliding his hands under it. His palms moved slowly over my abdomen and then up to my chest, pushing up the thin fabric. I shivered as his fingers found my left nipple. The little nub was already hard, but it got harder as he pinched it, and it wasn't the only thing. I jerked my hips as a flash of sensation traveled like an electric current from my nipple to my balls. I almost came.

"Fuck," I gasped, arching underneath him. "LT!"

"I want you to take a shower with me," he said, swiping his tongue over his lower lip. "I want you to come for me, and I don't just want to watch this time."

"Okay," I whispered, and he leaned down to kiss me again.

Holy shit, Brady, what have you just agreed to? Set some fucking boundaries before it's too late.

Who was I kidding? It was already too late.

CHAPTER NINE

I FELT like I was dreaming when Cam led me toward the shower. I felt like my mind was ten steps behind my body. I figured it would catch up at some point and voice an objection, but nothing.

I was doing this because I thought we were already dead.

I was doing this because, if we weren't, we'd be split up again as soon as Kai-Ren broke our connection.

Whatever this was between us, I wanted as much as I could grab.

My hands shook when I stripped. My T-shirt hit the floor first, and then my pants. I stood there in just my gray military-issue boxer briefs and cupped my hands in front of my aching cock.

Cam pulled his T-shirt over his head, and I watched the muscles in his abdomen ripple when he did. He was slender, but he wasn't scrawny. He had the long, lean lines of a runner, and in my mind's eye I caught a glimpse of a narrow, glittering beach. I could almost feel the sand between my toes as I ran, and twin suns beating down on my back.

"Did you ever get homesick there?" I asked him, not quite able to meet his eyes.

"Every day," he said. He hooked his thumbs over the waistband of his pants and his briefs.

My face burned as he bent over and shoved them down. I'd seen him naked before, but this was different. The first few times I'd seen him as a patient. After that, when we'd showered together, maybe I'd thought about sex—given the dreams we shared, it was impossible not to—but this was the first time I'd seen him undress for that purpose. It felt momentous.

You're not gay, my brain reminded me, but it wasn't an objection, exactly. It was more of a question I couldn't properly finish: *Not gay, so why does he make me hard? Not gay, so why do I want him? Not gay, so why can't I take my eyes off him?*

Not gay, but I don't care.

Cam stepped into the shower and turned the water on, and I watched the way it ran over him, slipping down the lean shape of his body in glistening paths, discovering every curve, every angle, every dip. The water made him shine.

He bowed his head under the showerhead, and water ran off the wet twists of his hair. He stepped free and shook his head like a dog drying itself. A corona of light exploded around his head like a halo, and then he ran his hands over his hair to get rid of the rest of the water.

His biceps bulged when he did that. I could see the muscles tightening under his tanned skin. Muscle, ligament, muscle, contracting and expanding. It was like one of those illustrations in Doc's dog-eared copy of *Gray's Anatomy,* intricate and beautiful. Miraculous.

I slipped my underwear off and tried not to feel like a skinny kid in comparison.

Dad once said I was still growing into myself, but that was three years ago now when I sent him a picture of me wearing a uniform that was way too big. I'd looked twelve instead of sixteen. Maybe I'd grown into myself since then, when nobody was paying attention. I guess my uniform didn't hang off me like it used to. I guess I'd filled out a bit.

Cam seemed to like what he saw. He smiled at me and held out his hand.

I swallowed. Couldn't believe I was going to do this. Couldn't believe I wanted to.

His hand caught mine: electricity, dizziness, and expectation.

"Close your eyes, Brady," Cam said and drew me into the shower.

Holy fuck.

He touched his lips against mine in a featherlight kiss, and my heart skipped a beat. Was this what I wanted, or was I only feeling his desire? Shit, did it even matter? Here in this moment I wanted it. I wanted it enough not to worry about how I would feel in the morning. I had a little over a week to live, a little over a week until the Faceless killed us all. Fuck regret.

"You're like starlight," Cam whispered, and his teeth scraped up my jaw. I shivered. "I could lose myself in you."

My cock was already hard. So was his. It jutted into my hip, and I thought I'd hate it. Didn't. It felt fucking hot. More than that, it felt right. I wished there was some way I could tell him that. I groaned instead, as his mouth found my pulse point. I dug my fingers into his shoulders.

"I'm not clever, Cam. Don't have clever words or nice things to whisper like you. But I want you."

"I know," he whispered. He leaned back and cupped my face in his hands. He showed me a crooked smile. "And you're smarter than you think."

"Whatever, LT," I said, tilting my head up for another kiss. "Let's just do this, and save the fucking pep talk for later."

He laughed, blinking water out of his eyes.

I was nervous now, as scared as all hell. There was a lump in my throat that I couldn't seem to swallow away. I liked Cam and I wanted him, but I didn't know what to do. In my dreams I knew, but this was real. I'd never done anything like this, and I was afraid of my inexperience.

Cam ran a hand over my head, his palm scraping against my prickly scalp. He smiled. "You'd look even hotter if you could grow your hair, Brady."

I made a face.

His green gaze met mine. "You can't take a compliment, can you?"

I didn't like the intensity of his scrutiny. "It's never really come up before, LT."

He narrowed his eyes and shook his head. "Don't be that guy with me, Brady."

"What guy?" I breathed.

He pushed me backward gently, until my back met the wall. His cock was still pressing into my hip, and now the rest of him was as well. Skin-on-skin contact, just like we both needed. One hand stroked my neck. The other one moved down my chest.

"The smart-ass," he said. He leaned in and kissed me again. He caught my lower lip in his teeth and nipped gently, and I groaned. "Don't be him, because I don't need him interrupting when I tell you that you're a decent guy, and you're smart, and you're fucking hot."

A shiver ran through me as his hand slipped down my flank.

"Hot?" I asked, screwing up my nose. He was right; I couldn't take a compliment.

"Yeah," he murmured. "Any other guy and I'd think you were fishing, but you don't even know it, do you?"

Heat rose in me, and it had nothing to do with the water temperature. Nobody had ever called me hot before, and I wasn't arrogant enough to think it myself. There were guys on Defender

Three who thought they were all that, but they were all big, ripped gym junkies, and everyone laughed at them. No fucking point being God's gift to women on a space station, right? Dicks.

I was nothing special: I was too pale since coming to Defender Three, and I had dark eyes. I looked like one of those pinky-gray geckos that lived behind the picture frames in my dad's house—pallid, furtive, and with big eyes. But I guess I wasn't ugly. With a bit of sun I might look half-decent. I just never thought I was anything special. Not until Cam told me I was.

I leaned my head back so Cam's lips could find my pulse point again. I liked that. "Maybe."

"You are," Cam said, his hand edging toward my pulsing cock. "You make me so hard, Brady."

Another flush of heat burned through me. This was definitely uncharted territory. I liked that he said that, but it was weird as well. Everything about this was weird, but not weird enough to make me want to stop. Not once Cam curled his fingers around my cock, anyway.

"Fuck, Cam!" I exclaimed. I jerked in his grasp, cracking my head against the shower wall. "*Ow!*"

"Are you okay?" he asked, releasing my cock and drawing me forward. He bit his lip like he was trying not to laugh. "Brady?"

I rubbed the back of my head, embarrassed. "Yeah, I'm fine. Sorry."

He smiled and wiped his dripping hair off his forehead. "So if I do that again, you're okay with it?"

"Hell, yes," I said, my chest constricting. My cock throbbed with anticipation. "Yes, please."

Cam traced a finger down my sternum. "But maybe I want to do something else."

I couldn't help pushing into his touch. "Like what?"

He flashed me a smile and went down onto his knees.

Holy fuck. No way! I didn't know whether to freak out completely or just celebrate the fact that Christmas had come early.

Cam held me gently by the hips. He looked up at me, blinking away water. "Try to keep your balance, hey, Brady?"

Something about his teasing tone relaxed me. Well, most of me. My cock was almost painfully hard. Jesus, it wouldn't take much to set me off. This would probably be embarrassing.

"I'll do my best," I managed.

"Me too," he said with a wicked grin and leaned in toward my cock.

Fuck. The first touch of his tongue, flicking against the slit in the end of my cock, was amazing. My whole body jerked forward reflexively, and his fingers tightened on my hips. Cam wasn't tentative. He'd had a lot of practice. I'd shared a fair amount of it, in my dreams, but this was new. I wondered why he'd only ever dreamed about giving head instead of receiving it. I mean, I knew he liked giving head, I knew he fucking loved it, but being on this end was *phenomenal*.

His lips found my cock. He opened them and drew my cock inside. His mouth was hot, hotter than the shower, and his tongue was clever. He knew exactly what spots to hit—not that there was a bad one, I guess, but Cam's tongue went straight to that really sensitive patch of skin under the head and played there for a while before laving against the thick vein on the underside of my cock.

I felt my cock nudge against the back of his throat, and I knew what he'd do. He'd done it in all his dreams, and the anticipation was almost enough to make me come on the spot. Shit, I don't know what stopped me, apart from the absolute fucking certainty that I really needed this to last because it was only going to get better.

Cam opened his throat and groaned as he took me farther in.

I wanted to close my eyes but couldn't. I needed to look at him too much. I needed to see the way the water ran down his naked back. I needed to see the way his dripping hair covered his face. I needed to see his head bobbing back and forth as he took me in his throat.

I reached out and touched a trembling hand to his head, and he groaned again. I twined my fingers through his hair, wondering if that was okay. Chris had done that, and Cam had liked it, but I wasn't Chris. I was just the guy in his head. I was the guy who was possibly hot, and the guy who was there, but I wasn't the guy he loved.

Cam groaned again, and a shiver ran down his back. I felt the vibrations in his throat in my cock, and I sucked in a shallow breath. "Oh Jesus, Cam!"

One of his hands slid around to my ass, his fingers moving gently down into my crease. And that felt good as well. His touch was so careful there, not demanding like his mouth. We were both wondering how I'd cope with his touch. We were both thinking of that asshole Wade, but this was nothing like that. This was good.

"You like that?"

His voice was in my head, and I almost burst out laughing. That was one good thing about telepathy, right? You could still talk while you were giving head.

"Yeah," I managed, jerking as his finger grazed right over my puckered asshole. "Feels good. You know it does."

I could even hear the smile in his voice. *"Tastes good too."*

My balls drew up tight. Everything centered there, between Cam's mouth and his finger. It was all heavy sensation now, building on itself over and over again. I gasped for breath.

"Gonna come," I said, squeezing my eyes shut.

"Then come."

Every muscle in my body tightened, froze, and I obeyed him.

My hips jerked wildly as I spurted down Cam's throat. I gripped his hair tightly, and he gripped my hips. I shuddered and cried out as I came. I think my toes even curled.

Coming so hard left me weak and dizzy.

Cam swallowed me down and then leaned back on his heels. He licked his lips and looked up at me. "You okay?"

"Yeah," I said, even though I was shaky on my feet now. "That was awesome."

Cam rose to his feet and drew me into an embrace. It felt good, because I knew I was blushing and didn't want him to see my face. I suppose it didn't matter since he could read my thoughts, but it felt good to be close to him as well. I leaned my head on his shoulder.

"Are you telling me nobody's ever given you a blowjob before?" he asked. "You're kidding me, aren't you?"

I pressed my lips against his shoulder for a moment. "Might be different in the officers' quarters, LT, but the enlisted men don't really go for that sort of thing."

He laughed, and his chest vibrated. "You just don't know where to look, Brady. But I wasn't talking about the military. What about at home?"

I shifted back and looked at his face. "My girlfriend gave me a handjob once, but that was all. But, you know, we were kids. Did, *um*, did you have anyone before the military?"

"A few casual things," he said. "Nothing serious."

And then there was Chris. Cam was remembering it, and suddenly I was *feeling* it.

It was on Defender Eight. It was in the lounge, after lights-out, and I felt his arms come around me. I felt the tickle of the soft hairs on his arms against my chest. I felt a hand slide up my torso, making me shiver, and then he pinched my hard nipple between his thumb and forefinger, and it was like a bolt of lightning had traveled straight to my balls. I could feel his hard cock pressing up against me, rubbing teasingly along the cleft of my ass. And I wanted it. Fuck, I wanted it.

Sure beat Kaylee's inexperienced handjob.

My eyes widened.

"Did you feel that?" Cam asked, peering down at me. He tightened his arms around me.

"Yeah," I said. "Full-on."

"It's the connection," he said. "It was the same with Kai-Ren. It's something in the drugs they gave me, something in the pod."

I tried to force a laugh. "Better than torture, right?"

He frowned. "Except it shouldn't have happened. It wouldn't have, if you'd opened the pod properly."

"It's not all bad," I said. Shit, nothing that led to a phenomenal blowjob in the shower could be all bad.

"I know," Cam said. "Just...just would have been nice to be alone in my head for once."

It was my turn to frown.

Cam smiled slightly. He brushed his lips against my forehead. "I like you. It's just been a long time since the only thoughts in my head were my own."

We both heard that sibilant hiss: *"Cam-ren."*

"Yeah," I said. "But he'll fix it, right?"

I still thought he'd kill us all, but now wasn't the time to bring that up.

Cam knew anyway. His smile grew, but it wasn't genuine. He must have read what I'd thought. He was uneasy. "Sure. He'll fix it."

Why did that sound hollow?

We stood there silently for a while, the water washing over us. And then I realized that I was being a selfish prick. I could still feel Cam's erection pressing against my hip, and it had to be the height of bad manners not to reciprocate, right?

I shifted, pressing my mouth to his throat. I liked being this close to someone. It was an intimacy I hadn't known before, not even with Kaylee. We'd been kids. This was all new to me, but it felt good.

I slipped a hand down Cam's chest, letting my fingers discover the shape of him. I liked the little dip underneath his pectoral muscle. I liked the valley where his ribs met his sternum. I liked the ridges of his abdomen.

"And until Kai-Ren fixes you," I said, "let me fix this."

I'd never touched another guy's cock before, and I don't know what I expected. Shit, my hand knew my own cock well enough, and this one wasn't that different. It was a little more curved than mine, I guess, but about the same size. Maybe a little thicker. It felt heavy, and the head bobbed against my palm as I moved my hand across it.

Cam gasped. "You don't have to do that, Brady."

"Can't leave you like this, LT," I told him. I moved back so I could actually see what I was doing. There was no way I could go by feel the first time. "And I want to."

Cam sure as hell had a lot more restraint than I did. God only knows how he managed to stay still as I handled his cock so awkwardly. I knew I was doing it wrong. Even if we hadn't been joined by some freaky Faceless science, I would have felt the frustration rolling off him in waves. He wanted it harder and faster, and I had no clue.

"It's not gonna snap, Brady," Cam managed at last as I ghosted my fingers up the hard, satin flesh. "Just...just do what you'd do to yourself."

"I would," I told him, "but normally I'm facing the other way."

His face split with a smile, and he squeezed his eyes shut. "You're real funny, recruit."

Right, no fucking mercy, then. I gripped his shaft tightly.

Cam shuddered. *"Do your worst, Garrett."*

"Yes, sir," I said.

His laugh turned into a groan as I stroked him roughly from the head to the base. I blinked water out of my eyes as I looked down at his cock. It was dark with blood. The plum-shaped crown was almost purple. I wondered how long it would take to make him come.

His hands came up to my shoulders. "Feels good, Brady."

His voice was raw with need, and a warm glow of pride spread through me. *I* did that. I did that to him.

This time I felt the electricity between us. It prickled my skin and stole my breath and suddenly I was in his head again.

I saw flashing lights. I felt restraints around my wrists. I heard Kai-Ren's sibilant voice in my ear: *"Cam-ren, Cam-ren. Come for me."*

No. That wasn't the way it was going to happen.

"Open your eyes, Cam," I told him, and he obeyed. "Stay with me."

He nodded, his body trembling. He ran his tongue over his bottom lip and gasped. "Keep going, Brady, please."

"I'm not stopping," I promised him. "But you gotta stay."

No fucking Faceless was going to steal my moment.

Maybe Cam heard that, because he bit his lip and smiled. "I'm here, Brady. All yours."

I stroked faster, and his cock jerked and twitched in my grasp. I liked that. I liked being in charge of Cam's pleasure. I liked it so much I tested it by slowing down until my hand was hardly moving at all.

Cam groaned and ground his hips against my fist.

I leaned in and pressed my mouth against Cam's. His lips were already open, waiting. I pushed my tongue into Cam's mouth at the same time I squeezed his cock tightly, and he gasped.

My own cock was hard again by then, so I shifted our position as we kissed so that our shafts pressed against each other. I couldn't get my fingers around both of them, so Cam dropped one hand from my shoulder to help. Our fingers twisted together and jostled for position, and then we were jerking against one another, back and forth in perfect rhythm like we'd done this a hundred times before.

We held our kiss for a moment longer, and then Cam's head dropped back. "Brady. *Oh.* Brady!"

I drew a shuddering breath. Yeah. He was here with me now. No Kai-Ren, no Chris, just us.

We thrust faster. Cam came first, gasping and trembling. I think it was the sudden wet heat against my belly and chest that sent me over the edge. He came on me. Cam came on my skin, and it was electric. I was only a second behind him, crying out, and then we were standing under the shower in a close embrace, letting the water wash us clean.

His breath was ragged in my ear. "Felt so good, Brady."

I traced my fingers down his spine. "Yeah. Fucking amazing."

I gave regret a moment to find me, but it didn't. That was interesting. Jesus, even if my brain told me I wasn't gay, and there was some debating that now, I was still Cam's medic. And I didn't think mutual masturbation was in any of the first aid manuals.

"Should be," Cam said, a smile in his voice.

I snorted with laughter. "Yeah. It fucking should be."

We stayed in the shower until the pads of our fingers had shriveled up like prunes.

CHAPTER TEN

DOC KNEW ALL MY SECRETS. He knew about that time with Wade in the showers even, because I'd been late to class, and he'd ripped shreds off me afterward. *"I expected better from you, Garrett,"* he'd growled. *"I stuck my neck out to get you put in the medical stream, so you don't have to run laps every fucking hour for the rest of your natural life, and you repay me by turning up late? Who the hell do you think you are?"*

"Sorry, sir."

"Drop and give me twenty, Garrett."

I couldn't even do three.

"What's the matter?" He hadn't shouted that. *"Garrett, are you hurt?"*

I lied and said I wasn't, but Doc ordered me to strip. I wish I could say that I don't know what was worse, the pain or the humiliation, but I wasn't that proud: it was the pain. It stung like hell when Doc examined me. Shards of pain as sharp as glass pierced me in the guts, and I threw up all over the floor when Doc's gloved fingers found where I'd torn.

"Who did this to you, Brady?" he asked me.

"Dunno," I lied.

But he must have figured it out, because Doc had never fucked up setting someone's broken leg as badly as he did with Wade when I finally got my payback that day on the wall. Turns out Doc wasn't above revenge either.

Anyway, he knew all my secrets. Still, I couldn't help blushing and stammering when he turned up the next morning for his regular visit and asked me what I'd done to improve Cameron Rushton so much.

"I dunno, Doc," I said at last. "Maybe it's just happening naturally, you know."

Doc looked at me sideways while he listened through his stethoscope to Cam's heartbeat. He knew I was lying to him.

"All right," he said. "You can put your shirt back on, Lieutenant."

"Sir," said Cam, and picked up his shirt.

I watched the way his muscles rippled as he pulled his shirt over his head. Fuck yeah, that was nice.

Doc looked at me sharply, and I'm sure I blushed.

"Well," Doc said at last, "since you're doing so well, how about we give young Garrett some time off?"

What?

"I think that would be fine, Major," Cam said. "I'm sure Garrett would appreciate the break."

And suddenly I wasn't allowed to have an opinion, because they were officers. Assholes.

I had an hour, Doc said. We knew Cam could go for up to two and a half hours without needing my touch to regulate his heartbeat, but that was when I was in the same room. He swore he was stronger than yesterday, but since when the hell did a patient know anything about anything? So Doc gave me an hour. And he gave it to me with a slap on the back, like he was doing me a favor. He was, I guess. If I'd been locked up with any other guy for four days straight, I would have been foaming at the mouth to get out of there. And I had, in the beginning. But I turns out I can be fairly tolerant of another person constantly encroaching on my personal space if they give me a blowjob whenever we hit the shower.

He'd given me another one that morning. I was still working up the courage to return the favor.

"You deserve some time off for good behavior, Brady," Doc said when he ushered me to the door.

I didn't want to go, but I didn't want to admit that.

"I dunno," I said. "What if something happens?"

"If something happens, I'll be here," said Doc. "And you'll have a radio. Take some time, Brady. Hit the wall, or have a round of paintball. I hear the guys from maintenance have a card game going, and there's always the gym."

I raised my eyebrows. The gym? It just goes to show how little there was to do on the fucking station. I hated the gym enough when we had to do circuits for training. I never went there in my spare time, which was probably how I'd ended up on Captain Lopez's shit list. I was always one of the guys with the slowest times. Never last—I wasn't dumb enough to let that happen—but I was hardly a star of the squad either. Not physically great, not academically great, not nothing great, but I kept my head down and shut my mouth. I flew just under the radar, or at least I had until I'd become Cam's human pacemaker. Now it made me nervous just how many officers knew my name.

"Take some time," Doc said, shoving the radio at me. "Take some space."

I looked over his shoulder to where Cam was sitting on the edge of the bed. He was picking at a thread on the knee of his fatigues. His hair curtained his face. Then he looked up and shot me a smile that made my heart beat faster. His too, maybe. He put a hand on his heart.

"I've got you here. I'll be okay."

"Go on," Doc said and pushed me out the door.

The first thing I noticed was that the armed marines were still there. Commander Leonski had every right to be worried that Cam was a security risk. It didn't say much for the regard he held me in if he'd been willing to lock me up with someone who might be dangerous, but since when does a lowly recruit count for anything? Not ever, that's when.

The marines stared at me like I'd grown a second head. Assholes.

I lingered in the hallway for a little while, half expecting my radio to crackle with an urgent call to get back to Cam's side. But nothing happened. I checked that it was on and waited some more.

Then it occurred to me that for the first time in four days I was free, and I was stupid to be wasting time just standing around in a hallway. I checked my watch. Maybe I'd give myself half an hour. That was a good enough compromise.

It was just past 2000. The mess halls would be empty, but the barracks wouldn't be. This was the time of evening that everyone liked best: free time. The hallways downstairs would be full of guys. There would be card games, like Doc said, and drinking and maybe even a movie playing in one of the rec rooms. I would have joined in, four days ago. Now I didn't want to. I didn't want to answer all the questions I knew would get thrown at me: *Where've you been, Garrett? What's with Rushton? What's going on with all the extra traffic? What do you know about the Faceless?* Because it would turn bad in a heartbeat: *What the fuck is going on? Why are you holding out on us, Garrett? Who the hell do you think you are?*

It's not that I didn't like any of the guys on Defender Three. I had a few decent friends, and I didn't make trouble. But the rumor mill in an enclosed environment like the station didn't take long to ratchet up into something ugly. Everyone would have been on edge since Cam reappeared. Everyone knew something big was going down, and everyone would want to know what it was. If they thought I was holding out, they'd turn on me. Recruits didn't count for much even among the enlisted men. Jesus, there were only five guys in my barracks who were lower in the pecking order than me, because they were newer. Three years didn't get you any respect, not from the guys who were near the end of their service. You were nothing to them but a snot-nosed kid, and it doesn't matter if you got there nine and a half years after them or a week after them. That's just the way things were.

So I roamed the narrow corridors of the officers' quarters for a while, steering clear of the lift that would take me back to my own turf. I found a vending machine around a corner, and I went to have a look. There were magazines, chocolate bars, and cigarettes, the same as on our level. I might have bought a chocolate bar—no point saving money if the Faceless were coming—but I'd left my wallet in the room.

I checked the back of the machine. It wasn't even bolted shut like the ones on our level, but you still needed a code to open it. Ours, you needed a screwdriver and a distraction.

I looked at the chocolate bar again, and my stomach growled. I could probably find a way into the machine, but it wouldn't be a good idea to risk getting caught stealing from the officers' quarters. Cam wouldn't be happy if we both ended up in the brig because of my sweet tooth.

Growing up in Kopa had kind of made me into a scrounger. You could tell the guys who came from places like that. We were always first in line in the mess hall like we were worried the food would run out. We hoarded extras from the ration packs, even those little packets of mayonnaise that tasted sour. Some of us volunteered to work in the kitchens. Some of us, like me, got smart and hung out in the med bay. And it didn't matter that the one decent thing about the military was that they never let you go hungry. If that happens enough to you when you're a kid, you don't forget it.

I bet Cam had never been first in line at the mess.

I left the vending machine and prowled around the hallways a little longer, checking my watch every five minutes.

I found the officers' club by accident. I rounded a corner, and there it was: a wide-open door that looked into a large room full of chairs and tables and couches and a wide-screen television. There was a bar. I could smell beer. There was also a guy on the door, and he looked at me suspiciously.

The lack of stripes on his shoulders said he was enlisted like me. I'd seen him around the place a few times, but I didn't know him. He was short but broad. He was ugly as well, with a nose that looked like someone had punched him and spread it halfway across his face. I wondered how he'd scored a job as cushy as this one.

"What are you doing up here, recruit?" he scowled.

"I've been assigned quarters down the hall," I said.

His disbelief showed on his face. "Fuck off. You're not allowed in here."

"Whatever," I said. I didn't want to go in anyway. I turned away and ran straight into a bunch of officers heading for the club.

"Watch it," one of the officers said, sidestepping me.

"Sorry, sir!" I pulled up sharply, snapped my shoulders back, and did my best to execute a decent salute. After almost three years in the military, you'd think I'd be better at them, but my habit of avoiding officers wherever possible meant that I didn't get all that much practice.

My sloppy salute got their attention, and so did my lack of rank.

There were three of them, and I didn't recognize them.

They were all of a height, all of an age, and they were all definitely cut from the same cloth. There wasn't that much to distinguish them at all. One was shorter, one was taller, and one was balder.

"What are you doing up here, recruit?" Shorter asked me, narrowing his dark eyes. "Have you got any reason to be in the officers' quarters?"

Yeah, hot date.

"Commander Leonski has assigned me temporary quarters here, sir," I said, wondering why that sounded so much like a dumb lie. "I wasn't trying to get into the club."

They didn't believe it, of course. They looked at me like I'd come up here just to try and break into their vending machines, slink around their hallways, and get drunk on the smell of their beer fumes. Like maybe they really thought all enlisted men were liars and thieves. Not that I was the exception to the rule. Jesus, I could be the poster child for scrounging, thieving bastards everywhere. I'd kept my head down on Defender Three because I didn't want to spend all my time in the brig, and because there wasn't much worth stealing, but back home in Kopa I'd done my fair share of taking what wasn't mine, even though my dad would have killed me if he'd found out.

Shorter raised his eyebrows, and Taller and Balder laughed.

I tried not to worry. What was the worst that would happen? They'd call the MPs who would call Commander Leonski or Doc, and it would all get sorted out. Still, how long would it take? I checked my watch: twenty-five minutes had passed since I left Cam.

Looking at my watch was a mistake.

"Got somewhere to be, recruit?" Taller asked me, jutting his chin forward.

"Yes, sir," I said, and he didn't like that answer much.

First they thought I was a liar; now they thought I was being a smart-ass. Officers call that insubordination. A big word like that looks better on the report.

"And where's that?" Taller asked.

I tried not to stare at the acne scars that pitted the lunar surface of his cheeks. "Major Layton is expecting me, sir."

Taller narrowed his eyes.

"You're the medic," Balder said suddenly. I didn't know them, but apparently they knew me. "You're Cameron Rushton's medic."

"Yes, sir," I said.

The look they gave me was the same one the marines had: *freak*. Balder blustered through it.

"Rushton is here in the officers' quarters," Balder said to the others, and there was something snide in the way he said it, like he didn't think it was right.

"That's right, sir," I said. "*Lieutenant* Rushton is here, sir."

They didn't like my tone, but that was okay. That's just how I'd intended it. Cam was still an officer until the war room said he wasn't, and they had no right to talk like he didn't deserve to be in the officers' quarters. He wasn't an interloper like me.

"He can't be a medic," Shorter said, looking me up and down. "He's still a recruit!"

I opened my mouth to explain that I would be a medic once I graduated in three months—that I wasn't some newbie fresh off the latest Shitbox from Earth—but Balder cut me off.

"It's not his qualifications Rushton wants him for," he said.

Shorter and Taller sniggered, and my cheeks burned.

"Hop to it, then, recruit," Balder said, and his tight smile slowly stretched into a sneer. "I'm sure the lieutenant's *missing* you."

It was his turn to emphasize a word, turning it into an insult.

"Sir," I muttered and turned away.

"I knew Rushton as a recruit," Balder said to the others as

they headed toward the doors of the club. He pitched his voice to make sure that I heard it. "He was always a faggot, even back then."

I tried not to show that I'd heard, but their laughter told me they saw the way I flinched when Balder said that word: *faggot*. I flinched, and I couldn't help the way my guts clenched and the bile rose in my throat.

"I wonder how long it took him to give it up for the Faceless!"

Fuckers. You don't know anything. Fucking assholes.

I headed back to my quarters, wishing I'd never stepped outside them. And I must have still had a mouth screwed up tighter than a cat's bum when I walked back inside, because Cam and Doc both stared at me.

"Brady?" they both asked at the same time.

"What happened, son?" Doc asked me.

Sometimes when Doc called me that, it took the edge off my homesickness. Sometimes it made it worse.

I crossed to the bed, shaking my head. "Nothing. It doesn't matter."

I sat down and began to unlace my boots. Fuck it. Those officers were just assholes. It didn't matter what they thought. If I only had a week to live, I sure as fuck didn't care what they thought about me. I'd see them in hell.

I pulled my boots off and then remembered I was a medic and not a fucking princess. I looked at Cam worriedly. "Sorry. Are you feeling okay?"

"A little tired," he said and sat down beside me.

Doc watched avidly as we clasped hands. Not our preferred method of contact anymore, but it did the trick.

Cam's heartbeat was a little tachy, but not too bad. It slipped back into a healthy rhythm quickly. He'd been better, but he'd also been worse. I shouldn't have left him, though. I wouldn't, in the future. It would be better for both of us.

Assholes.

"Does it bother you that much?" Cam asked quietly. He knew. I wondered if our connection was strong enough that he'd heard every word as it happened, or if he was only seeing the rerun in my whirling mind.

My eyes flashed open. "I don't care what they say about me. They need to show you some fucking respect, though, LT."

He smiled slightly at that and shrugged. "I don't care what they think, Brady."

It was the truth. He was calm, and I gradually calmed as well as his influence stole over me. It settled around me like an embrace, and all my anger and humiliation trickled away into nothing but a faint sense of regret.

"Brady?" Doc asked me in a quiet voice. I'd forgotten he was there. "What happened, Brady?"

I sighed. "It's nothing, Doc, really. I just ran into some asshole officers who called the LT a faggot. And me, I guess."

Doc frowned, his bushy brows drawing together. He crossed the floor to stand in front of me. He knew all my secrets. Well, until today he did. And it occurred to me that maybe he deserved to know this one as well.

"You don't have to do this, Brady," Cam's voice said in my head.

But I did, I think. Maybe it mattered. Because I'd never lied to Doc, except that one time.

"Who did this to you?"

"Dunno."

And that little lie had festered between us for a while, because Doc thought I didn't trust him enough to tell him, when in fact I trusted him more than anyone I'd ever met on the station. I just didn't tell him it was Wade because I couldn't bring myself to say that asshole's name.

I dropped Cam's hand. "Doc, it's, um...it's maybe not a lie."

Oh, that was smooth. Real smooth. "And I think it's why the LT is stronger," I mumbled, staring at my lap.

He put his hand on my shoulder. "Look at me, Brady."

Shit. My heart thumped as I met his eyes. I don't know what I expected to see, but it wasn't concern.

"Is this a conversation you'd rather have in private?" he asked me quietly.

"No point, Doc," I mumbled, jerking my head toward Cam. "He's living in my head."

Doc frowned at me worriedly for a while, and I knew he was thinking of Wade and the time I'd cried when he examined me. "Is this what you want, son?" he asked me. "Really?"

What I wanted was for the floor to open up and swallow me.

"It's not like that, not with the LT."

Doc was concerned, not surprised. Hundreds of guys locked in a tin can with no women: it happened. Sometimes it happened because of assholes like Wade, but it could be consensual as well. Not that I'd ever done anything like that before Cam. Shit, the most I'd done was jerked off with another guy a few times. At the same time, I mean, not actually touching. Because I wasn't gay, I'd always thought, and yet here I fucking was.

I stared at a hole in one of my socks and wiggled my toe through it.

"Okay, Brady," Doc said. "Just keep it safe."

My guilt spread across my face in a flush.

Doc sighed. "For fuck's sake, Brady, are you for real? You've *seen* STDs!"

"We've just messed around," I said, feeling like the dumbest kid in the class. "And we're both clean, right?"

"He is," Doc said. "You haven't been tested for STDs for six months."

"Well, I haven't picked up anything in six months except calluses," I shot back.

Doc lifted his hand off my shoulder and slapped me on the back of the head. "Watch the attitude, Garrett."

I made a face.

"I'll keep it off your records," Doc said. "You don't need the grief, Brady, and you, *Lieutenant*, don't need the charges."

Oh, yeah. *Fraternization* was another big word officers liked to use on reports. The military hierarchy didn't care what happened between two consenting adults, but they didn't like that shit to cross ranks. Being gay wasn't an offense, but fraternization could get you court-martialed. I'd end up in the brig, and Cam would end up stripped of his rank. They wouldn't discharge you for it—they needed the men too much—but they'd make sure everyone knew about it. And being gay may not have been an offense, but you'd still get the shit kicked out of you by guys you'd thought were your friends. You would in the lower ranks anyway, and from what I'd seen earlier the commissioned officers weren't exactly a shining example of tolerance.

Assholes.

Not that it mattered. Jesus, Cam and I had no future, not in any sense of the word. Even if the Faceless didn't wipe us out, it couldn't last. Because he was a lieutenant, and I was a recruit. Because they'd send him back to Eight, or back home.

And even if the Faceless didn't kill us all, Kai-Ren would break our connection. He'd fix Cam, and maybe that would be an end to whatever we had. Maybe he'd go back to Chris, and I'd go back to looking at girls with big tits in magazines, and we'd both be able to pretend it didn't mean anything.

We had as long as Kai-Ren gave us, that was all, to be together. Nothing else mattered except that. When fate's that big, you don't even have to fight it. It was almost liberating.

Cam reached out and took my hand again, and our fingers entwined.

Doc watched us quietly for a moment. "Tell me how he's in your head, Brady."

I closed my eyes briefly and then opened them to look out the window. Strange how the black didn't scare me that much anymore. Was it because Cam loved it so much? Or because I didn't feel so alone?

"I get feelings a lot," I said. "Sort of vibes, I guess. Maybe that's his unconscious. But sometimes I get his voice as well, a conscious response, except he thinks it instead of says it."

"Like this?" Cam smiled at me.

"Smart-ass," I muttered. "Sorry, Doc."

He only shrugged.

"So yeah," I said, trying to articulate to Doc what I couldn't properly understand myself. "I feel his physical and emotional reactions, and we share our dreams. I'm him in his dreams. There's no back-and-forth, there's no echo, I'm just him."

"It goes both ways," Cam said. "I've dreamed of your family."

We both thought of Lucy, and we both missed her.

"And the closer you are, the stronger the connection is?" Doc asked.

I blushed.

"I've been speaking to Commander Leonski," Doc said, turning his gaze to Cam. "Is this how the Faceless communicated with you?"

"Yes," Cam said.

He was still ashamed of that. My stomach twisted as well. But he wasn't ashamed of what had happened, I knew now. He was only ashamed of the way it made other men look at him. He didn't want their pity and their disgust. He didn't need it.

Doc wasn't one of those men.

"All right," he said at last. "All right, if this is how it is. But from now on you don't keep it from me, understand?"

"Yes, sir," Cam said.

I nodded. "Okay, Doc."

Doc frowned at me for a moment and then scrubbed his big hand over my head. "Look after yourself, son."

Did Cam feel how much my heart swelled when Doc did that? He did, of course. My miserable fucking life was laid out in front of him like the pages of a storybook.

Doc packed up his gear. "Come on, boys. I'm taking you to dinner."

I sat up straighter. "Dinner?"

———

THE OFFICERS' mess looked just the same as the enlisted men's mess: rows of steel tables and chairs and a long line for food. I was a bit disappointed by that, until I actually made it to the front of the line. Because the food was good. It was chicken Kiev that night. That's what the chalkboard said anyway. All I know is it looked good, and it smelled even better, and Doc laughed at me when I raised the tray to my nose to breathe it all in.

"*Bin scab.*" Cam flashed me a smile.

It was a nervous smile. We were getting more than a few sideways looks being in here. Me because I was a lowly recruit, and Cam because none of them knew what he was, but they sure as hell didn't trust it.

Cam was wearing a uniform that had been sent up from the Q-Store that morning. It had the patches on his shoulder that identified him as a Hawk pilot, another patch with "Def-8" on it, his stripes of rank, and his surname on his front pocket. I'd felt his cautious glow of pride when he'd dressed, as though he was pleased to be finally putting the right uniform on and afraid they'd take it away from him again.

They were almost treating him like an officer, instead of a

traitor. The only thing that made him stand out now was his faint tan and his hair. Nobody had told him to cut it yet, and he hadn't volunteered. Maybe he was waiting for the order. Maybe then he'd know they really thought he was one of them.

And they didn't. That much was obvious. Conversations fell to silence as we passed. When they picked up again on the other side, they were sharp with speculation. With fear.

We sat at a table with Doc, Captain Loh, and some guy with glasses I didn't know. The patch on his uniform said he was in logistics. It was probably him I had to thank for the chicken Kiev, then. He was reading a dog-eared novel and looked a million miles away. I envied him for that.

It was more civilized in the officers' mess. None of them ate with their elbows on the tables, hunched over their trays like dogs afraid their bowls would get taken away before they were finished. None of them were yelling at one another to be heard over the hundreds of competing conversations. None of them were stubbing out their cigarettes in the newbies' dinner for a laugh.

"Garrett." Captain Loh nodded at me as I sat down.

"Sir," I said.

Loh looked at me curiously for a moment, and I wondered if Doc had told him what Cam and I had been doing. He said he'd keep it out of our records, but what if he trusted Loh enough to tell him? I mean, medically it had to be interesting, right? Or maybe I was just paranoid. Maybe Loh, like everyone else in the room, was wondering if Cam was a traitor and if I'd caught it off him like a disease.

"This is more like it, hmmm, Brady?" Doc asked me, digging his fork into his mashed potatoes. "A change of scenery?"

"Yes, Doc," I said and dug into my chicken Kiev.

But it turned out he hadn't just brought me there for the view. He'd brought me there for career counseling.

"Now, you're graduating in three months," he told me over dessert.

Dessert! It was rice pudding, but it was sweet and milky, and I was going to filch Cam's if he didn't hurry up and finish it.

Cam glanced at me, smiled, and pushed the bowl my way.

Doc huffed into his mustache and cleared his throat. "You're graduating in three months," he said again.

I wiped my mouth with my sleeve. "Yes, sir."

Either graduating or already dead.

"I want you to enroll in the first training module on paramedic care," Doc told me.

My stomach flipped. "That's for interns, Doc, not basic medics."

I was training to be a medic, not a paramedic. Medics stopped bleeding, slapped on bandages, and sent guys to real doctors. Paramedics worked on a whole other level: cannulation, drug therapy, narcotic pain relief, intubation, sedation, sutures, and wound management. Paramedics could even assist in basic surgeries. Without a university degree, it was the first step to becoming a medical officer in the military. And Doc knew I didn't want to be an officer. Not for all the rice pudding in the universe.

Doc raised his hairy eyebrows. "We've got a shortage of paramedics on the station, Brady, and I've been asked to make recommendations."

I put my spoon down on the table. This was why he'd brought me to the officers' mess to ask. Doc knew he usually only had to bribe me with decent food to get me to do anything. But not this time. "No. I don't want to be a paramedic."

Which wasn't true, exactly. I just didn't want to be an officer. I wasn't going to commit another five years to the military. Not on top of the seven I had left. I had a life I wanted to get back to.

That I needed to get back to. My dad didn't have thirteen years left. Hell, he didn't have seven either.

Doc knew my situation. "You could be an officer in four years, Brady. It's good money."

"I know," I said.

The numbers would never add up right for me. Never. So what was the best choice? To hope that I could go home in seven years and find Lucy okay? Or commit to another thirteen years in the big black and start sending real money home in four? Whatever I did, I couldn't cover the gap that my dad would leave. It made the decision a lot easier.

"No," I told Doc. "Thanks, but no."

"Okay, son," said Doc, and he looked almost disappointed. And that stung me, because Doc's opinions had always mattered to me more than they should.

Cam's hand reached for mine under the cover of the table.

Yeah, I was an open book.

Fuck it. What did it matter that I'd disappointed him? He'd get over it.

Anyway, we'd all be dead in a week.

I ate Cam's rice pudding and didn't look up in case I met Doc's gaze.

CHAPTER ELEVEN

IT WAS the middle of the night, and I was bored. Cam had fallen asleep watching the Shitboxes—another four since last bell; things would be getting crowded on the station now—and I'd pulled the blanket up over him and watched him for a while. I didn't care about the traffic coming to the station. I wasn't a pilot. I couldn't get interested in watching them slowly maneuver on the Outer Ring until they got a docking lock. I couldn't tell the difference between a good docking and a bad docking, even though Cam tried to explain it to me. There was one Shitbox that was so out of line the pilot had taken it away for a fresh run-in, but all the others looked the same to me.

"He's misjudged the thrusters," Cam had said earlier. *"See?"*

But I hadn't.

Cam had talked a little bit about flying the Hawks, and I'd felt his yearning. He loved the big black. He looked at it and saw freedom, even after everything that had happened to him. I looked at it and saw asphyxiation. Doc should never have showed me that textbook on the vacuum of space. Those few guys who'd been rescued before they died described feeling the saliva on their tongues boil. You had minutes at the most. I figured I wouldn't even try and hold my breath. I'd want it over before I felt my eyes getting pulled out of their sockets.

I turned my back on the window. Fucking space. I hated it. It would take more than a trip down Cam's memory lane to change my mind on that. Maybe he liked to feel insignificant against the big black, but I'd felt that way my whole life, and the shine had worn off a long time ago.

Hawk pilots were all mad, Hooper used to say. Who'd want to fly something out into the black every day? There was no room for error out there, and that was even without going into combat.

Once, fifteen years ago, a squadron of Hawks managed to see off a Faceless ship. Not destroy it, but damage it enough so that it retreated. And that was pretty much the only fucking victory we'd ever had against the Faceless. So those guys were all heroes. The four who'd returned had been given medals and parades and the whole shebang. The sixteen who hadn't had been given solemn memorial services. Those are shitty odds, right? Who'd want to pilot a Hawk after that?

Crazy assholes like Cam, I guess.

Crazy assholes who talked about how being shot out of the Tubes into the black was amazing, and how the traps hadn't properly caught the Hawk once during a hard landing and Cam had almost crashed into the landing bay bulkheads. Crazy assholes who laughed when they told that story, like it was the funniest thing in the world.

Cam missed flying like I missed home. Hooper was right. Just fucking crazy.

When Cam slept, it gave me a break from his thoughts. I could tell his dreams were restless, like always, but unless I was sleeping as well, I didn't have to share them. Maybe that was the way we should have done it from the beginning, slept in shifts, but it was too late for that.

I lay beside Cam with my back to the window. I had one arm wedged up under my pillow and the other one lying over him. Sometimes I liked to put my hand loosely on his hip, but sometimes I liked to hold him closer with my hand on his chest and feel his heartbeat. And sometimes I liked to slide my hand down to his cock, just to feel it. I liked the way it stiffened under my touch even when he was asleep. The bonus was that whenever he woke up with a hard-on, he dragged me straight into the showers to sort it out.

My confession to Doc hadn't really changed anything. We still just basically jerked each other off in the showers, and Cam still gave me head. That was a favor I hadn't reciprocated yet. I was still working up to it, which seemed weird. I mean, either I was gay or I wasn't, right? I don't believe that shit about giving or receiving—either end of that equation is gay when it's consensual. So I was pretty damn sure I was gay. But I was also nervous as hell about sucking another guy off. Cam was good about it. He hadn't pushed.

Then again, we'd all be dead in a few days, right? What the hell was I waiting for? It's not like I'd have to be embarrassed for long if I completely flubbed it.

Doc had turned up the morning after my confession with a bag of condoms and lube. I'd stashed them at the bottom of my pack, and they just sort of lurked there. Lurked like the monster under the bed, daring me to face my fears.

We had days. It was going to happen. I'd die with enough regrets anyway. I didn't want Cam to be one of them.

My hand had found his cock while I'd been thinking, and it began to harden under my touch. Cam murmured something in his sleep and rolled over onto his back.

Once, when I was eight, I went to the river with a bunch of older kids. They used to play on the triangle, which was a rusted old handle on a bit of rope. I don't know why it was called the triangle, but it always had been. Anyway, you grabbed the handle and swung out over the riverbank. You had to time it right, because otherwise you'd land on the bank or in the shallows and break your neck. You had to let go right when the rope was at its highest and drop into the deep water. And everyone said I wouldn't do it, because I was too small and too scared. I did it just to prove them wrong, even though it was the most terrifying thing I'd ever done. I wasn't a coward, not then and not now.

Maybe I couldn't laugh off a hard landing in a Hawk, and maybe I couldn't look into the big black, but there was something I could do.

I climbed over Cam and knelt between his legs. He was still sleeping, and I managed to pull his sweats down without waking him. His cock lay against his thigh, not quite stiff, but not quite soft either. I moistened my lips with my tongue. My heart thumped as I leaned in close and inhaled. He smelled good. He smelled like soap and musk. I'd thought it would be gross, but it wasn't. It was Cam.

Why the hell was I scared of this?

I stroked him gently, and he moaned and shifted slightly. I even ran my thumb across his balls, and that weird wrinkly skin tightened as they drew up under my touch. His cock rose, and I'd never seen anything like it. Not from this angle, anyway. It thickened first and then began to stiffen. I caught it in my hand before it could press up against his abdomen, and moistened my lips again. A drop of clear fluid on the head of his cock gleamed in the dim light.

I put my tongue out and tasted it. Weird. Kind of bitter, but not exactly unpleasant. Just weird.

Cam shifted again, stretching, and then he was awake. Kind of. "Brady?" he mumbled.

"Don't move, Cam," I said.

"Am I dreaming?" he mumbled and then hissed sharply as I

lapped at the head of his cock again. His whole body jerked. "Brady! What are you doing?"

That was a dumb fucking question. I licked again.

"Oh Jesus, Brady! You don't have to do that!"

Something in the tone of his voice made me stop. I leaned back and looked up at him. His face was pale in the darkness. "Don't you want me to?"

"Come here," he said, opening his arms.

I slid up beside him, my stomach twisting. He didn't want me to. Why the hell not? Chris. Of course.

He tilted his head and kissed me gently on the lips. He ran his palm over my scalp. "I want you to, Brady, but not like this. Not just because you think you're going to die in a few days."

I sighed. "Whatever. I've told you I can't help what I think."

"I know you can't," he said.

I slipped my hand around his hip and pulled him closer. His cock was still hard. So was mine, just by being close to him. "Anyway, we've only got a few days whatever happens, right?"

He drew a sharp breath. His voice was low when he spoke. "What do you mean?"

"I mean even if we live, I'm a recruit, and you're a lieutenant," I said. I rocked my hips, fast losing track of what I was saying. "And I'm stuck here on Three, and they'll probably send you back to Eight, right?"

Cam frowned. "Yeah, probably."

I felt him pull away, and it took me a moment to register the fact that he hadn't actually moved. Not physically. Somehow he'd pulled his mind away, and the realization startled me.

"LT, what was that?"

"Nothing," he said and kissed me softly again.

Nothing? Yeah, right. He couldn't lie to me; I knew there was something he wasn't telling. He'd told me once before that he kept his memories of his family on lockdown. Is that what that sudden shifting disconnect between our minds was? Cam had put a space between us. That space gave him room to maneuver, to dodge. What the fuck was he hiding?

Traitor. Traitor. Traitor.

I pushed him away and climbed out of bed. I scrubbed my knuckles over my buzz cut and scowled at the floor.

"Brady?" he asked in a cautious voice. "Don't you trust me?"

I snorted with laughter at the same time my guts churned like I was going to be sick. "Fuck! You tell me, *sir!*"

"I've never lied to you," Cam said.

"Fuck you," I said. "What's the difference between a lie and a fucking secret?"

I sat down and pulled my boots on. I needed some space.

"Brady?"

"Back off, LT," I growled. "Get out of my fucking head!"

"I won't back off," Cam said. He knelt behind me and slipped his arms around my waist. "I've never lied to you."

And I knew it was the truth.

The fight went out of me. There hadn't been that much to begin with, I guess, just bluster and bullshit. I leaned back against him. "What's the difference between a lie and a secret?"

"You're not going to die, Brady," Cam said. He leaned his chin on my shoulder. "You're going to live. Everyone is, if Commander Leonski doesn't screw it up."

I closed my eyes. "Sorry. It freaks me out."

"I know that, Brady," Cam said. He tilted his head and kissed the side of my neck. "I know. But I'd never do anything to hurt you. Tell me you feel that."

I relaxed for a moment. It was true. I could sense it coming off him in waves. "Yeah, I do."

"I'm glad." He slipped a hand up and trailed his fingers over my chest. "So if I have to keep a secret or two for now, you have to know it's nothing that would ever harm you or anyone you care about."

I nodded. "Okay."

"Now come on," he said. "Come here."

"Okay," I said again, kicking off my unlaced boots and letting him draw me back down.

He brushed his lips against mine. "That's it, baby."

Baby? I'd make him pay for that.

"Go your hardest, Garrett," he murmured, and I smiled.

My lips found that place on his jaw that made his head fall back. I liked it when he exposed his throat like that. There was something primeval about that that spoke of trust and, on some level, surrender. It made my cock harden. His too.

I mapped his throat with my mouth and found my way up to his ear. "Will you let me blow you, LT? I want our time to count."

Cam shook his head slightly.

That stung. I tried to draw away, but he slipped his hand around to the back of my neck and held me there.

He leaned forward and brushed his lips against mine. "No, but I'll let you fuck me."

———

I DON'T THINK I'd ever been so scared in all my life. Not that time with Wade in the showers. Not when I first saw the Faceless pod. Not even when Cam said Kai-Ren was coming. Because those were things I had no control over. Those all fell into the "shit happens" category of my miserable life. This was different; this was something I wanted for myself, I *needed* for myself, and I didn't want to fuck it up.

My heart was thumping. I could hear the blood pumping behind my ears. My throat was dry, but I couldn't swallow. Maybe this was the time when other people would resort to small talk, but what use was that with Cam and me? He knew I was freaking out.

"It's okay, Brady," he said. "Relax, yeah?"

As if.

"Sure," I croaked, my fingers fumbling with my shirt. I was trying to grab the hem so I could pull it over my head, but I was all thumbs. *Shit. Shit. Shit.*

And then Cam was kneeling behind me on the bed and sliding his hands up my spine. His hands were warm, but I shivered like they were blocks of ice. I think my heart skipped a beat or two.

"I want you," Cam murmured, and then he had my shirt over my head and was laying a trail of kisses across my shoulders.

I looked out at the big black, and for once it didn't seem so frightening that it went on forever. Maybe I'd been looking at it wrong this whole time. Maybe eternity should have been peaceful like it was in Cam's memory, not terrifying. I wasn't alone in it now.

"Want you too," I managed.

Cam's teeth nipped the back of my neck, and a shudder ran through me. Starlight filled my vision. I closed my eyes and focused on sensation instead.

"I don't know what to do," I said as his fingers counted the knots in my spine. My cock was already hard, pressing up against my abdomen. I wanted this. Every nerve in my body screamed that I wanted this, but Cam's dreams hadn't exactly been specific when it came to preparations. I knew he wanted me inside him. I just had no idea what I had to do to get there.

"Do you want me to get myself ready?" he asked me, his breath hot against my ear.

Did I? *Days*, my brain reminded me. *Make them count.*

"I think I want to do it," I said, heat rising in my face. "Except you gotta tell me what to do."

"Days," he echoed, and his regret mingled with mine.

"Yeah," he groaned. "I'll tell you what to do."

I stood up and fetched the condoms and lube from my pack. My hands were shaking when I stood in front of the window and rolled the condom over my aching cock.

"You look so hot right now," Cam told me. His eyes were wide as he watched me.

I saw myself like he did, with the big black at my back. Framed in starlight. The juxtaposition made him breathless.

"Fucking pilots," I said.

He smiled. "Come here."

Lust rose in him, in *us*, and if the Faceless technology had a lot to answer for, it also had its benefits. I knew what he wanted. I knew what he needed. I could read his desires as clearly as I could read my own. Sharing a head space meant that neither of us had to explain. We'd never done this before, but it didn't matter. It was like finding ourselves in the middle of a dance and somehow knowing the steps.

Cam lay before me like something sacrificial, with a pillow under his hips. The dim light gleamed on his skin. It illuminated the planes of his body. It fought with the shadows when he shifted. It settled on him like water. His eyes were wide, and so were mine.

I knelt between his knees. I would have been afraid, lying so exposed like that. I think I would have, but maybe not with Cam. With anyone else, but not with Cam. He trusted me, and I trusted him. It flowed between us like electricity. It rose off us like heat.

The lube was cold in my palm, so I rubbed my hands together to warm it.

"You have to open me up first," Cam murmured.

"Okay." I tried not to let my voice waver.

He didn't have to tell me to go slow. He didn't have to tell me to be careful. I knew those things, even though I'd never been here before. I knew them because he did. I knew it would sting when I entered him however slow I took it, and I knew that was okay. He liked to ride the burn.

I slipped my hands up his inner thighs, feeling the taut muscles under the skin. His cock was as hard as mine, and his balls were already drawn up. My shaking fingers sought the entrance to his body and found it. I pressed against it gently, and Cam gasped as my fingertip slid inside. It was hot and tight, tighter than I'd expected. I didn't think my cock would fit in there.

"It will, Brady," Cam said, his stomach rising and falling as he breathed deeply. "Promise."

I pushed my finger in farther. I don't know which one of us was breathing heavier.

It was weird. I thought I'd be freaked out by what I as doing, or grossed out, but this was Cam. I could see what this was doing to him, I could *feel* it, and it was amazing. It was a fucking epiphany. I suddenly knew I had the power to reduce him to a quivering mess, and shit yeah, that's what I wanted to do.

"Fuck yeah," Cam gasped. "Do that!"

I drew back for a moment, feeling his passage tighten as he tried to keep me there, and then pushed two fingers into him. His cock bobbed madly, and his whole body trembled. All for me, I thought, all because of me. I crooked my fingers, looking for his prostate, and thanked all those medical textbooks I'd read when I found it. Cam jolted like I'd put a hundred volts through him, and squeezed even tighter around my fingers.

That's when my confidence rose to meet my ambition. I was doing this. He was already squirming. I could make this good. I already was.

I scissored my fingers carefully, and Cam moaned underneath me.

"Jesus...Brady! Put your cock in me!"

I'd never heard him sound so desperate, so ragged, and the sound of his voice almost pushed me over the edge. I closed my eyes and concentrated on breathing. I didn't want to come too soon.

"Please," he groaned. "I need it now!"

My heart thumped as I positioned myself. Funny how nature takes care of things. It was mostly instinct that guided me as I notched the head of my cock against Cam's puckered opening and pushed. There was a moment of resistance. Was that normal? Before I could worry about it, Cam wrapped his legs around me and urged me forward.

Oh fuck. He was so tight. So tight.

This was different from all those dreams. In those dreams I'd been Cam. Now I was feeling what Chris would have, and it was phenomenal.

I lost myself in sensation. I think we both did. I trembled as I pushed slowly into him, lowering myself over him. He raised himself up, and we kissed, and it wasn't just my desire I was feeling. It was his as well. We were closer than we'd ever been before. We were one heartbeat, one mind, and one being. I saw his universe.

This...this was what Kai-Ren had done.

"Not here," Cam whispered in my ear. "Not now. Just us, Brady. Just us."

And just like that, it was.

I pushed in until my balls came to rest against Cam's ass. I gasped for breath, feeling his muscles pulse and flutter around my cock. "*Cam!*"

"Fuck me," he urged, sliding a hand around the back of my neck.

I began to thrust.

Cam shuddered as the head of my cock dragged over his prostate.

We were sensation and sweat and short, sharp breaths. We were electricity. I couldn't tell his gasps and whimpers from mine. I didn't know it could be like that. Didn't think it was possible to be that close to another human being. The big black became small drawn, shrank into nothing. We were all that existed.

"Cam," I managed, desperate because I was going to come. Couldn't understand how I hadn't already. Fuck, I was teetering on the knife's edge. Every muscle in my body was tensed, coiled tighter than a spring, ready to go. "*Cam!*"

His eyes widened, and he came first.

I felt the sudden burst of wet heat between us, and I came as well. We shuddered against each other, shared our gasping breaths. When we finally stopped shaking, I collapsed on top of him, and Cam put his arms around me.

"Oh fuck," I murmured into his throat. His skin tasted salty with sweat. "Oh."

"*So good. So good, Brady,*" he said in my head.

Cam unhooked his legs from behind me, and we shifted apart for a moment so that we could settle more comfortably. He helped me removed the condom and tie it off, and then he lay on his back, and I curled up against his side with my head on his chest.

"Go to sleep," he murmured, stroking my cheek.

Regret washed over us again, but not for what had happened. *Soon.*

What a fucking waste, when we'd only just found each other.

I fell asleep with Cam's arms wrapped around me.

CHAPTER TWELVE

I SHOULD HAVE BEEN in a good place when I fell asleep with Cam's arms around me and my head tucked under his chin. He was warm, and it felt safe there. I shouldn't have been homesick with Cam holding me, but it still seeped into my dreams when my defenses were down.

But maybe I knew. Maybe I sensed it was already over.

I dreamed of Kopa that night. I was lying in my bed, staring out the window at the stars.

I'd got my letter that morning, and it was still shoved under my mattress. I'd read it once, and then I couldn't look at it again. I wanted to burn it or bury it, but I knew it wouldn't make a difference. My number had come up: I was being conscripted.

I had two days. Two days until I'd be leaving everything for the emptiness of the big black. I was old enough to be conscripted, but I'd never felt so much like a little kid before in my life.

I didn't want to go. I was afraid to go. I wanted my dad, and how the hell would I break this to him? Not that I had any decent future in Kopa, but at least I wouldn't be alone. At least I'd have Dad and Lucy, and at least they'd have me.

They were my whole world, and I'd always known it was so fucking precarious. I'd always been afraid of this moment. And now it was here, and everything I'd tried so hard to hold on to was slipping away from me.

"Brady? Brady? Are you asleep, Brady?"

Lucy slept on a mattress on the floor, or she was supposed to. Most nights she ended up climbing into bed with me. In the summer her body burned like a furnace, and we both woke up drenched in sweat.

"I'm awake."

She crawled up beside me. She smelled of carbolic soap. That was the only sort we could afford.

"Are you wishing on a star, Brady?"

"Yeah." Wishing I'd never seen them.

And then, in my dream, it was another night, and I wasn't there.

Dad pointed at the sky. "Wave to Brady!"

"Wish on a star!" Lucy said. "Is Brady in heaven, Dad? Is Brady dead?"

Is Brady dead? Is Brady dead? Is Brady dead?

I woke up with tears on my face.

I sat up, scrubbing my face with my hands. Cam was still sleeping. He looked beautiful when he was sleeping. A flicker of worry crossed his face as I watched, and I felt guilty. Had the tendrils of my dream ensnared him? And then he sighed, and it was gone. He was peaceful again.

You're all this place has ever given me, LT. You mean more to me than you should, so why can't I believe you when you tell me I'm not going to die? What are you keeping from me?

I checked my watch.

Shit, it was still the middle of the night. It was another four hours at least until the marines came with our breakfast. And then what? Then, in hours or days—who the hell knew?—the Faceless would come. We were already as good as dead, whatever Cam said.

I sat there for a while and tried not to hate it. It was what it was. It was more than I'd had any right to expect, wasn't it? If the Faceless were going to wipe us all out, at least I'd had Cam for a little while. And that would be some consolation, I hoped, at the end.

And if they didn't destroy us all? Well, at least I'd had Cam for a little while. At least when Hooper said all Hawk pilots were arrogant assholes, I'd be able to think of one who wasn't.

The dream was still lingering at the edges of my mind. It had been so vivid that I could almost smell the red dirt. Jesus, I was always homesick. Maybe everyone was. They told you it wore off after a few months, but maybe that was just when you learned how to hide it under false bravado. That was me, all bluster and bullshit, all the time.

Except with Cam. I couldn't lie to Cam. I had no secrets from Cam.

I looked down at him lying there so peacefully and wondered how it was that he had secrets. He'd had longer to get used to the whole Faceless mind-fuck thing, but that wasn't really the issue. I wondered what his secret was. Why didn't he trust me enough to tell me?

Even though Cam had promised his secret wouldn't hurt me, why couldn't I stop thinking of betrayal? He was keeping something from me, from everybody. That frightened me.

I looked out the window and wondered what Kai-Ren had done to him. Like Commander Leonski, I wondered if I could trust Cam when it came to the Faceless. He hadn't lied, I knew that, but what if we just hadn't asked the right questions?

"*Shithead,*" Linda said to me once, "*did you take ten dollars out of my wallet?*"

"*No!*"

"*You lying little shit!*"

I was ten and scrawny. She was bigger than me. The whole time she was laying into me, all I could think was: *I took twenty, you bitch.* And it was totally fucking worth it.

Later, when my dad got home, I promised him that I'd told Linda the truth.

"*I didn't take ten dollars! I didn't lie! How come you let her stay with us? How come you let her hit me? I hate you!*"

When I was I kid, I used to punish my dad, because I was too much of a coward to stand up to Linda.

Chalk up another regret: Linda had left before I'd ever got my own back. Not that it mattered. The only thing that mattered was that she'd gone.

I had a lot of regrets, I guess. But looking down at Cam, I decided that he was not going to be one. I might regret our short time together, but I'd never regret what we'd done. As if I could. I didn't have much to compare it to, but it had been amazing. It was even better than a blowjob, and that was saying something.

I bit my lip and tried not to laugh. Where the hell had Cam been all my life? A week ago I could count my sexual experiences on one hand—my right hand, if I was honest with myself. Kaylee and Wade and calluses: the good, the bad, and the ugly. Cam was like a revelation. And if I'd been at all religious, I would have been on my knees thanking God. As it was, I wanted to be on my knees thanking Cam.

I had to cover my mouth with my hand to stop laughing aloud.

It was a bit weird, though. I'd discovered a part of myself I never knew existed. I never thought I'd fuck a guy. And I never thought a guy like Cam—an officer and a gentleman and all that shit—would ask me to fuck him. Sometimes life is full of surprises. And so are officers.

I resisted the urge to lean down and kiss him. I didn't want to wake him. Not when he looked so beautiful sleeping. Not when I wanted to imagine he was dreaming about me for once.

My stomach growled, and I thought of the vending machine down the hallway. I could buy chocolate and cigarettes, the two things Doc refused to supply. What's the good of loving a man like a father if he won't score you nicotine and sugar?

I slipped out of bed and hauled on a pair of fatigues that might have been Cam's. I headed to the bathroom to dispose of the condom we'd left lying on the floor, and cleaned myself off with a washcloth. I headed back into the bedroom, pulled on my T-shirt, and checked my pack for my wallet. I didn't have a lot of cash. Most of my pay went straight to Dad, but I always kept a bit aside for incidentals, like alcohol and cigarettes and gambling. All those things a growing boy needs.

I didn't even bother putting my boots on as I crept outside. I was only going to be a minute.

There was a marine leaning against the wall. He pulled himself upright as the door slid open, then saw it was only Lieutenant Rushton's medic and slumped back against the wall.

"I'm going to the vending machine," I said. "Want anything?"

He didn't answer. Just fucking stared.

"Whatever," I muttered.

I slipped down the hallway. It was late, and the lights were still turned down. I made it to the vending machine without being spotted, and fed my coins slowly into the slot. I punched in the code, and a packet of cigarettes slipped into the tray at the bottom of the machine. That left me enough money to buy a thin bar of chocolate. It wasn't the same sort we got in our ration packs. This was the decent stuff that they sold in the shops back home.

I headed back toward the room. I heard the voices and foot-steps before I saw them, and realized what I looked like—a bare-foot kid slinking around the officers' quarters with chocolate and cigarettes. I looked like I'd been up to no good, for sure. I slipped my cigarettes and chocolate into my pockets and hoped maybe they wouldn't notice my bare feet.

Of course it was the first thing they noticed.

"What the hell is this?" one of them demanded, shaking his head. "Standards have slipped since I was last on Def-Three!"

There were three of them, and they had their packs on. They were also lugging a pair of footlockers between them.

I felt cautiously optimistic. I was wearing my plain gray T-shirt instead of my tunic with my surname embroidered on the pocket, and these officers obviously weren't from Defender Three, so they wouldn't know me. I might even be able to lie my way out of this one.

But they didn't even care if I was meant to be there.

"Is this level seven?" the one at the front asked.

"Yes, sir," I said.

The man put down his end of the footlocker. He pulled a bit of paper out of his pocket. "Where is room nineteen?"

I looked at the patch on his uniform. These guys were from intel. You'd think they'd be able to figure out that room nineteen was between rooms eighteen and twenty. Hell, weren't all the stations meant to be built on the same plan?

I pointed. "Down the hall, sir. Take your first left."

"Want to give us a hand here?" one of the others asked.

"Yes, sir," I lied.

"Thanks," said the officer on the other end of the footlocker I picked up. "I had to drag that here all the way from the Outer Ring."

If they weren't going to comment on my bare feet and the

fairly obvious fact I wasn't an officer, I wasn't going to be disrespectful.

"It's not a problem, sir," I told him and looked up.

Holy shit. I knew that face: those dark blue eyes, that olive complexion, the angle of the jaw, the straight, prominent nose, and the smile that was just a little lopsided. I'd seen it in all my dreams. It was Chris.

My stomach clenched, and my heart thumped. I felt all the color drain out of my face. My throat was suddenly dry, and my fingers, clasped around the handle of the footlocker, were shaking. I was dizzy.

"All right?" he asked me.

My gaze flicked down to his tunic and back to his face. Chris. Captain Varro.

I'd never met him before in my life, but I swelled with happiness. Chris was here. God, I'd missed him. I blinked back tears of relief.

"Yes, sir," I managed to croak, and we set off down the hallway.

Keep it together, Brady. Keep it together.

I concentrated on not dropping the locker on my bare toes. I tried not to look at him while we walked, and he kept shooting glances back at me. He was wearing a slight frown.

"All right?" he asked again, and I nodded and stared at the locker.

We reached their quarters, and I lingered there in the doorway, knowing I shouldn't but unable to turn away.

"Thanks, kid," Captain Varro said. "I can take it from here."

Kid? Asshole.

Crazy how I felt the sting of betrayal. I loved Chris. I wanted Chris. Wanted to touch him, to taste him, to ride him, and he was looking at me like I was nothing. I *loved* him.

Actually he was looking at me like I was crazy. "Is there a problem?"

My face burned. "No, sir. Sorry, sir."

I could feel his eyes on me as I walked away, so I had to wait until I'd rounded the corner before I smacked myself in the head. *You fucking idiot, Brady. He's never met you. He doesn't know you from a bar of soap.*

It wasn't fair. I *loved* him.

No, I reminded myself. I didn't love him. Cam loved him.

That brought me to a dead stop. Cam loved him.

It was over between us the minute Chris Varro had stepped on board Defender Three. All this time I'd been a poor substitute for Chris, and that was okay, but now it was over. Maybe it wouldn't hurt if Kai-Ren really did break our connection, but it hurt for now. It hurt like homesickness, and getting that letter from my dad saying he was sick, and the time I'd told Doc what happened to me with Wade. It hurt like my world was ending.

Which it would, one way or another, any day now.

———

THE SECOND I lay down beside him, Cam knew. He didn't wake up, but he knew.

"Chris?" he murmured, rolling toward me, and for once he wasn't mistaking us.

I twined my fingers in his and wondered if he'd feel the misery that was coming off me in waves.

Cam sighed in his sleep. "Oh."

Oh. Just one simple little exhalation of breath, and I couldn't tell if it signaled wonder or regret. I slid my hand up under his shirt and laid my palm against his heart. I tried to read him, but his emotions were as confused as mine. Maybe they were mine; I don't know. He was nervous, excited, and overwhelmed by the sudden onslaught of memories that now intruded on his dreams. I wondered which ones he was seeing as I relived them all myself, lucky me. Chris in the shower. Chris in the mess hall. Chris in their stolen moments together after last bell. Chris, Chris, Chris.

Cam frowned in his sleep.

I lay there in the quiet. I told myself I wasn't upset, and it wasn't a complete lie. I was glad Chris was here, for Cam's sake.

I brought Cam's hand up to my lips. I needed his touch as much as he needed mine, and I could feel time slipping away from us. Shit, who was I kidding? It was already over.

It's okay, I told myself. But it wasn't.

I dropped Cam's hand and turned away from him, not caring that it left me facing the window. Facing the big black and looking out into the cold, endless, awful vacuum of space. I felt like I usually did, like I always had before Cam—small and insignificant and afraid.

There was distance between us again. I wasn't sure if he'd somehow pulled away in his sleep or if I'd pushed him. It made no difference. I didn't want him to feel my misery, because it was unfair of me. Cam loved Chris, and he deserved to be happy. It was never going to work between us anyway. Not with the Faceless, not with different ranks, not with different stations, and not with me—a reffo piece of shit from the wrong end of Fourteen Beta. Cam deserved to be happy.

Cam shifted closer to me and slid his hand along my hip.

The electricity hummed between us, prickling my flesh.

Just a little longer, my brain told me. I could put up with the misery for just a little longer, and then, if the Faceless didn't kill us all, I could go back to my life. Maybe in time I'd even forget how close I'd once been to Cameron Rushton.

Yeah, right.

You don't owe me anything, LT. My throat ached.

I wanted to sleep, but I didn't. I lay there and stared out at the big black. And it turns out that you don't have to be as brave or arrogant as a Hawk pilot to look at it and not be scared. It turns out that you can feel so fucking miserable that even the thought of asphyxiation doesn't seem so bad.

CHAPTER THIRTEEN

THE LIGHTS SHOULD HAVE COME on at 0600 like they had every other morning, but not today. I thought I hadn't slept, but I must have, because when the lights flashed on at 0415, it took a while for my brain to catch up. For a second I didn't know where I was or what was going on, and it was the longest second in the world. And then there was a face right in mine. And it was faintly amused and faintly disgusted, and I faintly recognized it from my foray into the corridors earlier that night.

"Make yourself decent, recruit."

I was wearing sweats, so I was hardly indecent, but I climbed out of bed, pulled a uniform out of my pack, and headed into the bathroom. That's what the military does to you. Some guy with stripes on his shoulders tells you to do something, and you do it, and you don't ask questions even if it's still the middle of the night. Especially if it's still the middle of the night.

"Brady? Brady?" Cam was awake now, and his voice was pitched higher than usual. He was afraid.

A low voice said something I couldn't make out, and Cam fell silent.

I leaned against the basin in the bathroom for a moment and turned on the tap. I splashed water on my face. It stung my eyes; I was too tired. I stripped off my sweats and pulled on my fatigue bottoms and a T-shirt. Then I realized I'd left my boots outside.

I slipped back into the bedroom and discovered that this was Cam's interrogation.

It was the three officers from a few hours ago, the ones from intel. And one of them was Chris. They stood around the bed and regarded Cam stonily. Funny how it only took three guys to make a fucking wall like that.

Cam was sitting on the edge of the bed, still wearing just his sweats. Still smelling of me, probably. His hair was mussed up from sleep. My dad used to call those twists of hair elflocks.

"My name is Major Durack," said the first officer to Cam. "This is Captain Lutkus, and you know Captain Varro."

"Yes, sir," Cam said. His eyes flashed to Chris and back again. Nothing passed over his wary face, but I felt his heart skip a beat.

Major Durack turned his head to look at me. He was sallow-faced, and he had bags under his eyes. He looked like he hadn't slept either. His gaze slid over me, and then he turned back to Cam. "Do you need the recruit here, Lieutenant Rushton?"

Cam hunched over slightly. "Yes, sir."

"And why is that?" Major Durack asked.

Cam looked at the floor. "His heartbeat regulates mine, sir."

The three intel officers exchanged looks.

Yeah, I wanted to tell them, *it's exactly as fucked-up as it sounds.*

"And how does he do that?" Major Durack asked. He looked at me again, as though expecting to see something other than a skinny recruit with a bad haircut.

"By touch," Cam said. He was still looking at the floor. Avoiding Chris's gaze, I knew.

And how shitty was that? They'd sent Cam's boyfriend to

interrogate him. I was no expert, but surely there had to be a conflict of interest there? Except, I thought as I sifted through Cam's memories, maybe it had been a secret. There was nothing there to indicate they'd been out and proud, although there was nothing to indicate they hadn't been either. It was just their most private moments that Cam remembered and dreamed about, as though they'd been the only two people in the whole universe. They were the moments I envied.

No, I was better than that. Cam didn't owe me anything.

He glanced up at me quickly, and I flashed him a smile. *"It's okay, LT."*

Major Durack frowned at me. "You may stay, Recruit Garrett."

"Yes, sir," I said. "Thank you, sir."

I slipped between the three officers. I sat on the bed beside Cam and half turned away from him. It gave the pretense of privacy, I guess, even though everyone there knew I was listening to every word.

Captain Lutkus handed Major Durack a folder. Durack opened it and began to flick through the paperwork inside. Meanwhile Chris moved away and took out a notebook.

Glorified secretary, I thought. That's not what he imagined when he took the intel entrance exams!

Cam's lips quirked, and he lowered his head until his hair curtained his face. *"No, it isn't."*

I slid my hand across the mattress, palm upturned, and Cam pressed his hand against it. We didn't link fingers, not this time. Neither of us wanted to show that much intimacy in front of Cam's interrogators, but I couldn't resist looking up at Chris.

His lips were pursed tightly as he watched us.

I wavered between jealousy and pity, and then looked away again. I couldn't hate Chris any more than I could hate Cam. Cam loved him, and even the echo of it that welled up in me was powerful. And horrible as well, because Cam loved him, and very soon he was going to confess terrible things to him.

"Cam-ren, Cam-ren." Kai-Ren and his sibilant hiss, and his restraints and his drugs and the way he'd laid Cam bare and then fucked him. My guts churned just thinking about it, but my cock twitched as well. Fear and lust mingling together, into something weird and transcendent. Into something mind-blowing. Into communication, into understanding, into that heart-stopping moment when those sibilant hisses had coalesced into words and made everything that had come before worth the price.

Chris wouldn't get that. Nobody could, except Cam and me. And hell, even I struggled with it. This would be fucking horrible.

Major Durack consulted his notes for a while longer.

In the Middle Ages kings used to build the doorways to their throne rooms low so that everybody who came inside had to bow. That's what Durack was doing now, standing above us. He'd told me to go and get dressed, but what about Cam? He was keeping Cam lower than him, keeping him in nothing but his sweatpants, and keeping him waiting to remind him who was in charge here. He'd pulled him from sleep to catch him off-kilter. And his first comment wasn't even directed at Cam. It was directed at me.

"It's not our usual procedure to allow third parties in on interviews," he said in a conversational tone. He had sharp eyes, though. He wouldn't give an inch.

"Yes, sir," I muttered. Maybe he'd be considerate enough to let me hold Cam's hand when they water-boarded him. Asshole.

Cam's fingers dug into my palm briefly. *"Relax, Brady."*

"You won't give us any trouble, will you?" Major Durack asked me.

"No, sir."

Chris clicked the end of his pen.

For all his stand-over tactics, Major Durack asked exactly the same questions that Cam had already answered a hundred times before: *Who is Kai-Ren? What is a battle regent? What does he want? What did he do to you?* They were the same old questions, but Cam wasn't inured to them yet. His gaze dropped, and his voice snagged in his throat when he answered that last one. And then clarified it when that asshole of a major asked him if he'd capitulated. *Capitulated*, like it was a fucking euphemism for gagging for Faceless cock.

"No, sir." Cam's voice wavered. "I was restrained and drugged."

Then there was that awful silence where they faltered between revulsion and compassion and came down in some uncomfortable place in the middle. I looked at Chris. He was still writing down what Cam had said, but his jaw was clenched. That was the only sign he was at all affected by what he had heard.

Screw them, and screw what they thought. I curled my fingers through Cam's and squeezed his hand. "It's okay, LT."

Major Durack pounced on that. "Keep your mouth shut, Recruit Garrett."

"Yes, sir." I fixed him with a stare that didn't match my respectful tone. "Sorry, sir."

Major Durack narrowed his eyes at me.

My brain reminded me that it wasn't a great idea to make enemies of these men. My gut told me I'd be dead in a few days and it didn't matter.

"Brady," Cam murmured. His hand trembled in mine.

A wave of nausea hit me. "LT?"

He was pale. His skin was clammy.

"Another word and you're out, Garrett," Major Durack growled.

"He's sick, sir," I protested. I put my free hand on his chest. It was covered in sweat. His heart was thumping wildly. "Last time this happened he arrested."

"Well, he's not going to play possum today," Major Durack said.

My jaw dropped. Play possum? "Sir, his heart stopped!"

Major Durack exchanged a look with Captain Lutkus.

"I'm okay," Cam managed. "I'll be okay. I'm stronger now."

"Glad to hear it, Rushton," Major Durack said, like he didn't give a damn either way. "Are you strong enough to tell me what you know about the Faceless' weapons systems?"

Cam raised his eyes. "I don't know anything, sir."

"You were with them for four years," Major Durack said. "I don't believe you."

Cam smiled slightly and shrugged.

I closed my eyes as a rush of memories washed over me. I saw the usual flashing lights and heard the usual hisses, but this time his memories showed me something new: I was standing on a platform and looking down into what appeared to be a spinning turbine. And the hell if I knew what it was, but I knew Cam's memory had snagged on it because Durack had asked about weapons systems. It was something. It was something important. And then I saw Cam's hand—*our* hand—on Kai-Ren's shiny black suit, that impenetrable black suit. And I saw Kai-Ren peeling it off his skin. His skin was like porcelain: white and cold and *hard*.

Jesus, the things Cam could tell intel. So why wasn't he?

I looked at Cam, wide-eyed.

"Cam-ren, you will obey me in this. Cam-ren..." The memory of that voice sent chills down my spine.

"Why?" I wondered. *"What does Kai-Ren have over you?"*

Cam's green eyes couldn't meet mine. *"It's not like that, Brady."*

I turned away again, and Captain Lutkus, who hadn't done much up until now, suddenly spoke up.

"You have a telepathic link," he said. "Is Rushton telling the truth?"

"Yes, sir," I lied.

You can't bullshit a bullshitter. Lutkus knew I was lying.

"Stand up, recruit," he said, narrowing his eyes.

I obeyed nervously.

"Turn around," he said. "Hands behind your back."

Fuck me. Really? Cold metal cuffs snapped closed behind me. I pulled my wrists apart reflexively, and the cuffs rattled. I turned back to face Lutkus and bit my lip to stop from burying myself even further in the shit.

"Maybe they'll let you hold my hand when they water-board me instead, LT. Fuckers."

But I wasn't water-boarded. I guess they didn't want to make a mess. The thing with Captain Lutkus, though, was that he'd read more medical books than me. He knew all about the pain withdrawal reflex and just how to work me like a fucking puppet. Sudden pressure on my collarbone forced me down onto my knees, and then he bent down and gripped my cuffed wrists. He dug his fingers right into my ulnar nerves, and I almost ripped my arms out of their sockets trying to pull away.

"Leave him alone!" Cam was outraged. "He's just a recruit!"

I whimpered like a kid. *Fucking asshole.* I couldn't even wipe the tears away.

Captain Lutkus leaned close to my ear. "Is Rushton telling the truth?"

"Yes," I said through gritted teeth.

He dug his fingers in again, and I tried to wrench away again. It was a fucking mistake. Again. Apparently I just didn't learn. I whimpered on the floor for a bit, and then he dug his fingers in under my jaw, and the pain propelled me back up onto my feet. I think I saw white.

"Is he telling the truth?" Lutkus asked again.

"Yes!" Fucking amateur, this guy. Half the guys in Kopa could have given him some decent pointers. They also could have warned him that you couldn't beat an admission out of Brady Garrett. I was always way too stubborn to give in.

"Major!" Cam exclaimed. He tried to get up, but Durack held him down by the shoulder. "Jesus! What the hell are you doing? He's a fucking kid! *Chris!*"

"Major," Chris said in a worried tone.

Durack let Lutkus have one more go first.

Solar plexus this time.

Fucking hell.

"Is he telling the truth?"

"Yes!" I was crying like a scared kid by then, but it didn't mean I'd break. And the fucked-up thing was if they'd taken me aside and asked me quietly, maybe I would have admitted Cam was lying. Because I hated the Faceless, and I was scared of them, and I didn't owe Kai-Ren anything. But the moment Lutkus hurt me, I hated him more.

"Let him go," Durack said.

Fucking assholes. The second Lutkus uncuffed me, I turned around and threw a punch. And that was pretty fucking dumb of me. For a start, he was an officer. Secondly, my shoulders were killing me, and I could hardly make a fist, so he blocked the punch easily and knocked me onto the bed like I was nothing.

"Stay down and shut up, Garrett," Major Durack told me.

"Assholes." It was Cam who said it, not me. "Fucking assholes."

I'd only ever heard him swear before when he was close to coming. I was a bad influence on him, apparently. He reached over and caught my hand. "He's my medic. He's not my fucking whipping boy!"

"Let's begin again," Major Durack said.

I curled up on the bed and cried. I hurt. Worse than that, I was humiliated. I was a kid all over again. Whenever Linda belted me, I took off for a while and then sneaked back into the house when she'd drunk herself to sleep. Sometimes I went into the kitchen and opened the drawers to look at the knives. Once I made it as far as Dad's bedroom, as far as the edge of the bed, but I couldn't do it. Most times I just slunk off to my room and crawled under my bed and fell asleep there.

And then Lucy was born, and Linda left, and for a long time it was okay.

Then I got conscripted, and it all went to shit again.

If it hadn't been for Dad and Lucy, I wouldn't have given a fuck if Kai-Ren wanted to kill us all. He would have been doing me a favor.

Major Durack went through exactly the same questions he'd already asked, and got exactly the same answers. Cam wasn't ashamed anymore, though. He was angry. I heard the waver in his voice as he tried to control it. More than that, I felt it. Every muscle in his body was tense, and every nerve was on edge.

"I'm okay, LT. Promise."

But he didn't relax.

My tears stopped eventually, and I felt a bit better. I was tired, though, and I ached. I wanted to crawl under the blankets and sleep. But Durack kept going with his questions, and Cam kept answering them in a voice that was just on the right side of respectful.

Nobody had ever stuck up for me before. Not even Dad. That wasn't his fault, not really. Most times he wasn't even there, but all the other times it was her word against mine. And Linda had a problem with the drink, Dad said. I hated her more when she was sober. At least you knew what to expect with drunk. When she was sober, I think she was ashamed of herself, and that just made her angrier when she got drunk again.

Anyway, it was nice that Cam had stuck up for me. It hadn't made a difference, but it was still nice.

"All right, Rushton," Major Durack said. "That's enough for tonight. We'll talk again soon."

Talk? I buried the face I made in the mattress.

Cam didn't answer.

As soon as the door closed I shifted. Cam's arms came around me, and I buried my head against his bare chest.

"I'm so sorry, Brady," he said. "I'm so sorry."

And warned me: *"We're not alone."*

Shit. I pulled away, scrubbing my face with my hands, and looked around. Chris Varro was still standing by the door, and he was wearing a troubled frown as he watched us.

Cam leaned down and picked up his T-shirt from the floor. He pulled it on and ran his hand through his hair. His heart beat faster when he looked back at Chris.

I didn't hate Chris, but I sure as shit hated Durack and Lutkus, and Chris was with them. I wanted nothing more than to slide my arms around Cam again and see how much Chris liked that. But Chris didn't really deserve it, and Cam certainly didn't, so I stared at my lap and picked at a thread in the hem of my shirt instead.

"Sorry about that, Cam," Chris said. He sounded concerned, and it sounded genuine. "It's just... It's the Faceless, you know?"

"Garrett has nothing to do with any of this," Cam said, shaking his head.

Chris.

My throat constricted with tears, because Cam was remembering the good times, and so was I. Chris was a good guy. Cam had always thought it, until now.

"I said I'm sorry." Chris frowned.

"Yeah," Cam managed. "Well, it's not like we could grab a drink and catch up anyway, is it?"

"No." Chris sighed. "I suppose not."

"So you might as well fuck off," Cam said.

Even I flinched at his tone.

"LT?"

"Okay," Chris said. He flashed an uncomfortable smile at Cam. His gaze fell on me, and his dark blue eyes narrowed. "I'll leave you alone to your nice digs. And your nice company. You should thank Leonski for assigning you a fuck buddy."

Cam put a hand on my shoulder to calm me. To calm us both. "It's not like that."

"Don't bullshit me, Cam," Chris said. "I know you too well."

"Not anymore," Cam said.

"And how long have kids been your thing?" Chris asked.

"I'm nineteen," I growled and tacked on a belated, "Sir."

"Was he always such an asshole?"

Cam squeezed my shoulder. *"I've got this, Brady."*

"It's been great to see you again, Chris," he said. "Maybe next time you can actually remember you've got balls and speak up before your colleagues torture an innocent recruit."

Chris opened his mouth to say something, but Cam must have hit his target because nothing came out. He shook his head, looked at Cam helplessly for a moment, and then turned on his heel and left.

The door slammed shut behind him.

Cam buried his face in his hands.

I shifted closer. "Cam? You okay?"

"I'm fine," he said, which was a complete lie. He sighed and sat up. "I mean, I will be fine."

"You didn't have to say those things to him," I said warily.

Cam frowned at me. "Of course I did."

I linked my fingers through his. "But he's a good guy. And, you know..."

"What?" Cam asked. He narrowed his eyes and stared at me intently. "What?"

I shrugged, trying to pretend it didn't hurt. "And you love him."

Cam's face went blank for a moment, and then his eyebrows shot up and disappeared under his messy hair. "I *love* him?"

I flushed. "You can't lie to me, LT. Don't try, please."

Cam caught my other hand. "No, Brady. Four years ago I loved him. Four years ago he was a good guy. But it's been a long four years."

My face burned. "But you dream of him all the time."

Cam showed me a lopsided smile. "Brady, the sex was great! Of course I dream of it! And I did love him, but we broke up before I got captured. Months before."

"Really?" My heart skipped a beat. I wrinkled my nose. *"Really?"*

"Yes," Cam said. "He transferred to Defender One to get a position in intel. I wanted to stay on Eight and keep flying. A few memories and dreams don't tell the whole story."

It took my brain a little while to process that. "So you don't want Chris?"

My heart beat faster. We were down to days, but Chris was out of the equation. And it was enough. I'd take it. I'd take anything Cam could give me.

"Maybe you're not smarter than you know," Cam said. He leaned forward and brushed his lips against mine. "I should think it's obvious that I want someone else."

"And who's that?"

"You don't know him," Cam said. His lips found my throat. "Some smart-ass medic with a foul mouth and a bad attitude."

"Yeah?" I pulled back so I could look him in the eye.

"Yeah," he said softly. "You didn't say anything to them, Brady. Thank you."

For being a traitor?

"It's gotta be like this," Cam said. "If they think we can fight back, if they try, we're all dead. You understand?"

Yes. No. I don't fucking know.

"I don't want anyone else to die," Cam said. "I don't want it to be for nothing."

"They think you're a traitor." I bit my lip. "Chris thinks it."

"It doesn't matter," Cam said, even though we both felt the sting. "It doesn't matter what anyone thinks, as long as Commander Leonski signs the treaty."

"Does it matter what I think?"

"Yeah." Cam's smile was shaky. "That matters. You matter."

I curled my fingers through his. "Yeah, right."

Cam lifted his free hand. He ran his fingertips along my jaw. The intensity of his gaze shocked me.

"You're my heartbeat, Brady."

CHAPTER FOURTEEN

ON SOME LEVEL I was happy, I guess, or the closest I'd ever been in the black. It was weird. It wouldn't last—Kai-Ren was coming—but it was almost a relief to know that. That way I didn't have to wait for the other shoe to drop because I knew it was any day now. Cam and I didn't have a future, *nobody* had a future, but we had a now. I didn't have to hold my breath. I could spend the rest of my life eating officers' rations, lying around on a real bed, waiting for the world to end.

Cam and I lay facing each other. He reached up and touched my face. "For a long time I was scared, and then I was lonely."

Not too many days ago my thoughts would have screamed at him to shut the hell up. Not now. If Cam wanted to tell me, I wanted to listen.

"It was so hard." His voice dropped to a whisper. "I would have done anything just to have another human being to talk to. To touch."

That's when he learned to put his memories on lockdown. They were slipping out past his defenses now, in tiny flashes of color and light: his parents, a house with a backyard that sloped down to a canal, that backyard strung with party lights and filled with people. Cousins, uncles, aunts. Friends and neighbors.

"You look so handsome in your uniform, Cameron! When do you ship out?"

"Next week."

The woman—Aunty Dee—left a lipstick print on his cheek and went to get another drink. And Cam turned his face to the night sky.

He would chase starlight until he caught it.

Until it caught him.

I just want to go home.

We both thought it at the same time.

When this was done—if the Faceless didn't kill us, if Cam wasn't a traitor—how much would it hurt to let him go? Cam wasn't the only one who'd been lonely. Wasn't the only one who ached to touch.

When our connection was broken, would I miss him? Or was this just biochemistry?

I was his heartbeat. I was his fucking universe.

Now I was, but soon I wouldn't be.

I would miss that, miss being important.

I would miss having someone.

"Me too," Cam whispered.

I leaned closer for a kiss.

It was the middle of the day. The lights were up, and I didn't care. The knock at the door sure caught my attention, though.

"Shit." Cam rolled away from me, and we both scrambled for our clothes.

I was fumbling with the buttons of my tunic when those assholes from intel entered the room.

"Get out, Garrett," Major Durack said, his gaze raking me up and down. "You no longer have my permission to be here when I interview Lieutenant Rushton."

I stood my ground and appealed to a higher authority.

"I'm here on Commander Leonski's orders, sir," I told Durack, jutting my chin out.

Captain Lutkus's eyes widened at my audacity. I got the feeling he saw it as a personal affront. Apparently he hadn't taken me down hard enough last time. All I knew was that I didn't want to leave Cam alone with these assholes.

But they weren't on their own this time. This time Doc was with them.

"Take a break, Garrett," he told me. I knew the frown on his face wasn't directed at me. He was as unhappy with this as I was. "And take a radio."

I shot a look at Chris Varro as I left. *Hurt him,* I hope that look said, *and I'll fucking gut you.*

His stormy blue eyes narrowed, but at least he didn't laugh. Hell, who was I kidding? I wasn't an attack dog by any stretch of the imagination. I was probably something between a Chihuahua and a Pomeranian. But at least he didn't laugh.

I took the radio from Doc and headed outside. They closed the door behind me.

It was strange to be on my own again, and I didn't like it. For a moment I stood in the hallway, just around the corner from the room and out of sight of the marines, and leaned against the wall. I felt alone.

I wondered if I could reach him. I concentrated. *"LT?"*

"Hey, Brady." I even heard the smile in his voice.

I ran my fingers over the radio hanging on my belt loop and smiled as well. Wouldn't be needing that. *"You okay, LT?"*

"I'm okay. Still with you."

Heat rose in my face. I'd been just as worried about being alone as I had been about Cam's welfare, and he knew it. But it made us both smile, so I guessed it was okay. I hoped it was. What the hell did I know about relationships?

Or whatever it was we had. It felt like more than just biochemistry, but I didn't know. I had nothing to compare it with. I had no frame of reference.

I moved off toward the lifts. I figured I'd head down to the barracks and see if Branski was there. Branski worked in the Q-Store and ran the black market. He always had a good supply of magazines and cigarettes at reasonable prices, and I was still in credit from the last handful of oxycodone tablets I'd smuggled his way.

Food wasn't the only benefit of working in the med bay. A busy shift, guys going in and out, sometimes drugs got misplaced. Branski was always after me to try for more, but I didn't want to end up in the brig. I didn't want to disappoint Doc either.

The first thing I noticed when the lift doors opened down-stairs was the smell. The week upstairs had spoiled me. Back down in the enlisted men's quarters it stank. Even the hallways smelled of old socks, sweat, and urinals. No wonder most of the officers looked at us like we were filthy animals.

The place was mostly empty. I checked my watch. It was just past 0900, and I think it was a Monday. I passed a few guys in the hallway, but everyone would have been at their duties by now. I should have been at PT, getting yelled at by Captain Lopez for not giving 110 percent. And then, after he kept me back to abuse me for a while longer, I'd break my neck trying to get to class on time.

In between all the shitty jobs, the military gave us an educa-tion. In theory, anyway. In practice you had guys like me who'd left school at twelve, you had guys who'd been on track to go on to higher education, and you had guys who couldn't even write their own names. So the classes were a bit of a joke.

My barracks wasn't empty. Carter was still in bed, snoring. His foot, encased in plaster, extended over the edge of his cot. He was on light duties, and he was milking it.

There was someone in the shower room as well. I could hear the water running and smiled a bit at that. Lukewarm showers, if you were lucky. Jesus, being back in this place was almost enough to make me want to bag a commission. Or another commissioned officer.

A pair of shirkers were sitting on a bunk playing cards. I gave them a nod as I walked past. One of them was Harris, who was okay. The other one was Prietz, and I hated him because he was a buddy of Wade's. Branski wasn't around, which sucked.

It felt strange to be back in my barracks. It had only been a week, but it was like I was looking at the place with a stranger's eyes. I was a different person now, and it had nothing to do with sex. It had everything to do with Cam, though. If I'd had someone like that from the beginning, maybe I wouldn't have been so homesick on Eleven.

I headed back for the door at the moment Cesari appeared out of the shower room with a towel around his waist.

"Hey, Garrett," he said around his toothbrush. "I hear you've got a sweet gig babysitting Cameron Rushton."

The words were light. The tone wasn't.

"Yeah," I said. "Something like that."

Cesari was wearing nothing but a towel, and his skin was shiny and damp. A silver crucifix hung from a chain around his neck. It gleamed, and I wondered if he really thought it made any difference.

He stared at me. His jaw worked, but he didn't say anything.

He wanted to know, but he didn't. Something in my eyes warned him that he really didn't.

Yeah, Cesari, we're all going to fucking die.

Cesari raised his gaze to the ceiling as the alarms started to blare. "Fuck it!"

"This is a drill. Proceed to your evacuation point. This is a drill."

Harris and Prietz headed outside. Carter woke up long enough to shove a pillow over his head.

Cesari, struggling to haul his pants on before heading to his evacuation point, gestured toward my bunk. "You got a letter, Garrett. It came on the last Shitbox."

"Thanks," I said.

Cesari left, carrying his boots. His wet shirt stuck to his back.

The letter was lying on my cot. The envelope was wrinkled and stained, but nothing ever arrived at Defender Three in a pristine condition. There were a lot of miles between Earth and the station. Even as I reached down to pick it up, I knew what it was. I knew it, because only one person ever wrote to me, and the handwriting on the envelope wasn't his.

My hand wasn't shaking, which was weird. Maybe I had a surgeon's hands after all. Doc always said he liked that about me. My steady touch, and the fact I didn't panic in a crisis. *"No fucking point in panicking,"* I'd told him then. I told myself the same thing now.

I turned the envelope over and saw the return address: *Denise Clark, c/o- Post Office, Kopa township, Fourteen Beta.*

I opened the envelope and took the letter out. It was dated five weeks ago. *Dear Brady, I'm sorry to tell you that your father died last night...* I folded it back up and slipped it into the pocket on the front of my tunic.

Biology took over.

My body was flooded with epinephrine. My heart rate increased. My blood vessels constricted. My muscles tightened. There was a buzzing in my ears. I sank down onto my cot. All I could hear was that buzzing, like my brain was off-line or something. I recognized the symptoms of an acute stress response from Doc's textbooks. No fucking point in panicking, but you can't reason with physiology.

We were on our outer orbit. We were weeks away from

Earth. And the Faceless were coming. And if they didn't kill us all, I still had seven years to go on Defender Three. Nothing I could fucking do, stuck in a tin can in the big black. I'd always known this day would come. I'd always known I wouldn't be there for Dad, or for Lucy. I'd always known I'd feel this helpless.

And it didn't matter. It wouldn't make a fucking difference if I dropped to the floor and started crying like a baby. No point in panicking. No point in breaking. No point in anything at all.

That's life for you, isn't it? It fucks you every which way from Sunday.

I closed my eyes and thought of my Lucy. Denise couldn't look after her forever, and my wage didn't stretch that far. There were some good people in town, people like Denise and Kaylee, but there were plenty of assholes as well. And a pretty little girl would slip through the cracks so easily with nobody to watch over her. Maybe it would be better if the Faceless did blow the stations away and poison the Earth. Maybe Lucy wouldn't suffer so much then, because there was nothing I could do to help her from all the way out here.

For a second I really hated my dad for not being strong enough to hold on until I got back, but it wasn't his fault. It was just life. And life just sucked.

I sighed and it caught in my throat. Tears stung my eyes, but I refused to let them come. *Harden the fuck up, Garrett.*

I hunched over and fought for a breath. I held it in my lungs until I felt the burn. And then I held it some more. I'd show my body who was in charge. My vision swam before I let it out.

I stared at the metal floor.

And breathe.

Metal that maybe my dad's hands had touched, once upon a time in the factories and smelters of the town. Metal that had been manufactured by the industry that had fucking killed him.

And breathe.

That's all the stations were: cold tombs. Useless fucking monuments to the people who died building them.

And breathe.

It was my voice in my head reminding me to breathe, not Cam's. I ached to hear Cam's voice in my head again. *Still with you*, he'd said when I left him, but where was he now? I needed him now. And then I hated myself for that, because I was the one who was supposed to be looking after him, not the other way around.

I stood up. My hands were shaking by that time, so I shoved them in my pockets. Maybe it was a good thing he wasn't in range.

"LT? LT?"

Nothing.

It's the distance, I told myself, or he's distracted, or *I* am, but I suddenly felt sick to my stomach. I swayed as dizziness caught me, followed by a wave of nausea. My stomach churned, and saliva flooded my mouth as though I was about to vomit. And my medic's brain told me that these weren't my symptoms. Shit. These belonged to Cam.

"Garrett?" Carter asked me, peering at me from under his pillow as I raced out of the barracks.

My throat was dry. My chest ached. *Mine or his? Mine or his?*

There was traffic in the hallway now. Guys were heading for the passageways to the evacuation points on the Outer Core. They'd done too many drills over the past couple of days to be in any hurry about it. Even the blare of the siren couldn't get their blood up anymore.

"This is a drill. Proceed to your evacuation point. This is a drill."

"Get out of my fucking way!" I tried to shoulder-charge through a pair of them.

"What the fuck?" An ugly face swung around and split with a leer. "*Garrett?*"

It was Wade. Great.

I backed off. My heart beat faster. My whole chest hurt now. "Get out of my way, Wade."

"What's the rush, Garrett?" Wade asked me. He narrowed his eyes and swaggered toward me. He still had that limp, though. He'd never lose that.

"Been on the wall lately?" I asked him, resisting the urge to check if the passageway behind me was still empty. Never engage an enemy without an exit strategy, they told us in class, but Dad always said you should never turn your back on a wild dog.

Wade's face twisted into something uglier. "Fuck you, Garrett!" And then he realized what he'd said and laughed at his own joke.

"Get out of my way, Wade," I said. "I haven't got time for this shit."

And neither did Wade; he was just too fucking stupid to realize the trouble he'd be in if he wasn't at his evac point in minutes.

Awooga, awooga, awooga.

"*This is a drill. Proceed to your evacuation point. This is a drill.*"

I wasn't the same scared kid I'd been three years ago. I was Wade's height now. Sure, he was built like a Shitbox, but I had a lot more mongrel in me these days. Particularly today, particularly right now. I reckon I could have taken him, and Jesus, it would have felt good to punch that asshole in the face.

"Take a fucking shot," I offered.

"*This is a drill. Proceed to your evacuation point. This is a drill. Proceed to your evacuation point. This is a drill.*"

I drew a deep breath. My chest hurt, but I was running on adrenaline now. I wasn't the sniveling kid Wade remembered.

Even if I couldn't get through him to Cam, I would make Wade hurt like hell for stopping me. Another part of me almost wanted Wade to beat the living shit of me, to make me hurt as well. Maybe I wanted to taste my own blood to remember that I was still alive. Still alive, when my dad had been dead for five weeks.

And I was angry. I knew angry. I liked angry.

"Go on," I snarled. "Take a shot! I fucking dare you!"

He must have read the pure rage in me, because Wade did something I'd never seen him do before. He stepped back.

"Fuck off, Garrett," he sneered.

I was already gone, my boots slamming on the metal floor and echoing in the hallway like a wild heartbeat. I rounded the corner and raced for the elevator.

Don't be a wait. Don't be a wait. Don't be a wait.

The doors were already open. I punched the button and leaned against the wall. Every breath felt like a knife in my lungs now, and it wasn't from running. My heartbeat was too fast. My blood pressure must have been off the chart. I could feel it pounding in my skull, like the roar of the ocean. It would drown me in a minute.

My radio squawked. *"Garrett? Garrett?"*

My hands shook as I reached for it. "On my way, Doc!"

When the lift doors opened, the marine from the hallway was waiting there. He grabbed me by the wrist and hauled me out of the lift. We raced down the hallway together.

The sirens were still blaring all over the station. *"This is a drill. Proceed to your evacuation point. This is a drill."*

"Brady! Hurry up!" Doc shouted into the radio.

I shook off the marine and pushed past Captain Lutkus into the room.

My heart seized when I saw Cam. He was lying on the bed. He wasn't moving. Doc was kneeling over him, pressing the pads of the defibrillator onto his chest. Chris Varro, crouching on the floor, was holding his limp hand.

Major Durack was standing by the window, watching on with a grave expression. I wondered if he still thought Cam was playing possum.

"No pulse," Chris Varro said.

What the hell was wrong with me that a part of me was glad he hadn't been holding Cam's hand after all?

I pushed Chris out of the way. I took the chance to get an elbow in too.

Doc turned on the defibrillator. "Stand clear."

"Turn it off!" I laid my hands on Cam's chest before Doc could protest.

Doc unhooked the machine but left the pads in place. He met my eyes, and I knew he was wondering the same thing as me: how many times until my touch stopped working? Maybe this time.

I didn't feel the familiar crackle of electricity where my palms touched his chest, and panic thrilled through me.

"LT?" I asked.

His eyes were closed, but he wasn't gone. He couldn't be gone.

"LT?" I ran my hand down his sternum. "Cam?"

Doc looked at me worriedly from under his shaggy eyebrows. "Brady?"

My throat was dry. "I don't feel it."

"Okay," said Doc. "We'll defib."

My head snapped up. "No. *I'm* his battery."

That was the one thing I knew with any certainty. I'd known it when we'd cut him out of the pod, and I knew it now. I closed my eyes and breathed. I placed both hands over his heart, spreading my fingers out. I would feel his heartbeat in just a second. I would. Because this was not going to be the day that I lost everyone.

A part of me wondered how long they'd let me stay like that if my touch didn't bring him back. Until he was cold? Oh God, not that. Not today.

"Brady?"

I heard his voice in my head before I felt his heartbeat under my hands. *"Cam?"*

His eyes flickered but didn't open. *"What happened?"*

"I don't know," I said. My throat ached. *"I got back as soon as I could."*

His heartbeat grew stronger under my touch.

"He's back," I heard Doc tell the room.

I resisted the urge to stroke Cam's hair. I just kept my hands on his chest and hoped that made him stronger.

"Do you think they'll go away if I keep my eyes closed?"

Relief washed over me. I bowed my head. *"Try it and see."*

His lips quirked for a fraction of a second. *"Okay."*

———

WHEN EVERYONE LEFT, I fell asleep beside Cam, and I dreamed of home.

"Dad? Dad?" I sat across from him at the kitchen table.

Dad curled his swollen, scarred fingers around his mug, trying to keep the heat in. It got cold in Kopa sometimes, late at night.

I'd waited up for Dad to get home from his shift. Lucy was in my bed with all our blankets lumped on top of her. I was cold, but I had to show Dad the letter from the Conscription Office.

My dad already had an old man's face: thin, hollow, gray. He was thirty-eight.

"Brady," he said, "it's not right."

I couldn't speak around the ache in my throat.

"You were supposed to look after your sister," he said.

"I know."

He wasn't blaming me. We both knew there was no way around that letter.

My dad's gray eyes filled with tears before he blinked them away.

"I'm sorry, Dad," I said.

He looked out the window, out at the night sky, like he was already searching for me in the heavens. "Brady."

I woke up to find I'd been crying. So had Cam. His dark lashes and his cheeks were wet. I reached out and traced my fingers through his tears, and then I looked across him, out the window at the big black.

"I'm sorry, Dad," I told the starlight.

I was sorry he couldn't hold on. I was sorry I couldn't go home. I was sorry that between us we'd left Lucy alone. And mostly I was sorry that his life had been so hard. He hadn't deserved to live like that. Once he'd been a boy, in love with a girl who owned a hardcover edition of *The Complete Shakespeare*. My dad had deserved more than a life in Kopa, a job in a smelter, a dead first wife, an alcoholic second one, and nothing but kids and debts.

I sat up and pulled Denise's letter out of my pocket. I brought it close to my face so I could read it in the gloom.

Dear Brady, I'm sorry to tell you that your father died last night. Your sister is living with me now. I have taken her out of school because of the cost. I am very sorry, but even with your pay coming in I will not be able to look after Lucy past the New Year. They are cutting back jobs, and Dave's hours have been reduced. I hope you will be able to make some arrangements for her before then. I hope it will give you some comfort to know that Steven spoke of you at the end. Denise.

Arrangements? My lip curled, but I knew it wasn't Denise's fault. She was doing more than most people would. But Jesus, what arrangements could I make? If my pay wasn't enough to keep Lucy in Denise's care, it wouldn't stretch any further anywhere else.

I closed my eyes and prayed to my nightmare. *Kai-Ren, kill us all and make it quick. Please?*

And it was no good aiming for a discharge. I'd seen guys in the med bay before who thought they could get the next Shitbox home for the cost of a few fingers, but they never did. Nobody got discharged. They just found you a shittier job to do to teach you a lesson. Assholes.

There were only two ways off the stations: ten years older than when you arrived, or in a body bag. Neither of those would help my sister. If it was just me, I would have slit my wrists years ago. Right after Wade, probably. But I didn't have the fucking luxury of suicide. That had never been an option. But fuck, it sounded good.

I looked at the stars.

It is an ever-fixèd mark, that looks on tempests and is never shaken; it is the star to every wandering bark, whose worth's unknown, although his height be taken.

And that was love, but love wasn't enough. If it was, the fierceness of my love would have stopped my dad from dying. It would have made him happy. And it would save my sister from halfway across the galaxy. Love might have been an ever-fixèd mark, but it wasn't enough to make a difference.

I laid my palm on Cam's chest and felt his heartbeat.

Cam could chase the starlight all he wanted, but he'd never catch it.

CHAPTER FIFTEEN

YOU CAN'T HIDE a secret from the guy who can read your mind.

But you can try.

"You okay, Brady?" Cam traced an invisible pattern on the scratched tabletop.

I watched his hand and wondered if he'd started to reach out and touch me and then remembered we were in public.

"You freaked me out, LT," I told him, shoveling mashed peas into my mouth.

We were in the officers' mess, sharing a table with Doc and nobody else. Cam was like a contagion nobody wanted to catch. And maybe I was too: Brady Garrett and his Bringing Back the Dead routine. We were getting a lot of looks from the officers at the other tables. Chris was sitting somewhere nearby, with Lutkus and Durack, but I was doing my best not to look at them.

Cam was still weak, and paler than I'd ever known him. I wondered if every time his heart stopped, it was like an infarction. Did the tissue die? Was every episode damaging his heart and bringing him closer to a death he couldn't come back from?

Doc was reading a medical journal. He had it open at a diagram of the heart, which I guess was no accident. But I also guessed he wouldn't find his answers anywhere in that journal. Cam and I had defied Doc's medical knowledge, and the medical knowledge of anyone on Earth. What the hell was in that pod that had made Cam this way? And could Kai-Ren really fix it?

"Sorry," Cam said with a slight smile. "I'll try not to faint next time."

"You didn't faint," I told him. "You *died*."

I didn't like the way the word sounded. I didn't like the way I had to force myself to say it, and I didn't like where the associations would lead. My hand crept up to the letter in my pocket, and I felt a jolt of pain.

No. Don't go there.

Cam frowned at me. "Brady?"

I didn't want to share this, not with Cam and not with anyone. It wouldn't do any good; I wasn't a sniveling kid anymore. I could keep my mind from seizing on it. I could keep distracted. My fear and homesickness could read exactly the same as they had the day before to Cam, as long as I didn't dwell on it. It didn't have to signify.

"You died," I repeated and channeled all my grief and anger into that.

He frowned at me, trying to pick the tangled threads of my thoughts apart. "I'm back now," he said.

I glared at him. *"For how long?"*

He smiled slightly and lowered his gaze. *"Yeah, I know."*

And that was the kicker, wasn't it? Cam might live, but we wouldn't be together. Maybe once Kai-Ren fixed him—or killed us all; I was always the pessimist—I wouldn't feel this need to have him close. Maybe that was part of the biochemical link between us, like symbiosis. He needed me to live, so part of the process was that I felt a need to constantly touch him. Maybe that need was nothing more than something artificial placed there by a Faceless scientist. Maybe it would vanish when our connection was safely broken. Maybe it would drop off like a gecko's tail, when it had served its biological purpose. And maybe I was an idiot sitting there and trying to think it through when I should have been making the most of our remaining time together.

It felt so good for Cam when Chris had fucked him. Did I want that? I think I wanted that. And I knew Cam would be patient with me. I trusted him. If I was going to do this, I wanted it to be with him.

Except why the hell was I thinking of fucking at a time like this?

"What's wrong, Brady?" Cam's gaze fixed on me. *"What happened?"*

"Leave me alone."

As if that would work.

"Brady?" he asked quietly.

I didn't want to think about Dad or Lucy, but why had I thought about fucking instead? Thought about being fucked, about coming, when my Dad was dead and Lucy's sky had fallen. What the hell was wrong with me?

"Fuck you," I said. "Seriously, LT, fuck you."

That was some first-class insubordination right there, right in the middle of the officers' mess. Right in front of a bunch of assholes with enough brass stars to fill a galaxy. Right in front of Commander Leonski.

He was watching, narrow-eyed and lantern-jawed, from a few tables away.

Put me in the fucking brig, asshole. See if I fucking care.

I wasn't dumb enough to say it out loud, but Cam heard it. His eyes widened.

"Garrett," said Doc. He scowled at me. "What's your problem?"

Where do you want me to start? Fuck off.

"Brady," Cam said, his voice low. "Brady?"

I pushed my chair back so fast it crashed to the floor. "Get out of my fucking head!"

It turns out that officers don't like it when recruits come into their mess and eat their rations and then cause a scene. I don't know which one of them grabbed me first, but it wasn't Doc, and it wasn't Cam, because they were still staring at me, shocked.

Some asshole who smelled of aftershave and boot polish. He got me on the floor in seconds, which was no accomplishment really since he was built like a Shitbox. My problem, everyone always said, was my mouth.

"Get off me, you fucking asshole!"

That's not a smart thing to say to a guy twice your size. Especially when he's an officer. He mashed my face into the floor, and it felt good. That sudden surge of pain and humiliation ripped right through the dull ache in my chest and tore it apart. It shattered like glass—sharp, bright, fierce—and left cold, shining anger behind. Felt so good.

Hurt me. Hurt me again.

I struggled so he did.

On the periphery of my losing battle I could hear raised voices. Doc, I think, and Cam were the only ones objecting. Nobody else cared that a lowly smart-ass recruit was learning a lesson. Not even the recruit. Because this way I wasn't thinking about Dad, wasn't thinking about Lucy, and wasn't thinking about that letter in my pocket that was as heavy as lead.

Except of course I was, and of course Cam heard it. He must have told Doc, because before I knew it Doc was ferreting around in my breast pocket and pulling out the letter.

I went quiet then, and the officer released me. Cam knelt beside me and helped me up onto my knees, and I hunched there and kept my gaze on the floor, because I could feel every asshole in the place just staring.

"Come on," Cam said at last, drawing me to my feet. "Come on, Garrett."

My face burned as he and Doc led me away.

Because everyone would know. They would ask Commander Leonski why I wasn't being hauled straight to the brig, and he would tell them. Everyone would know that poor little Brady threw a tantrum like a kid because his daddy died.

Fuck you. Don't you fucking pity me, assholes. Fuck you, and fuck this place. I hope this place burns. I hope we all do.

"Come on," Cam said as he ushered me down the narrow gray corridors of the station.

The lights buzzed. The air was stale. Nothing fucking changes in the black.

When we got to the room, I sank down onto the floor.

"Brady," Cam said, dropping onto his knees in front of me. "I'm so sorry, Brady."

You also can't use the silent treatment on the guy who can read your mind.

"It's okay," I said in a monotone. I couldn't trust myself to meet his eyes. "Shit happens."

That was the motto of my life, apparently. And Dad's.

"Hey," Cam said. He pulled me forward until I was resting my head against his shoulder. His hand was warm on the back of my neck. "I've got you, Brady."

But who's got my sister?

I didn't deserve his sympathy. She did.

"Brady," said Doc. He leaned down and put a hand on my shoulder. "I'm so sorry, son."

I was nineteen years old, for Christ's sake. I didn't need their sympathy. It was so sickly sweet, so fucking cloying, that I thought it might choke me.

I pulled away and leaned back against the wall. I got my elbows out as well, just in case Cam thought he could hug me.

"I'm okay," I said over the buzzing in my ears.

I thought of Lucy. Fuck, what did it matter? I wasn't there for her five weeks ago when her world fell apart, and I wasn't there now. I'd never felt so far from home in my whole life.

And there I was feeling sorry for myself. My father was dead and my sister was alone, and I was feeling sorry for *me*. Fucking selfish asshole.

"If you need anything, son, call me," Doc said at the dull edges of my hearing.

I nodded. I didn't want to open my mouth, because I was afraid I would cry, and tears are always pointless. So is shedding them over something that happened five weeks ago and a million miles away. Tears don't do anyone any good. They just make the guy you're fucking feel responsible for looking out for you, when it's not his fault your life is shit either.

Cam leaned forward and didn't seem to notice my elbow in his ribs.

"What can I do, Brady?" he asked me, his lips scraping over my buzz cut. "What can I do?"

His closeness sent my mind straight to the gutter.

I grabbed a fistful of his shirt. *"Make me feel good, LT. Fuck me. Do it now."*

"What?" Cam's green eyes flashed wide open.

I'd caught him off guard, and I took advantage of that. I stood up and hauled him to his feet. Then I pushed him onto the bed while he was still surprised, and crawled on top of him. I straddled his hips and stared down at him. "Fuck me, LT."

I didn't recognize my own voice. It was still that monotone. It was still afraid to break.

"This is not a good idea, Brady," Cam said. He put his hands on my hips like he was going to push me off him.

"Don't move." I narrowed my eyes at him and dug my fingers into his shoulders. "Remind me I'm alive."

That's true. I remember reading that in one of Doc's psych books. He wasn't a psychologist, but he had a shitload of books on the subject. When I read it, I thought it was weird, but it didn't feel weird now: grief can make you want to fuck. Doc's books said seeking sex could be a legitimate response to shock and grief. It could also be avoidance, but whatever.

Cam shook his head.

"I'm having a shit day," I said, "in a shit week, in a generally shit life. Make me feel good."

"No," he said in a shaky voice. "You don't want this, Brady. Not now."

I didn't need to be able to read him. His emotions were written right on his face. Lust and sadness and compassion and worry, and even self-disgust because he wanted it as well. I seized on his want.

I leaned forward and nuzzled into his throat. Because he liked that, and so did I. My lips mapped his skin and found his fluttering pulse point and fixed on it.

"Fuck me, LT. Please." I got a hand between us, then down his pants. My fingers found his cock, and it was already hard. It was already leaking. So there. His argument was moot. I called bullshit on it.

I ground myself against him.

"No!" Cam gripped my wrists and bucked his hips suddenly, and then I was lying on my back on the mattress, and he was on top of me. Which was also okay. His hair hung down around his flushed face. "No, Brady, okay?"

I wriggled. "You gonna fight me, LT? Because I could go for rough right about now. Come on, fuck me!"

He frowned at me helplessly. "No, Brady. I won't let it be like this your first time."

"You know it isn't." I scowled. How come he had to bring Wade into this?

"I'm not counting that prick," Cam said. He held my wrists more tightly when I tried to shift. "And neither should you."

"Asshole," I muttered. "Can't you forget for a second what a fucking mess my life is and just fuck me?"

He shook his head and slowly lowered his face to mine. The kiss was almost chaste. "No, Brady. I like you too much for that."

The fight went out of me. It usually did with Cam, and I wondered why that was. I would have screamed with rage if someone else had held me down like that. I had, only minutes ago. I would have kicked and bitten and ripped until I was free or until I was beaten. But not with Cam. Never with Cam. And so I lay there, with Cam holding my wrists while my erection subsided, and felt like a fucking idiot. A dumb, needy kid who'd made an idiot of himself.

Maybe he thought I should have been crying. Maybe he didn't understand the sort of guy who cried with Captain Lutkus dug into his pressure points, but didn't when his dad died. But shit, I've never been that complicated. Physical pain gets a physical response. Everything else is nobody's fucking business.

"You can let me go now," I said. I couldn't meet his eyes.

"Maybe I won't," Cam said.

"Whatever." I didn't bother to struggle.

Was he timing this? The awkward seconds stretched out into excruciating minutes. And all that time Cam was staring into my face, and I was staring at his throat. He wasn't going to get any eye contact. It's not like he needed it. He knew I was burning with humiliation.

You throw yourself at a guy, and he turns you down. But he doesn't let you go. What the fuck was that about?

I closed my eyes. We had hardly any time left at all, and this was how he wanted to spend it? Fine. Whatever. What the hell did it matter? We were all dead: me and Cam, my dad and Lucy. The entire human race, not that I gave a shit about most of them.

I could have saved myself a lot of grief by opening my wrists after Wade. I wished I had.

"You don't mean that."

I opened my eyes. "No, I wouldn't kill myself. But I fucking envy the bastards who do it."

Cam loosened his grip on my wrists. "Brady, you've been running on anger for the past three years, haven't you?"

Something about that almost made me smile. "It's been way longer than that, actually. Way before the black."

"How do you even sustain that?" His voice was soft.

"No shortage of assholes in the universe, LT."

"Jesus, Brady," he murmured. He shifted off me, lying beside me and pulling me into an embrace I didn't have the energy to resist. "It doesn't have to be like that. It's harder to hold on to hate than you think. It doesn't make you stronger, you know."

Whatever.

"I mean it," he said. "And maybe this is just the latte-drinking faggot city boy speaking, but nothing that pushes people away can make you strong. You just don't see it. You need to give yourself a break."

I inhaled. Cam smelled so good. And it was only sweat and soap, but it was uniquely him. I'd miss it when the end came. "I don't mind that you're a latte-drinking faggot city boy."

"And I don't mind that you're an ignorant reffo," he said. He brushed his lips against mine, and a shiver ran down my spine. "But I mean it. You need to give yourself a break. You need to let people in."

I frowned. "No offense, LT, but the last person I let in was you, and that's all over in like a minute."

"Yeah," he murmured. He kissed my eyelashes, and it tickled.

"And it will hurt, but in the end the times you remember will be the good ones."

"Like with Chris," I said. I pressed my lips against his jaw.

"Like with Chris," he said.

"I can't do that," I said. My stomach twisted.

"Why not?"

I shook my head. "Because I can't even look after my sister. She's gonna be out in the gutter, and there's nothing I can do about it." My voice cracked, and I hated myself for it. "Do you think I deserve anyone after I do that to her?"

"Brady," he said in a soothing tone and held me more tightly. "It's not your fault. I know you've done everything you can."

I burned at that—*patronizing fucker!*—and elbowed him in the ribs to put some distance between us. "Fuck you! I'm not talking about some old wreck of a dog you have to get put down! I'm talking about my sister! She's a little kid!"

"Fuck," Cam growled. "Nobody gets a chance with you, do they? What do you want me to say? I'm *sorry?* Well, it's not my fault either!" He lifted himself up onto one elbow and ran his fingers through his hair. "I was trying to make you feel better, Brady!"

I hauled myself off the bed. I was fucking livid. "And did it ever occur to you, city boy, that there is nothing in the whole fucking big black that can make this better? Fuck you!"

I stormed into the bathroom and slammed the door shut.

"Go on, then," he said in my head, as clear as day. *"Run away. You're good at that."*

"Fuck off!" I yelled at the door. I slid down onto the tiled floor and put my head in my hands. My whole body shook with tears.

Fuck him, fuck this, and fuck everything.

And if I didn't touch him and he died, fuck that as well.

CHAPTER SIXTEEN

CAM and I weren't talking. Not aloud, anyway. And I was doing my best to ignore the sympathy that came off him in waves and threatened to drown me. I was hurting, and he wanted to help. Well, fuck him. I didn't need his pity.

I lay in bed almost the entire next day, curled up on my side so he couldn't get too close. It was bad enough how he rested his hand on my shoulder to regulate his heartbeat, because I liked his touch too much. I wanted it, and I needed it, but not with all the shit that came along for the ride. If he wanted to blow me, that would be fine. If he wanted to fuck, that would be fine. But he wanted to help.

I knew I was being the asshole. I knew I was being angry because it was a better alternative to falling apart, and I knew it wasn't fair I'd turned that anger on Cam. I was old enough to know better, but it turns out I was still a stubborn teenage shit where it counted. Brady Garrett hates his miserable life; therefore he hates everyone who tries to worm their way into it. Stupid.

"You should eat something, Brady," Cam said.

An hour later he said it again.

"Brady, you have to eat."

I stared at the wall.

He slid his hand from my shoulder down my arm. "Brady, please."

"Fuck off, LT."

I knew I should never have relented and come out of the bathroom the day before. I hated that we had to touch. I hated how much I wanted it. Cam needed it to stay alive, but what was my excuse? I was just pathetic.

"Do I have to pull rank on you, Recruit Garrett?"

His cold tone of voice caught me by surprise, and I snorted. "I'd like to see you try."

Cam's fingers ghosted against the sensitive skin on my wrist. "Eat something. That's an order."

I ignored him.

"I could put you on report," he told me.

"Yeah," I muttered. "And I'd love to tell my career officer how I got to fuck a lieutenant up the ass. He'd probably get a laugh out of that."

"Are you threatening me with blackmail, Garrett?" His voice was still stern, but his touch was gentle.

I tensed as his other hand slid up under my T-shirt, following the knots in my spine. "I'd be in less trouble for disobeying your order than you would be for blowing a recruit, *sir*."

I tensed again, because I felt the shiver of pleasure that ran through him. He liked snarky Brady. He liked the way I called him sir like it was an insult.

"You wouldn't last twenty minutes under my command," he said.

I closed my eyes as his warm palm swept across my back, and the electricity crackled between us. "Yeah, I bet you were a real asshole to recruits."

"Only the ones who deserved it."

There was something in him I couldn't get a fix on. I resisted the urge to move either way, to run or to yield to his touch, because then he'd know he'd won. But I couldn't read him, not exactly, and that worried me. He was turned on by our close contact, but no more than me. And he was still angry as well, but there was something behind all that. Was it amusement? Because if he was laughing at me, I'd punch him.

He had my T-shirt rucked up under my arms now, and every sweep of his hand made me shiver. "So, are you up for the challenge?"

"What challenge?" My breath caught in my throat.

"Twenty minutes under my command," he said.

I sighed, imagining him ordering me to eat my lunch. How fucking pedestrian, when his touch had promised something so much better. "I'm not hungry."

"You will be," he said. "Afterward."

Fuck. Maybe I was on a promise after all. My twitching cock thought so.

"I'm not gonna do push-ups for you, LT," I muttered. *Tell me. Tell me what you want to do.*

"Twenty minutes," he said, his voice so low that I had to struggle to hear it. "You're mine for twenty minutes. And that's all I'm saying."

It was all he was thinking as well, the prick. He was better at shielding his thoughts than I was. He'd had four years of practice, I guess.

"One question," I said. "Do I get to come?"

His breath was warm on the back of my neck. "Not until I say so."

Shit. I swallowed. "All right."

"All right, what?"

My cock leaped. "*Sir.*"

He pulled away from me.

I rolled onto my back and scowled at him to mask my nerves. "What now?"

He stood up. "Watch your attitude, recruit."

I searched his face for a smile, but there was nothing. He looked the part, all right. He looked like one of those officers who wouldn't know a sense of humor if he tripped over one. And more than that, he looked commanding. Jesus. My cock had never responded to authority before, but apparently it was good to go even if my brain was still catching up.

"Get up," he said and didn't even give me time to move before he was berating me. "Up, recruit, now! Don't make me repeat myself!"

He sounded so much like the real thing—he was, I guess—that I automatically reacted like the lowly recruit I was. I hauled myself off the bed and flushed. "Yes, sir. Sorry, sir."

Cam's gaze flicked over me dispassionately. "Strip."

Now there was an order I was happy to obey. I wasn't dumb enough to smile, though, because I wasn't sure of the rules of this game. I pulled my T-shirt over my head and slid my pants and boxers down. Somehow I felt more exposed than I ever had, and looked nervously at Cam.

"Eyes front." He walked around behind me. I heard him moving, and then he was pulling my arms behind my back. My shoulders still hurt from Lutkus, and I tensed, but Cam was careful not to wrench them. He bound my wrists with something. It felt scratchy. A sock?

"Really? We're going for restraints after your buddies from intel?"

"Watch the attitude, recruit," Cam said. Then he slipped my T-shirt back over my head and twisted it. He adjusted it so that my nose and mouth were unobstructed, but it remained firmly over my eyes. I couldn't see shit.

Well, at least Lutkus didn't blindfold me. I tried to find this amusing, but I couldn't, not really. I didn't like being like this, naked, bound, and not knowing what the hell was going to happen next. I didn't like being helpless. And he knew it, the asshole. I opened my mouth to tell him he'd won, but I didn't get the chance to speak.

"Sixteen minutes."

I swallowed. Okay. I could handle that. I was stubborn enough for that. And then I realized Cam was probably counting on that, and wondered what the hell he was intending. I took a deep breath and held it.

Don't freak out. Don't freak out.

His low, amused voice was very close to my ear. "No, Garrett. Don't freak out."

He said it like it was a challenge. He knew all my buttons.

I held my breath until my lungs started to burn, and then I held the burn. I needed something to distract me from thinking. I didn't know why I was so nervous.

He'd knotted a sock around my wrists, for Christ's sake. A sock. Nothing scary about a sock. Except when I finally let my breath go in a rush, it sounded almost like a whimper.

He wasn't touching me. Why wasn't he touching me? Was he still close? I turned my head blindly.

"Eyes front." He was behind me.

The sound of his voice calmed me down, and the part of me that recognized that resented it. But the rest of me told me that I'd be okay, as long as he was still here. As long as he hadn't walked away. But I didn't like this. I didn't like how I wasn't in control. I didn't like how hard it made me, how fucking obvious and needy.

I was eleven when Linda first called me a sniveling faggot. At the time I'd only thought she was right about the sniveling part.

Maybe she wasn't as dumb as she looked. Jesus, wouldn't she fucking laugh at me now?

I didn't realize my breathing was so fast and shallow until Cam laid a hand on my back between my shoulder blades. "Shoulders back. Chest out. It's not your first day, is it, recruit?"

I swallowed and pulled my shoulders back as far as I could manage without pain. "No, sir."

It was a game. It was just a game. He couldn't really pull rank on me. Not like this. But it felt real, and I wanted it to be real. I wanted Cam to take control, to tell me what to do and then praise me for doing it. I wanted it, and I hated it. Most of all I wanted to cry, and I didn't know why. My throat ached, and there were tears just waiting to come. My entire body was on edge.

The seconds ticked by into minutes, but I'd already lost count. I'd lost everything, standing there with my wrists bound and my shirt over my eyes. Being bound, being blind, had reduced me to nothing but a frantic heartbeat and nerves that were screaming for something to happen. My cock was hard as hell, throbbing and already leaking. I was nothing but competing sensations. And all my brain could hold on to was Cam. I needed him to touch me again, to talk to me, to reassure me he was there.

My chin dropped.

"Eyes front."

I jerked my chin back up. Okay. I could do this. I just had to hold it together until the clock wound down. I just had to stop from freaking out completely.

"I warned you I don't like to repeat myself." His voice was very close to my ear, and I flinched. "You can't even hold your position. I shouldn't have expected anything better from an ignorant piece of trash from Kopa."

I clenched my jaw and scowled.

"Something to say, recruit?"

"No, sir," I managed through gritted teeth. Latte-drinking

faggot city boy. Chardonnay socialist. Bleeding-heart liberal. Hypocrites, every last one of them. Save the trees. Save the oceans. Save the climate. Save us from ourselves, but don't bother to save the little reffo kids. Fuck, I hoped the Faceless killed those assholes first.

My breath snagged in my throat. All my rage, all my hurt, was all right there, just below the surface. I was already so fucking helpless, so why did I let Cam put me there as well? Why did I let him tell me I was a piece of trash? I didn't need to be bound and naked for that. I could get the same from any other officer on Defender Three and most of the people at home.

And then his hand was on my chest, and my whole body jerked in response. My balls tightened. I think I even whimpered.

"Something to say now, recruit?"

"Yes, sir," I said. His breath was warm on my lips. "Please keep touching me, sir."

"You're not in charge here, recruit." He drew back. "Twelve minutes."

Fuck, *really?* This was proper torture. I squirmed.

"Do you know what your problem is, Garrett?" He moved around behind me and grazed my ass with his fingers.

I made a face under the shirt. I needed to come. My cock was aching now, and my balls were tight. "No, sir!"

His hands found my hips, and he pressed himself against me. His erection nudged my ass, and I shivered. The scratch of his zipper and the promise of his body heat made my heart race. It took all I had not to push back. Cam leaned his chin on my shoulder. "You have a bad attitude, Garrett."

A bad attitude was better than no attitude at all.

"You've got no respect for your superiors," Cam said.

I bit my lip. Holy hell. I was going to come in a second, from nothing more than the feel of Cam rocking gently against me and the electricity that crackled between us.

"You need to shut your smart mouth and learn to take orders." Cam pulled me closer, and the sudden movement made me tremble. It made me squeak as well, like a kid, and at least that sudden flush of shame was enough to put the dampers on my impending orgasm. For a couple of minutes, maybe. But not if he kept rubbing his erection against me like that. "Are you hearing me, recruit?"

Hell, no.

"Yes, sir," I managed.

He slid one hand up from my hip to my chest and found my sternum. "Do you want to get fucked, recruit?"

I squeezed my eyes shut under the blindfold as a jolt ran through my body. "Yes, sir!"

He ghosted his palm across my nipple. "And what does that make you?"

"Yours, sir," I said.

I don't think that was the answer Cam was expecting, because I couldn't read him at that moment. His sharp intake of breath told me I'd surprised him, but he recovered quickly. "Damn straight, Garrett. But you've got to earn it."

I shivered as his hand slid over my chest.

He didn't say anything for a long time. He just touched my abdomen lightly and never let his fingers stray too low. Nowhere near where I needed them. And I just stood there, trembling and trying not to move my hips. I fought my frustration. I needed more, but Cam was in charge.

Cam's breath was warm against my ear. "It's not your fault."

I stiffened. What the hell? What happened to that asshole officer who was playing with me? Yeah, not fun anymore. My erection flagged, and I was suddenly cold. I wanted to push him off, and I don't know what was stopping me.

"Eight minutes," Cam said.

Or I could just end this now.

Cam linked his arms across my chest and held me there.

Shit. I felt like an idiot. Had he done all this just to get me in a position where I couldn't escape his embrace? What did my erection make me, then? A pervert, probably. A sick fuck getting turned on by power games when my dad was dead and my sister was next.

"Are you listening to me, recruit?"

His voice and his touch were my anchor in the darkness. I had no choice but to listen. I hated this, though. My guts churned, and bile rose in my throat.

"Yes, sir," I rasped.

"You need to give yourself a break," Cam said. His voice still held that note of command I'd responded to in interesting ways. "And that is a fucking order, Garrett."

My mind went blank. I shook my head, but I couldn't come up with a single coherent thought, let alone voice one.

"It is not your fault, recruit." He touched his lips to my naked shoulder.

I felt it, but I was numb.

"Answer me!"

My lips worked for a second before anything came out. And it wasn't a voice so much as a croak. "Has to be someone's fault, sir."

"You're wrong," Cam said. "You're just an ignorant fucking kid from Kopa. You don't know shit."

Maybe. I squeezed my eyes shut tightly under my T-shirt as tears stung them. Shit happened, but that didn't absolve me from my responsibilities. I couldn't let it. If I did, I'd be just as bad as Linda. She'd walked away with a spring in her step, hadn't she?

"So you will eat," said Cam. His voice had a hard edge to it. "And you will talk, and you won't shut down, because this is not your fault. You hear me, recruit?"

My chin jerked up and down.

"I didn't hear that." Cam tightened his grip.

That was when I realized he was never going to let me go.

"Yes, sir," I managed, and then tears overcame me. It was like letting the air out of a balloon. My legs went first, the rest of me followed, and the next thing I knew I was on the floor sobbing while Cam fumbled at the sock around my wrists.

When he ripped the shirt off my head, the room felt brighter than normal, and my tears gave the lights glowing coronas like starlight. My arms went straight around Cam's neck like it was the most natural thing in the world, and I howled like a fucking baby.

"You're not weak, Brady," he told me, and I think I almost believed it. "You're stronger than you think."

"Doesn't matter," I said into the hollow of his throat. "Doesn't make a difference."

"Maybe not." He rubbed my back gently. "But you have to know it."

I choked on a sob. "I don't want Lucy to die!"

He rocked me back and forth. "I know, Brady. I know."

"Is it really so bad in the north?"

"City boy."

"Yeah," he murmured. "I also don't know shit."

It took a long time, or it seemed like a long time, but at last I dragged myself out of his embrace. I leaned back against the bed and scrubbed my eyes. I looked at Cam warily, and he looked back.

"You tricked me, LT," I said at last. "I thought I was on a promise."

Cam's lips quirked in a smile, and he reached forward to link his fingers through mine. "You still are, Brady. We've still got time."

We had no time at all.

I sighed. "I guess you were right. I didn't last twenty minutes under your command."

Cam raised my hand to his mouth and kissed my knuckles. "No, but don't beat yourself up. I did go fairly hard on you."

"Yeah," I said. "I felt that."

His green eyes shone. "Smart-ass."

I frowned at him. "How come you give a damn, LT?"

He raised his eyebrows. "Maybe I'm just being selfish. When you feel bad, I feel bad. Or maybe, even though you had no choice but to let me into the crazy world you call your head, I kind of like it there, and I want to make it a better place while I'm stuck there."

I shrugged uneasily, and we both thought the same thing: *Days.*

Either we all died when the Faceless came, or we didn't. If we didn't, our connection would be broken anyway. Cam wouldn't be staying on the station. They'd sent him back to Eight, maybe, or back home, and I'd be alone. But not as alone as Lucy.

I closed my eyes for a moment. I could get mad, or I could break down again, or I could try and forget Lucy had ever existed. None of those options helped. Nothing helped, and nothing ever would. Over time she'd just be another regret of mine, just another thing inside me that I couldn't face. Another failure.

"Do you know what happens to kids in Kopa who are on their own?" I asked, opening my eyes.

Cam's face was grave. "No."

"They die," I said. "No school, no doctors, no chance. And it's better if she dies. You understand? Because it could always be worse."

"Don't make me paint a picture, Cam. Don't make me tell you what happens to some kids."

Cam nodded.

"And it's not fair," I said. "Shit, I've been saying that my whole fucking life, and it doesn't change a thing. I kind of hope Kai-Ren blows the whole planet away."

"You're running on anger," Cam said. He reached out and laid his palm on my cheek. "And I get that now, Brady. I really do. But I meant what I told you. It's not your fault."

And around and around we go.

I sighed. "That doesn't make it better."

Cam leaned forward and brushed his lips against mine. "I know that too."

I would have begged him for help, but it would have been pointless. Nobody ever thought Cam was coming back from the Faceless. First thing they do when you die? They stop your pay. Cam was in no position to help.

I thought of the way I'd carried Lucy in a sling. How I'd felt her heartbeat against mine, and how I'd put her down in her cot at night and wiped the wisps of hair off her forehead. My heart still swelled when I thought of her. Swelled until it broke, every fucking time.

"You feel that?" I asked him.

He nodded. "Hurts."

That's love for you.

In a few days our connection would be broken. Cam didn't owe me anything. I was the one who was supposed to look after him, and what had happened to that? He hadn't asked for a front-row ticket to the shitty drama of my life. And he sure as hell hadn't volunteered for audience participation. It wasn't fair on him.

I forced a smile. "Sorry."

Cam leaned in until our foreheads touched.

I closed my eyes. My breath shuddered out of me.

His closeness worked where words were fucking useless.

Just another thing that would hurt when it was gone.

CHAPTER SEVENTEEN

MY FIRST WALK-THROUGH of a UV chamber in weeks.

I left my uniform in a heap by the doorway and pulled on a pair of goggles. I blinked behind the smoky panes as I looked around. Jesus, even the officers' UV chamber was nicer than ours. Ours smelled like sweat and rust and ammonia. This one didn't smell of anything at all. Also, none of the tubes were cracked, so you didn't get a headache from the flickering lights.

I squinted at the timer on the wall. The fifteen minutes had already ticked down to twelve while I was getting over how big the chamber was. Maybe the fact I wasn't walking around the painted circuit on the floor with twenty other guys wearing just their underwear had something to do with the feeling of wide-open spaces. It was just Cam and me. We kept our distance. The whole point of being in a UV chamber was to expose as much skin as you could to the light.

I turned in a slow circle, my arms out, soaking up the light and the heat.

"You look hot," Cam said in my head.

I snorted. "Real funny, LT."

He flashed me a smile. "I wasn't joking, recruit."

I raised my eyebrows and hooked my thumbs into the waistband of my underwear. "You want some of this, sir?"

His smile widened. "Careful, Brady. There are some places you don't want to get a sunburn."

Ouch. I made a face and began to pace the circuit out of habit. The floor was already warm underfoot.

This weird, flirty banter between us was, yeah, it was just weird. A part of me was still numb, still shut down, making the rest of me feel like I was playacting. I was putting on a show for Cam: the smart-ass, horny recruit with the bad attitude and the filthy mind. But I wasn't that guy, really.

Really I was hollow.

Except it wasn't that simple. I was that horny recruit, and I was also that guy carved apart by grief. I was both those guys at the same time, and I flipped between them with absolutely no fucking control.

Grief should have been all-consuming. I hated myself that it wasn't. But sometimes I forgot. Jesus, how could I fucking forget? Sometimes I went for minutes without remembering my dad was dead, but that whole time it was regrouping so it could hit me all over again.

"Okay?" Cam asked me quietly.

"Yeah."

We circled each other on the floor.

"I'm in your head, Brady," he said. "Don't lie."

"Well, don't ask dumb fucking questions."

"Okay." Cam stopped pacing. "I'm worried about you."

I knew that. I was in his head as well, and the worry had been coming off him in waves ever since he found out my dad was dead.

Dead. Shit. My dad was dead. Each time I remembered, shock bit at my guts. And it was stupid. My dad was dead, but I knew that. I fucking *knew* it, but it was like my brain kept pushing it away. The only other time I'd experienced anything like this was—

Fuck. It was Wade. Numb shock, my brain off-line, and something so big that I couldn't process it. This can't be happening, I told myself, and I must have believed it so much that I couldn't face the truth. Like a coward.

"No," Cam said. "It's shock. Don't think it's anything else. Not then and not now."

I moved farther away from him. At least we'd always have that in common: psychological trauma. Although who the hell was I to think that what happened with Wade or my dad's death in any way compared to what had happened to Cam?

I didn't realize Cam was that close until he grabbed me by the arm and wrenched me around to face him. "What the fuck, Brady?"

My stomach clenched. "What?"

"Stop doing that!"

I frowned at him. "Doing what?"

His grip relaxed, but he didn't let go of my arm. He frowned. "Stop thinking you're not important! You matter, okay? What happens to you *matters*."

"To who?" I asked, my voice snagging in my throat.

"Brady." Cam cupped my cheeks in his hands and pressed his forehead against mine. Our bulky goggles knocked together. "How can I get it through this thick skull of yours? To me. You matter to me."

I closed my eyes. "I'm just the guy in your head. You could've got anyone."

He sighed. *"Do you think that's all this is? Biochemistry?"*

"I don't know," I whispered. I shrugged. "You don't even want to fuck me."

Cam ran his fingers over my buzz cut. He sighed. "I've wanted to fuck you since the first time I saw you."

My cock hardened. "So why haven't you?"

"It's not the right time."

I frowned. Because of my dad? Because of Kai-Ren? Because Cam was in my head? We were never going to get the right time. Never. Either Kai-Ren would kill us all, or he wouldn't and Cam would be sent back to Eight, or back to Earth. Whatever happened, this was the only time we had.

"I don't know if you're ready," Cam whispered. "*You* don't know if you're ready."

I drew a deep breath. "How will we find out if we don't try?"

———

IT WAS the middle of the day, but that counted for shit in the black. I turned down the lights and made it night in our room. Just Cam and me and the starlight he loved.

"You sure you want to do this, Brady?" Cam's eyes were wide in the darkness.

"Yeah," I said, my heart beating faster.

"You're scared," he said.

"Doesn't mean I don't want to do it." I checked that the door was locked and closed the distance between us.

Cam splayed his hand against my chest, holding me back. "Because I'll be gone soon, like it never happened, and you don't have to do this. You can, you know..." He trailed off.

I didn't need to read his mind to know what he was thinking. "You think I can pretend that all this faggot stuff never happened so long as you haven't put your dick up my ass?"

Cam's eyebrows shot up. "*Faggot* stuff?"

"I'm still working on the terminology," I told him. "Anyhow, it's no big thing. I'm pretty certain the fact I sucked your dick means I can't really get any gayer."

Cam shook his head. "Do you ever listen to how much crazy shit comes out of your mouth?"

"Nope." I hooked my fingers into his waistband and pulled him closer. "Nobody does. That's why I remain undiagnosed."

He snorted with amusement.

"No time for laughing, LT," I said. "Get your clothes off and fuck me."

His face became serious. "Brady, are you—"

"I'm sure," I said, popping the button on his fly and sliding a hand down into his underwear. His cock, hot and already hard, jerked against my fingers. "Want your cock inside me."

Hell. Those were five words I never thought I'd say in a blue fit. But I said them, and I didn't choke on them, and they were true. All that anxiety and skittishness that Cam could read, that was nothing. That nervousness was mine to overcome, not his. Wasn't fair that he could read it.

"Please," I whispered.

I wanted Cam. I wanted this.

Except, except, except...

Except the last time I had a cock in my ass, I was begging in a whole other way, a jumble of words and tears and snot: *"No, no, no, please no."* Except fuck that. That was years ago.

My heartbeat raced in both of us.

"But you're scared," Cam said.

"Doesn't matter." I lifted my face for a kiss.

Our lips brushed. The kiss was soft, featherlight. The tenderness was new. The slowness was. But he didn't push, and I didn't rush, because for once we both knew where we were going.

Our bodies knew each other. Our dreams did. Buttons and bootlaces came undone under our touches. Cam's fingers were electric, slipping under the elastic of my underwear. No other touch would ever be like that, and right now I didn't care if the chemistry wasn't really ours, if it really belonged to the Faceless. What did it matter? His touch sparked every nerve ending in my body, and I knew mine did the same for him. I could feel it, and it took my breath away.

I climbed up onto the bed, my heart thumping. I dragged my pillow down to shove under my stomach. Worried about making a mess on it, seizing on that thought because I didn't want to think about how this would hurt. Probably it would hurt. Wade had made it hurt.

"It's okay," Cam whispered. He straddled my thighs and dug his thumbs into my shoulders. "Just relax."

"Yeah, right."

"I heard that," Cam said.

"I know." I squeezed my eyes shut.

Cam worked at loosening the muscles in my shoulders and neck. It hurt at first; then the ache faded, and pleasure crept in. Cam's touches became less solicitous. He started to tease. He stroked his fingers down my spine, the electricity between us tickling my skin, and I could feel his amusement when I shivered.

"Feels good," I whispered. My cock was already half-hard from anticipation. Yeah, my brain was worrying that this might hurt, but at least my cock was an optimist. And why the hell not? It's not like Cam had ever done anything to prove it wrong.

I *trusted* Cam. Everything else counted for shit.

Cam shifted off me into the gap between my knees that had opened up for him. He ghosted his hands across the cheeks of my ass, and my cock jerked and filled some more.

"Okay, Brady," he said, his hands on my hips. His gentle touch drew me up and back, onto my knees, and I went with it. Wasn't going to fight this now.

I rested my forehead on my crossed arms and tried not to feel stupid like this or, worse, exposed. I *trusted* him, remember? I trusted him.

Cam's fingers, slick with lube, found the crease of my ass. When he circled them against my opening, I bit back a whimper and reminded myself not to freak out.

"You're okay," Cam whispered, pressing one finger gently inside me. Fuck. *Inside* me. "Just tell me to stop if you want."

"Keep going," I mumbled. It didn't hurt. Felt weird. Felt like I seriously needed to shit. How the hell was that supposed to be hot? Maybe he was doing it wrong. Maybe there was something wrong with me.

I heard the smile in Cam's voice. "Just give it a minute, Brady. It's new. Of course it's weird."

He got another finger inside me, and I groaned at the fullness. It still didn't hurt, but it was pretty fucking overrated. Shit, if I wanted a cavity search, I'd get in a fight with an MP. And if I wanted a prostate exam—

"*Fuck!*"

Cam twisted his fingers again. "You were saying?"

I groaned and pushed back. "God."

"Just breathe," Cam said. "I'm just going to do this for a while, just to get you good and ready."

Okay.

I never knew. Even with all Cam's memories and dreams taking up space in my skull, I never knew it would feel this—not good, not *all* good anyway—this *intense*. It was a lot. It was a bit too much, maybe, and I started to whimper and squirm. I needed it to stop, or I needed *more*, or something.

Fuck, I didn't know.

"Brady?" Cam's voice was low, strained.

I sucked in a breath. "Fuck. God."

"You okay, Brady?"

I whimpered into the mattress.

I don't know. I don't know. It aches. I think it does, but fuck, I need more. I want to come. Please. Cam, please.

"Gonna fuck you now, Brady."

Okay. God, okay. Do it.

And there was the pain I was expecting, just a teasing flash of it as the head of Cam's cock breached me. I hissed, and Cam held still. He ran his hands down my spine and rubbed my lower back. The pain melted away, but the pressure remained. The fullness. This didn't feel so good anymore.

I bit my lip.

Maybe, shit, maybe I would never be ready for this.

Cam reached underneath me and curled his fingers around my cock. I jerked, my breath leaving me in a shocked *whuff*. My cock filled, throbbed, and I was so full of competing sensations that I could hardly breathe. Cam pressed forward inside me, stroking my cock until pleasure and need drowned pain, or until I couldn't tell the difference anymore.

"Cam," I whispered, my voice straining.

We moved in counterpoint. I pushed back to meet every gentle thrust and then pushed forward into Cam's hand.

"So tight, Brady. So good."

I mumbled something into the mattress as we picked up the pace. Then we were fucking, properly fucking, hard and fast. It felt good. It felt better than good. Every time his cock rode over my prostate, I thought I was going to come. I wanted to, and I didn't want to.

I wanted this to last forever.

It didn't. It couldn't.

Nothing ever did.

I gasped into the mattress as I came all over Cam's hand, all over my stomach and chest, and all over the sheets. Cam was only a second or two behind me.

"Fuck. *Fuck.*" His fingers dug into my hips as he followed me over the edge, both of us shuddering and shaking like the electricity between us had been amped up to a few thousand volts. "Brady."

I closed my eyes.

"You still think I wasn't ready?"

Cam laughed breathlessly and slid a hand down my sweaty spine. "Yeah, you were ready."

We disengaged slowly.

I lay curled on my side on the mattress, staring out at the black and wondering if I should feel different. Starlight filled my vision, and my fear competed with Cam's wonderment.

Cam padded back from the bathroom with a washcloth. He settled down beside me and wiped the cloth over my stomach. Then he dropped it onto the floor and raised his hand to my face.

Our gazes locked.

We didn't need words.

Didn't need telepathy either. The truth was right there in our faces.

Could have been something, except it would be over before we knew it.

It already hurt.

CHAPTER EIGHTEEN

WHEN KAI-REN CAME, it happened fast.

I thought we still had time. I was wrong.

It wasn't a dream, and that was the worst part.

We were in the shower, touching, tasting, both of us right there in that moment. Just us, just the beat of the water on our skin, just the sound of our breath, our moans, the small, urgent noises we made. Just us, like we'd somehow managed to leave all our fucking baggage in the other room.

"Cam-ren. Cam-ren." There was a hint of amusement in that sibilant voice. *"What are you doing, Cam-ren, my pet?"*

"Holy fuck!" I leaped away from Cam like he was poisonous and almost slipped. I caught myself awkwardly, and pain shot through my shoulder. I barely noticed it. I just stared at Cam, the water dripping off my nose, and tried to get a breath. "That wasn't a memory!"

I threw the words at him like an accusation, which wasn't fair. It wasn't his fault.

He stared back at me. "No. He's close enough to read me now."

I looked into Cam's eyes and wondered if Kai-Ren was watching me through them. "For real, LT?"

He nodded.

And that was the end of shower time. I stepped out of the stall and grabbed a towel.

Fuck that. It was bad enough with Cam in my head. I didn't need anyone else in there. Especially not a Faceless. Holy shit. Please, not a Faceless.

My heart beat faster. So, I guess, did Cam's.

God. We were so well cocooned in our room that it was easy to ignore what was happening in the station. The daily drills had increased, but there was no more traffic, and Cam could tell by the position of the stars that we were on the outer edge of our ellipse. It all added up, but we'd thought we still had time before Kai-Ren's little mind trick had chilled me to the bone.

I dressed.

We ate dinner in silence, both of us sitting cross-legged on the bed. I kept my back to the black, and to Cam as well. I couldn't shake the feeling that Kai-Ren was there in the room with me, wearing Cam's face. But it didn't matter if refused to look at Cam, or refused to look out the window. The Faceless ship was coming. I could feel it getting closer, and I didn't have to see it to know what it looked like. Cam knew, so I did.

I remembered the flashing lights in its interior that cast colors over the strange, bowed walls. I remembered the hum of the power conduits inside those dark, ridged walls, like veins in flesh. If it was a metal, we had nothing like it. If it was organic, it grew how they wanted it. If the pod had looked like a beetle's carapace, the Faceless ship was like a hive.

When Cam had first opened his eyes in that place, he hadn't been able to breathe. He'd been naked, hanging by his wrists, and his fear had choked him.

The memory of it choked me now.

"He's closer," I whispered.

Cam's gaze slipped off my face to the black at my back, and I *knew*. I knew even without turning around what I'd see there, but I turned around anyway.

With a field of stars behind it, it was a black shape. It was the absence of light. It was a thing carved out of the never-ending night. It was dark space.

It was my nightmare, and it was coming for me.

Kill us all, Kai-Ren, and please make it quick.

But another part of me whispered, *No no no no no.*

"Brady." Cam's arms were around me, pulling me into his embrace. "You'll live, Brady, I promise. Promise."

I buried my face in his neck and breathed in his scent and felt, for the first time in forever, almost like a kid. Like I could almost believe him, like it was almost the truth. Except I didn't. I couldn't.

Once, I'd knelt in the red dirt with my arms around Lucy, forcing a smile I didn't believe. *"It's okay,"* I'd said. *"You and Dad will be okay without me, and I'll be home real soon, I promise."*

Promise, promise, promise.

I wondered if Cam's lie tasted as bitter on his tongue as mine had.

I didn't hate him for telling it.

I hoped Lucy didn't hate me.

———

THERE WAS no night in the black. No day, no night. The clocks on the station were set to an arbitrary twenty-four-hour cycle, so how was Kai-Ren to know that it was three o'clock in the morning when he arrived at Defender Three?

The alarms sounded just after midnight, a deafening wail that echoed through the narrow metal arteries of the station.

Three hours later red strobes still flashed intermittently, but someone had turned off the Klaxon. We didn't need it to remind us that we were on red alert.

That we were dead men.

The Faceless ship was bigger than anything I'd ever seen. It was at least a quarter of the size of the station, and it bristled with jagged edges and points and things that might have been antennae. Insect-like.

There were no exterior lights and no portholes. It was just black. The same inky black as Cam's stasis pod. The Faceless ship attached to Defender Three like a parasite, its black skin reflecting the station's lights back as though through a dark mirror or an oil slick.

Logic told me that the Faceless ship wouldn't blow us out of the sky as long as it was still attached, but logic took a backseat to breathless fucking panic.

I closed my eyes. I couldn't look out the window, down onto that massive, parasitic thing. I couldn't look at Cam either, too afraid that Kai-Ren was looking back at me through Cam's brilliant green eyes.

Oh God.

Fuck. Was there a God? It seemed the kind of thing I should have thought of before now. All this time waiting for imminent death, and how come I'd never asked myself that question?

My heartbeat stuttered.

The truth landed as heavy as a stone in my gut: because the question was stupid.

No God. No afterward. No forever.

We're born. We die. Nothing but a quick spark, quickly extinguished. Nothing but the black left behind.

Once, I took a copy of *The Myth of Sisyphus* from Doc's bookshelf. It had a big red rock on the cover that reminded me of the color of bauxite. I think that's why I liked it. *"You don't want to read that, Brady,"* Doc had said, but I did anyway. That book said that life was meaningless. Seemed like a strange thing for a doctor to have on his shelf. And I could even get how that was meant to be liberating—like Cam looking into the big black—but I didn't feel it. Maybe I would have, on my own, but Lucy didn't have the consolation of philosophy.

"You're not going to die, Brady," Cam told me. "And you're too angry to be a nihilist."

Yeah. I took a deep breath and held it for a moment. Yeah, that was probably true. I closed my eyes and breathed. While I could, I breathed.

And when the marines came to get us, I just climbed to my feet and followed.

There was nowhere to run, nowhere to go except where the marines led us: out of the officers' quarters and into the Core. In the red-lit halls everything seemed strange and dreamlike. My heart raced, and so did Cam's, and adrenaline coursed through me. Through us.

We reached the Core and stepped into an elevator.

"I'm scared, LT. You feel how scared I am?"

We ached to touch, but the marines were staring, beetle-browed.

"You'll be okay, Brady. This will all be okay."

Cam's silent voice sounded hollow.

The elevator whisked us upward.

The doors opened on a massive circular room I'd only ever seen on the station maps: the Dome. The Dome was where politicians and diplomats came for photo ops. It was where officers wore their dress uniforms, and it was full of officers today: Commander Leonski, Lieutenant Commander Chanter, Major Durack and Captain Lutkus, and Chris Varro. Doc was there as well.

When they showed pictures of the stations on the shiny

pamphlets back home, they always showed the Dome. Floor-to-ceiling windows gave a three-sixty view of the big black. Starlight caught in my vision from every side. But for once it wasn't the big black threatening to suck the air out of my lungs that made me want to hide.

It was the Faceless.

My heart stuttered as he turned to look in our direction.

Kai-Ren was tall, just as tall as in my nightmares. He stood head and shoulders over the tallest man in the room. He was covered in black: latex-thin but as hard as steel. The mask showed the vague shape of his face—a brow, a chin, the ridge of a nose—and nothing else. I might have thought that was his skin, but I'd seen Cam's dreams. I'd seen flesh as white and bloodless as porcelain underneath.

How did he see? How did he *breathe?*

There was a Faceless on Defender Three. How the hell were any of us still breathing?

That shining, formless face turned toward us, toward *me*, and I shouldn't have been able to tell because of the mask, but a jolt of *something* went through me when Kai-Ren fixed his gaze on mine. It was fear. It was anticipation. I don't know what the fuck it was, but it was as electric as any time that Cam and I touched.

That thing looked right into my fucking brain.

"You're okay," Cam said, but all I heard was the whine at the back of my throat that I tried desperately to swallow down.

The Faceless turned its masked face to look at Cam and said, in a sibilant voice that sounded almost pleased, "Cam-ren, my pet."

"Kai-Ren," he said in a soft voice.

"No warm greetings, Cam-ren?" Kai-Ren asked.

"It is difficult to know what to say," Cam said. Waves of regret rolled off him that translated to fear as they caught me in their wake. Cam was hiding something.

"Cam?"

He ignored me.

Commander Leonski cleared his throat. "Please, Lieutenant, if you could limit yourself to translating?"

"Yes, sir," Cam said. His nerves hummed as tightly as guitar strings. His heart raced. "Kai-Ren was merely greeting me."

What? I blinked. *Fucking what?* Holy crap. I'd understood what the Faceless said. It hadn't been in English, but I'd understood. The blood drained from my face. It wasn't just Cam I had in my head. Kai-Ren was there as well.

That black-masked face turned toward me, and my stomach clenched.

No no no no no.

"It's okay, Brady," Cam thought.

I stepped back. I tried to believe Cam, tried to read him, but I couldn't. The more I tried, the more I couldn't get a fix. My mind wouldn't focus. It felt a little like a headache, like a hangover, like a mental blank. That was it: a mental blank. I knew it was there. I could feel around the edges, but I couldn't see what was inside. I kept coming up empty, and I *knew*. The thing that Cam was hiding, that's where it was.

I exchanged a look with Cam.

"Sorry, Brady." His smile was so fleeting I could have imagined it.

I stepped back again, bumping into a dress uniform. It was Doc.

"Something's wrong," I whispered to him.

Doc reached out and wrapped his fingers around my wrist. For comfort, his or mine, or to keep me from making a scene like the last time I'd been surrounded by officers, I don't know. My pulse fluttered under his blunt fingers.

"Something's wrong," I whispered again, a little louder this time.

"Nothing's wrong, Brady," Cam told me. "I promised, remember? You'll be okay. You'll survive, and you'll go home. You all will."

I saw the truth for the first time.

"But what about you?" I whispered.

"I'll be okay too," Cam said in a low voice. He reached out and touched his fingertips to mine. "I'll just be a long way away."

———

IT WASN'T A BETRAYAL. It stung like one, but it wasn't. Cam was a hero. When people found out about this, they'd know that. And maybe it was because he had a famous face, a face that looked good on posters, that I thought all his heroism would be like that: big moments, breathless moments, framed forever by the lens of a camera. A careless smile to take the edge off that heroic determination.

That wasn't heroism. That was artifice. Every poster I'd ever seen with flags flying behind Cam's smiling face, they were manufactured so that I would look at them and know he was a hero. Except his heroism, in real life, wasn't full of color and light.

Cam was pale. There were dark shadows under his eyes. He translated quietly as Commander Leonski and Kai-Ren spoke, and I know I should have been watching this historic moment wide-eyed, drinking in every detail, whitewashing the fear off the faces of every man in the room, but all I could see was Cam. Cam and, when a particularly strong wave of misery hit me, Kai-Ren. He turned toward me every time like a hound that had picked up a sharp scent, and terror spiked my senses.

"He's going with him," I whispered once, and Doc gaped.

When Cam announced it, there were no cries of protest. Commander Leonski didn't pick that treaty up and rip it apart in his fists. There was only silence, and a room full of men who couldn't meet Cam's gaze. Chris Varro didn't even object. Asshole.

And hell, neither did I.

I turned away and stared out into space.

Time loses meaning in the black. Off planet, time meets the place between mass and light and turns into a whole weird thing that I don't understand. It turns into physics, into philosophy, into shit that my brain can't get around. I know this: looking into the black is the same as looking into the past.

You'd think I wouldn't be so scared of it, then.

"I never lied." Cam's silent voice cut through the entire Dome to find me.

"I know."

"We never had a future."

Time was meaningless, except each moment was a countdown to the end. I wondered if we'd already had our last touch, and I hated myself for wondering that. Who the hell was I to think about touching him when I didn't even have the guts to turn around and face him?

"I know."

I fixed my eyes on the past, on a past so distant that maybe that bright star went supernova a million years ago. Maybe the blast was still hurtling toward us, and we wouldn't know until it hit. Like moths dancing in headlights, dazzled, who didn't see the truck until it was right there with them in the exact same point in space and time. Splat.

I closed my eyes. *"This would be easier if I was angry."*

I heard the smile in his voice. *"You are a bit angry."*

"Maybe." I balled my fingers into fists. *"But not with you."*

I was angry with the universe, with fate, with a God I didn't really believe in, but not with Cam, because Cam was a hero.

Regret washed over both of us. I wiped my nose on the back of my hand.

"*Feral reffo.*"

Cam made it sound like affection, but I couldn't even pretend to smile. I turned back. My gaze found his pale face.

It was wrong. It was fucking wrong, and nobody was going to even try and stop it because Kai-Ren could blow us out of the sky. Kai-Ren could destroy the Earth. If Cam was the price of survival, we couldn't jettison him fast enough. We might mourn him later, we might even honor him at some point, but in the meantime let's tie a ribbon around him and throw him back to the Faceless. Enjoy! Merry fucking Christmas!

Kai-Ren turned his masked face in my direction. "*What is Christmas, Cam-ren?*"

Oh fuck. I pressed my back against the window, almost wanting it to break and suck us all out into oblivion. I remembered how Cam had laughed at me that time.

"*What I don't like is knowing there's only a thin sheet of glass between me and a fucking vacuum.*"

"*It's not glass, Garrett.*"

I wished it was. I wished it was paper-thin, because Kai-Ren was in my head, and he was staring at me—had he been listening the whole time?—and suddenly all I could think about was the way Cam had hung from his wrists the first time Kai-Ren fucked him. And it wasn't only fear that made my breath hitch.

Kai-Ren knew it. "*The noises this one would make under my hand, my pet, would be exquisite.*"

Cam's heart beat faster.

"*Do you want him, pet? They would give him, if I asked.*"

"No." Cam's gaze met mine. "*I don't want him.*"

I squeezed my eyes shut and thought of red dirt and sunburn. *God, please no. Please.*

I heard Kai-Ren's sibilant laughter in my mind.

"Brady?" Doc leaned close. "Are you okay, son?"

"Don't let him take me, Doc," I whispered. "Please don't."

"No one's going to take you anywhere," Doc said, but his gruff voice was distant, just an echo of Cam's: *"He's not going to take you, Brady."*

"I need to get out of here," I said, panic clawing at my throat. He was still looking. Kai-Ren was still looking, and I could fucking *feel* it. "Jesus, Doc, *please.*"

Doc only had to look at my face to see that I was about to lose it. He put an arm around my shoulders and walked me toward the doors.

"Brady. Brady?" It was Cam's voice, but I couldn't turn around again. I had to get out of there, because every time Cam said my name, Kai-Ren echoed it with a hiss, as though he was testing the taste of it on his tongue: *"Bray-dee."*

Doc got me outside and halfway to the elevator before I leaned over and vomited all over his boots.

CHAPTER NINETEEN

THE LIGHTS WERE DIMMED in the med bay, but it was one of the few places on Defender Three where they weren't flashing red. You can't have that, not in the med bay. Doctors are under enough pressure not to fuck up. They didn't need red strobes and alarms when they were up to their elbows in some guy's guts.

Doc maneuvered me onto an examination table.

"Fuck." I sucked in a shaking breath and watched as Doc carefully pried my fingers off his shoulder. "He was in my head, Doc, in my fucking *head*."

Doc scrubbed his big, square hand over my hair. "Rushton?"

"The fucking Faceless," I whispered. I wanted to vomit again. "I'm a fucking coward. Didn't even say good-bye."

One more useless regret. I'd find a way to drown it, like I did all of them.

"I'm sure he understands," Doc said.

The platitude rang hollow, but it didn't matter. It made the silence less stark.

The sting of a syringe brought me back.

"What the hell, Doc?"

Doc drew his bushy eyebrows together. "It's a mild sedative, Brady. It'll help you sleep. You want to crash here?"

I looked around the med bay. "And get woken up by some asshole having a psych episode in the middle of the night?"

"That was one time," Doc growled. "And it's already the middle of the night."

"Nah, I'm good."

A lie, but what I really wanted was a shower, a clean uniform, and cigarettes. I could only get two of those things in the med bay, and it was suddenly the cigarettes I wanted the most.

Doc sent me on my way with a sympathetic pat on the shoulder, into the flashing red strobes. I headed up to the officers' quarters to find the door to the room I'd shared with Cam locked open. The bedding and the mattress were gone—I guess I was evicted—and my pack was sitting on the floor with a bunch of condom packets strewn around it like confetti.

I looked around for whichever asshole with the sense of humor had left those out in plain sight of everyone who walked past, but there was nobody there to see the look on my face. Fuckers.

I gathered up the condoms and shoved them in my pack. I kept my back to the window, to the black, and to the massive Faceless ship that hugged the Outer Ring of Defender Three like a leech.

My throat hurt, and my chest was tight, but there was no point crying over a fucking room. It didn't matter if it had been the room Cam and I shared. It was empty now. It was cold.

I shouldered my pack and headed for the elevator.

The whole world was red. I tried to blink it away out of instinct. I'd seen a Hawk pilot with acceleration stress do that. He just sat in the med bay and blinked, trying to clear his redout when the blood vessels behind his eyes had burst. When the elevator doors creaked open in my barracks level, I was still blinking as well.

The place seemed mostly empty. With the station on red alert, guys would be at their emergency posts. A few of them were moving back and forth down the wide corridors. One of them was Cesari.

"Garrett, hey." Cesari's face was guarded, wary. The red lighting swallowed the sharp edges of door frames and bulkheads and softened the planes of Cesari's face. "They done with you upstairs?"

"Yeah."

Cesari's eyes widened. "You know what's going on up there? With the Faceless?"

"No idea, man," I lied because, holy fuck, where to start?

"Okay." Cesari chewed his lip. His hand went to his neck, and I remembered the crucifix he wore under his shirt. "Good luck, yeah?"

"Yeah, you too."

My barracks was empty, blankets pushed back from cots or dropped onto the floor where the guys had left them when the alarms sounded. I dumped my pack on my empty bunk and rifled through it for my cigarettes. The smoke stung my throat.

I wondered if Cam could still hear me. I wondered if I'd feel it when Kai-Ren fixed him. Would Cam simply slip away from me, or would the separation be as sharp and brutal as a battlefield amputation?

I closed my eyes.

"Cam? You still there?"

I felt nothing. There was no answering voice in my head. Nothing except the sting of my own misery, and what the hell did that matter? I'd known it couldn't last.

I stubbed my cigarette out on the floor and lit another one. I watched the curling tendrils of smoke and ignored my sore throat. I figured I'd smoke them until I ran out. Despite the sedative, I didn't want to sleep.

I don't know what I wanted.

I didn't like being alone.

I thought of this one guy I saw in the med bay once, after he'd slit his throat with his razor. He was dead by the time they got him there, and the guy who'd tried to save him, some newbie covered in blood, just stood there, shaking, repeating, *"He said could I pass his razor."*

I felt sorry for the newbie, but not for the guy who killed himself. I envied him. I never believed that shit about where there's life, there's hope, but where there's life, there's responsibility, right? I had to keep trying until it was over. Couldn't quit on Lucy. I owed her more than that.

"I will hold on," I whispered to myself. "I will hold on."

"Hey, Garrett!"

Fuck. I knew that voice. I spun around on my bunk to find Wade standing in the doorway. He had two of his asshole buddies with him. I was outnumbered.

"Your faggot friend Rushton brought the Faceless down on us."

My heart beat faster. Did his? Was he still with me?

Wishful thinking.

"You don't know what you're talking about, Wade."

"I know you're a faggot," he said. He sneered, but it didn't cover his fear. "I think I've proved that."

I tried not to sound scared. It didn't work. "Fuck off."

My palms were sweaty. I wiped them on the canvas bunk.

"Come over here and say that." He grinned.

And fuck, there was nowhere else to go.

I rose to my feet, flicking my cigarette onto the floor. I crushed it under the toe of my boot and tried to look casual. "What the hell do you want, Wade?"

Which, in hindsight, was exactly the wrong question to ask a sadistic fucker like that.

Assholes had me pinned against the wall before I even had a chance to get past them. Simple as that.

Then they started in on me.

"Cam? You there, Cam?"

Fucking hard to form a coherent thought when Wade was trying to make me vomit up my own guts. His first punch broke my nose. His second one broke my ribs. After that I wasn't really up to keeping a tab on my injuries.

Stomach, face, and balls.

Those are the three places I tried to curl up to protect, but those assholes were having none of it.

I was on the floor at that point, and every time I curled up, one of them delivered a kick that stretched me out again. These guys weren't as precise as Captain Lutkus and the way he played the pain withdrawal reflex, but I'm sure they had a future in intel if they wanted one.

Who would have thought that I could lose Cam and have a Faceless talk directly into my brain, and it still wouldn't be the worst thing that happened to me today? That's the definition of *fucked-up.*

Round about the sixth kick, my smart-ass attitude abandoned ship and left me with nothing but the hurt.

"Cam?"

God. This wasn't just a beating.

Laughing, one of them crouched down and drew my arm out, and I didn't have the strength to pull it back. Drowning in blood from my busted nose and from a punctured lung for all I knew, I couldn't even pull away when one of Wade's laughing buddies took at running jump at my arm.

I felt my ulna snap when he landed, and all I could think was the next time it would be my head.

These assholes were actually going to kill me.

———

I DROPPED out of school when I was twelve to look after Lucy.

The school in Kopa wasn't a government school. It was run by a church. I don't know which church it was, but they said the Faceless were God's punishment for the sins of mankind.

At my school, the teachers said we would be judged.

I believed that.

Judged and then condemned.

I wondered if whoever judged me would look like my dad.

"Brady," he said when Lucy cut her foot open on the old water tank, *"you were supposed to look after your sister."* And he shook his head at me and sighed.

I'm so sorry, Dad. I'm so sorry.

Lucy had Dad's gray eyes. God, I could see them now.

"Brady? Brady, carry me!"

I heard laughter.

"Yeah, go ahead and cry, you little fucker!"

If I was crying, it wasn't for me.

But maybe it was. For Dad, for Lucy, and for me. For all three of us, and for the bad luck we'd all had to be born in Kopa and because we'd never caught a break. For not asking much, and not getting it anyway. For the cold, black universe that tore us apart.

For everything.

"What the fuck, man?" I recognized the voice. It was Branski. Branski, who ran the black market on Defender Three, and who was supposed to be my friend. "You can't do this shit in here! You gotta get rid of him!"

Fuck you, Branski.

Someone lifted up my legs and started to drag me. My eyes rolled back in my head, and a strange noise escaped me. It oscillated somewhere between a whimper and a howl.

"Fuck," Branski said again. "Go and get a fucking mop!"

"Relax." Wade laughed.

"Relax? You want to go to trial for murder, you fucking idiots?"

I always liked Branski because he was smart and he ran rings around the officers he worked for at the Q-Store. There was nothing that Branski couldn't get away with. Too bad he was on Wade's side.

"And where the fuck am I supposed to get another contact in the med bay?" Branski demanded.

Is that all I was to him? Hell, it wasn't like we'd sworn eternal brotherhood or anything, but it would have been nice if Branski had been at least a little more concerned about my imminent death than his supply lines.

"Don't," I tried to say. "Don't, please, Branski."

I don't think the words were words, exactly.

It hurt when they moved me, just when I thought it couldn't hurt any more. I thought there must be a point where it hurt so much that my pain receptors couldn't send any more information to my brain, but that was wishful thinking. Instead of the pain climbing higher and higher until it hit the same pitch that only dogs could hear, when they moved me, it hurt in all new, different ways.

I whimpered as they dragged me down the hallway.

My blood vanished under the red lights.

I blacked out once, maybe twice, and woke up again when

they dumped me on a floor. A gray metal floor reflecting the red flashing strobe above the door. Even though the walls and the ceiling were covered in light tubes, it took me a while to realize where I was.

A UV chamber.

Fuck Wade, fuck his buddies, and fuck Branski most of all for being smarter than the rest of them. I didn't even have the strength to stand up to check if the door was locked, but of course it was. And one by one, the tubes in the walls and ceiling began to glow.

I opened my mouth to call out—to scream, to beg, or something. No words came. Just sounds. Just blood.

I couldn't get out.

With the entire station on red alert, nobody would even come near here. It would be hours. And if I remembered the orientation vid the officers made us watch every time they sent us into the UV chamber, without protective goggles I had twenty-five minutes before I went blind. I had forty-five minutes before I died. I guess all the forensic evidence of my murder would have burned off me long before then.

I tried to move, but I couldn't even roll over onto my side. Too much broken, too much bleeding. Too much white pain tearing at the fuzzy edges of my consciousness.

Lucy, so sorry, baby.

I had one final thought before I let go. It was the thing I should have had the guts to say when I was in the Dome, instead of running: *"Good-bye, Cam."*

———

"BRADY? BRADY?"

I struggled to open my eyes.

There were lights shining in my face. I was on a gurney.

"Brady?"

Doc was bending over me, shoving a syringe into my bloody arm—fuck, was that the bone sticking out?—but it wasn't his voice I'd heard.

"Cam?"

"Right here." His pale face appeared above mine, framed by hair.

I couldn't feel a thing at that point. I knew I was dying. I'd seen the amount of morphine Doc had injected into the vein in my elbow. And I couldn't breathe. My lungs were too heavy. They were filling with blood. Something in me had busted. It was something irreparable, because you only ever injected a guy with that much morphine if you were giving him an intentional overdose. Easing his pain, the textbooks called it. Putting the poor bastard out of his misery, Doc said.

I always thought morphine would make you float. It didn't. It just made me slowly sink. Very slowly and very gently, and I didn't mind much.

"Can you hear me, Brady?"

Cam was there, and that was nice. He was holding my hand, I think, or someone's burned, blistered hand. I couldn't feel it, but my bleary eyes told me it was attached to my arm. So that was nice as well. And meanwhile my chest cavity filled with blood that shouldn't have been there. It was drowning me, I suppose, but I trusted the morphine to take me first. Doc wouldn't give me time to hurt, or time to be afraid. At least I'd slip away free of pain, wrapped in only my regrets.

Lucy.

"It'll be okay."

It was hard keeping my eyes open.

Lights flashed overhead. They were wheeling me somewhere, and I didn't know what the hurry was. No point fucking hurrying. No point to anything at all.

I felt a twinge of regret at the unfairness of it all. Nineteen years old, and I was going to die. And that was a selfish thought. I should have been thinking of Lucy, but I was too tired for that. I just felt vaguely cheated. It wasn't right, and it wasn't fair, but I was too sleepy to rail against it.

"Hold on," Cam told me.

My lungs were filling with blood. My internal organs had been ruptured. Morphine was taking me gently down. Didn't he know there was nothing to hold on to?

The lights changed. An air lock hissed closed behind us, and then we were somewhere different. The ceilings weren't gray like they should have been. They were darker than that. Lights flashed, and I remembered them from Cam's dreams.

I was on the Faceless ship. I closed my eyes. As much as I hated Defender Three, at least those gray metal walls were familiar. Maybe, once, my dad's hand had touched them in the factories back home. I didn't want the last thing I saw to be something alien.

"Wake up, Brady. Wake up!"

I forced my eyes open at his pleading tone, and that was when I saw it: a stasis pod. A giant, black gleaming beetle with the skin of its sac pulled back.

I tried to shake my head. I tried to make words that wouldn't come: *No. Please no.*

They stripped me and lifted me, and then I was lying in the pod.

No no no!

I tried to struggle, and the only thing that broke free was a wave of pain. And I tried to scream and sprayed blood instead.

"Brady!" Cam held me down. "Brady! It's okay, Brady!"

I was in a fucking Faceless stasis pod. How the fuck could that be okay?

"Cam-ren," Kai-Ren hissed. "It must lie still!"

No. I didn't want this. I didn't want Kai-Ren to lock me in the bug. I didn't want to get carved up by some Faceless scientists. I wanted to die in the med bay instead, in the only place on Defender Three I'd actually fucking liked. Why had Commander Leonski given me to Kai-Ren? Why was Doc helping?

I remembered what Kai-Ren had said in my head in the Dome: *The noises this one would make under my hand, my pet, would be exquisite.* And I remembered what Hooper had said that night we'd been drinking moonshine in the storage bay, back before my life turned crazy: *"The Faceless will take you apart cell by cell. Cell by cell, and you'll feel every cut."*

No no no no no.

I tried to call out for Doc and choked.

Other hands held me down then. Doc was there, and so was Captain Loh. What the fuck had I ever done to them that they'd sell me out like this?

"Cam! Cam! Don't let him take me!"

And then Cam was back, and he was naked, and he was climbing up beside me. "You're okay, Brady."

He held me down.

"Still," Kai-Ren hissed. "It must remain still."

The unit buzzed with power, and the skin slowly drew across the pod. It was like liquid at first, and then it coalesced. And then the pod began to fill with fluid.

Cam held me tight, wrapping his arms around me. "Stay still, Brady. You can breathe it in. Don't fight it."

I was drowning, first in blood and then in weird Faceless amniotic fluid. I coughed and choked, and then the fluid covered my face. I sucked in a breath and got the fluid instead. It burned as it forced its way into my ruined lungs. And then I realized that I wasn't choking. Why wasn't I choking?

I turned my face to look for Cam under the milky fluid.

He pressed his lips against mine briefly and relaxed his grip.

I exhaled, and for a moment the fluid was bloody.

"You're okay, Brady," Cam said in my head. *"You'll be okay. We're going to sleep now. Close your eyes."*

So I did.

CHAPTER TWENTY

I OPENED my eyes to sunlight. "Where are we?"

Cam flashed me a smile. "No idea. It's okay, though."

Shit. I knew. We were sitting on a paddock of red dirt dotted with clumps of scrubby grass. About fifty meters away, cockatoos screamed in the line of trees that marked the riverbank. Follow that riverbank east, and around the bend you would see the stacks. You would see the smoke pouring from them and hear the bash of metal on metal as it reverberated through the town and rattled the walls of the fibro shacks.

Follow the riverbank west, and you would hit the mudflats, the mangroves, the rotted pylons of the old jetty, and the rusted croc traps half-submerged in the saltwater.

This was Kopa.

Cam looked different in the sunlight. I saw a hint of freckles on the bridge of his nose that I'd never seen on the station. His skin glowed. His eyes looked greener than ever before.

"Are we dead?" I looked down at my hands. They were as pale and pasty as three years on Defender Three had made them. The big black had leeched all the color from my skin.

"No." He reached over and took my hand in his, his warm fingers slipping between mine. "Promise you won't freak out, Brady?"

Fuck. I managed a sharp nod.

"We're in stasis," Cam said. He wrinkled his nose. "This isn't real. This is something the pod found for us to watch. I've never been here before, so it must be yours."

"It's Kopa," I said. The cockatoos screamed. I could taste red dirt on the air. "Please make it go away."

"Don't you want to be here?" Cam asked, frowning slightly.

"It's not real." I'd rather live in a real nightmare than a fake dream. What if I saw Lucy? What if I saw my dad? Please no.

"Close your eyes," Cam said.

I shut Kopa out.

"Can you see us?"

"I don't know," I said, but then something inside my brain shifted, and I could. My heartbeat ratcheted up.

We were in the pod, floating. Not drowning. How were we not drowning?

Cam's arms were wrapped around me.

"Am I dying?" I asked in my head.

"No."

I was mending.

As I lay suspended in that weird fluid, my bleeding stopped. My burns healed. My bones knit.

I lost all sense of time, of place. All sense of everything except Cam. We fit together, my face tucked under his chin, arms around each other, legs entangled. I could feel his heart beating.

"Please don't let them cut me up, Cam. Please."

His voice was calm. *"That's not going to happen, Brady."*

"I need to go home. For real. For Lucy. Please."

In the pod, his arms tightened around me. *"I'm so sorry, Brady. I'm so sorry. This was the only way to save you."*

"Then you should have let me die."

Something in the fluid held the thought, and I felt the echo of it washing over us for a long time, drowning us both in regret.

————

I DON'T KNOW how I knew he was there, but I knew. When Kai-Ren put his gloved hands on the surface of the pod, it bowed inward slightly, and the increased pressure felt like a caress. Cam's hand lifted. So did mine. Two little puppets dancing when Kai-Ren pulled our strings.

Awareness prickled the edges of my mind. Fear followed it.

I opened my eyes and stared up through the milky fluid, through the skin of the sac, and into the black formless mask of Kai-Ren.

"Bray-dee," he said in my head.

My heart raced, but I couldn't pull my hand back down. I wasn't just myself; I was somehow also a component in this machine, and my body had been programmed for a task. I spread my fingers. My stomach clenched as Kai-Ren put his hand over mine. The smooth skin of the pod rubbed between my palm and his glove.

His other hand was on Cam's.

We glowed. Gleaming characters curled up our flesh, flickering and changing as Kai-Ren stood above us. Our vitals, I suddenly realized: heart rate, temperature, blood pressure, and respiratory rate.

Kai-Ren shifted his hands, drawing ours with him, and then stepped back.

Vibrations shuddered through the fluid in the pod, though me, though Cam, and the lights on our skin disappeared. Above us, the skin of the pod began to dissolve. In moments I would be delivered into the hands of my nightmares.

No no no no no.

Maybe I would choke first, like Cam almost had. Except this time the pod worked like it was supposed to. I tried to move, to struggle—I *wanted* to—but instead I was flooded with a calmness so sudden, so pure, so all-encompassing, that it could only be chemical.

The fluid began to drain away.

There should have been a moment—even my addled brain knew it—when my body switched between breathing in fluid and breathing in air and thought that it was drowning. I should have panicked, convulsed, but I didn't. I lay in the pod, my arms still wrapped around Cam, and felt the fluid dribbling out of my numb lips. I felt the air touch my face, fill my lungs, but there was no violent moment of transition. The fluid flowed out, and the air flowed in as the skin of the sac melted away.

I gazed at Cam and marveled at how dilated his pupils were. They'd almost swallowed his green irises. His hair, dripping with slimy fluid, stuck to his face.

"So sorry, Brady."

I struggled to keep my eyes open as Kai-Ren loomed over us, but the drug was stronger. I whimpered, and Kai-Ren lifted me; my nightmare lifted me. I saw lights in the gleaming ceiling. I heard hissing noises. I felt Kai-Ren's fingers curling around my throat.

"Cam... Cam..."

It wasn't Cam who answered.

"Be silent, little thing."

I wondered if my sudden burst of fear blasted him like radio feedback. That's the pitch it hit in me. Was he going to kill me? Was he going to fuck me like he had Cam? Was he going to cut me apart cell by cell just to listen to the sounds I made?

The room Kai-Ren carried me into was dark. He lowered me

onto the floor and slid a gloved hand down my chest. He splayed his fingers across my abdomen and made a hissing noise.

I tried to fight the drug that was pulling me toward sleep and wondered why the hell I was. Unconsciousness was a gift, right?

I whimpered as Kai-Ren rose. For a second he was framed in the dim light from the hallway outside. The looming Faceless, covered in his black battle armor, tall and silent: the thing from all my nightmares, from the nightmares of every human being who existed.

And then he was gone, the door sliding shut behind him.

My dad used to sing to me. He had a voice that was wrecked by cigarettes and by working in the smelters. It was cracked, gravelly, but on certain notes it was perfect. When I was scared of the dark, it was Dad's growly voice I listened for. Some of the songs he sang had words in strange languages. The songs had come down from his father, but Dad didn't know what the words meant or what lands they were from. The meaning was long gone, but the sounds were left behind. An echo.

I whispered the songs to myself in the Faceless ship, in the middle of the big black, in places those words had never been whispered before. I thought it might comfort me, but it didn't. It only reminded me of how small I was, and how far away from home.

In the blackness, I didn't know how long I slept or even if I slept at all. Maybe I lay there until the drugs wore off, or maybe I just dreamed I did. I only knew that at some point I could move again.

I flexed my fingers and toes, checking for injuries. After the beating I got from Wade and then my time in the UV chamber, I should have been dead. I couldn't even feel a twinge now. I remembered seeing the bone stick out of my arm. Not even a scar.

The fluid from the pod had dried on my skin. It flaked off like dry skin as I passed my shaking hands over my body.

Tears stung my eyes.

I should have died on Defender Three, where I might have been surrounded by sadistic fucking assholes, but at least they were sadistic fucking asshole humans. Shouldn't have been given to the Faceless, however much Cam wanted me to live. What about what I wanted?

It was so dark that I didn't have to close my eyes to see her: a grubby little face, fine, flyaway hair, and eyes that changed between blue and gray depending on the sky. Three years was a long time for a little kid. I was her whole world once, but did she even remember me? It would be better if she didn't.

I scrubbed my eyes with my hands.

"Why are you sulking, my pet?"

Shit. I ripped my hands away from my face, expecting to see Kai-Ren standing above me again. Nothing. The door was still shut. I was still lying alone in the dark. My heart thumped.

"I'm not sulking, master," Cam said.

Jesus. I could hear them. Not in my head, or not *just* in my head. I could hear their spoken words, even though they weren't anywhere near me. I closed my eyes, and in that second I *saw* them as well, the same way that Kai-Ren had seen Cam and me in the shower.

They stood in a large round room. The bridge, instinct told me. Instinct, or that part of me that was in both their heads. There were no control panels here, no buttons and displays. Instead there were alcoves filled with strange glowing lights that reminded me of bioluminescence. Faceless technology was *alive*.

Cam was agitated. He folded his arms over his bare chest. He was wearing a pair of military-issue cargoes he must have got on Defender Three, and his feet were bare.

"Don't you want your own pet, Cam-ren?" Kai-Ren's sibilant voice sounded amused.

Cam stared into that formless black mask. "No," he said, but his voice was strained.

Kai-Ren hissed, and I couldn't tell if it was in amusement or displeasure. "Don't lie."

Cam closed his eyes for a moment. His chest expanded as he drew in a deep breath. "Not like this. He's scared."

I shivered in the darkness.

"You were scared."

Cam reached up and touched Kai-Ren's shoulder. "It's different, master."

I hated that word. I hated to hear it coming from Cam's mouth. Cam was clever and brave. Cam chased starlight. He wasn't a fucking pet with a master.

Cam slid his fingers up behind Kai-Ren's skull, and I knew what was coming next. I balled my hands over my eyes, but it didn't help. I could still see.

I could see the room I lay in: small and dark.

I could see the bridge.

I could see Kai-Ren through Cam's eyes, and I could see Cam through his.

Cam unfastened Kai-Ren's black mask and revealed the face of the nightmare.

Flesh as white and cold as porcelain pulled tightly across a sharp, angular skull with prominent cheekbones and brow. His eyes were lashless, the irises yellow. Kai-Ren's nose was narrower than a human's. Underneath it, his thin, bloodless lips curled into a smile as Cam reached up and stroked his hollow cheek.

"God, Cam, don't. Don't touch it."

If either of them heard me, they didn't react.

"How is it different?" Kai-Ren asked, the words escaping his thin lips like a hiss of steam.

Were those sharp teeth I glimpsed? I didn't want to watch, but I couldn't get out of my own fucking head.

"I was scared for me," Cam said. "He's scared for more than himself."

Kai-Ren narrowed his eyes.

"I know you don't understand," Cam said. He smiled ruefully, and I remembered what he'd told me days ago: *"He is honorable, in their sense. But he also really does think we're lower than pond scum."*

Kai-Ren growled and slid a gloved hand down Cam's spine, and I felt it. I felt it as if he were touching me. I felt how the touch teased Cam into arousal, and how it did the same to me.

My heart racing, I hauled myself up onto my knees and retched. Nothing came out, but at least I somehow managed to jam the connection between Cam, Kai-Ren, and me. If my flesh prickled and I shivered, that was because I was naked on a Faceless ship in the middle of the black, not because Cam was getting touched and he liked it.

Because if that was the reason, I was totally fucked-up.

———

I HAD no more idea of the passage of time in this room than I had in the pod, except I didn't need to piss yet, and I wasn't hungry, so it couldn't have been too long. I lay on the floor and tried not to notice how it felt more like skin than metal, and how small vibrations passed through it. The thrumming of an engine, maybe, or maybe a pumping lymphatic system. The hell if I knew.

The door slid open. "Brady?"

Relief flooded over me. "Cam!"

"It's okay," he said.

Another fucking lie, but I tried hard to believe it. I think I almost did for a second; then the whole thing crumbled.

Cam sat on the floor with me and held me while I cried. He stroked my face, rubbed my back, and let me burrow as close as a tick.

"*It's okay,*" he thought, and every time he wrecked it with what he really thought: "*I'm so sorry.*"

"*I know.*" I tried not to think about how the Faceless had touched him. Tried not to think about how much further they'd gone when I managed to shut them out, and whether or not Cam liked it.

He did. I knew he did.

Fucking telepathy.

I wished I had some clothes to wipe my nose on. I sniffed instead. "Why are we still connected? I thought he was going to fix that."

"He was," Cam said. His eyes were large in the gloom. "But he wants you to be able to communicate with him, Brady, yeah?"

I shrugged.

Cam rubbed his palm over my buzz cut. "And you remember how he does that, right?"

Fear stabbed me.

Technicolor flashback to the first time Cam awoke on this ship.

Cam had twisted his head from side to side, but he couldn't see. He was blindfolded. Naked. He was chained, wrists and ankles, and he couldn't move. His arms were pulled above his head. His shoulders hurt. His bare feet scrabbled on the floor but couldn't get purchase. There was nowhere to go. There nothing to do but take it.

I squeezed my eyes shut.

"So maybe it's okay if I stay in your head awhile," Cam said. "Be your intermediary."

"Yeah." My breath shuddered out of me. "Yeah."

We sat together in the darkness.

Fear fades.

You think it does, but sometimes it's just regrouping.

Cam held me until I fell asleep. When I woke up again, I was in chains.

CHAPTER TWENTY-ONE

I SCREAMED.

I was in the room with the flashing lights, with the restraints, and Kai-Ren was standing right in front of me. He wasn't wearing his mask. He narrowed his yellow eyes as he gazed at me.

I struggled, even though I knew it was pointless. My hands were chained above my head. There were straps around my ankles, keeping my legs apart.

"Don't!" I begged, twisting my body. "He said you wouldn't! He said you wouldn't!"

Kai-Ren hissed. "You do not understand, Bray-dee. You do not *listen*."

"I'll listen. I'll listen!" But I knew that's not what he meant, not really.

My connection with Kai-Ren wasn't as strong as my connection with Cam. Cam had called himself an intermediary. Maybe that wasn't good enough for what Kai-Ren wanted, although why the fuck he wanted to communicate better with a filthy reffo from Kopa was anyone's guess. Cam was a better ambassador for humanity than me.

"I hear you," I said. My heart rate spiked in panic, and adrenaline coursed through me. *Fight or flight?* biochemistry asked me, and I couldn't do either. I could only beg. "I'll listen, please!"

Kai-Ren hissed again, and something in his tone sounded almost affectionate. "Soon you will, little thing."

Kai-Ren moved behind me. His fingernail—his claw?—scraped gently down my spine, following the knots. My skin turned to gooseflesh, and my guts turned to water.

No no no no no.

Was that my voice in my head or the memory of Cam's when he'd been in this exact position? I couldn't tell, and what the hell did it matter anyway? His, mine—it hit the same brittle, panicked pitch.

"I'm not him!" I whimpered. "I'm not the same as him!"

If Kai-Ren expected that after this, I'd understand, he was wrong. Cam might have been able to understand that Kai-Ren was alien, that the violation was incidental to the purpose, but I couldn't, and I wouldn't. Cam was smarter than me. Cam didn't have the same reserve of anger boiling in his guts that I did. Cam couldn't hold a fucking grudge.

Nothing, *nothing* would make me stop hating Kai-Ren for this.

And fearing him.

And wishing I was dead.

This wasn't just biochemistry. This was *me*.

"I'm not the same as him!" I said again, my eyes stinging with tears, my nose dripping. "We're not all the same!"

But who can tell the difference between insects, right?

Kai-Ren touched my neck. A sudden, sharp pain stung me.

The drug was instantaneous. Calmness stole over me. My heartbeat slowed. My breath slipped out in a sigh. Fear died.

Sensation replaced it as Kai-Ren's hands ghosted over my skin. His touch wasn't warm, but it was as electric as Cam's had ever been. I hated the way he touched me like he owned me. I hated the moan that escaped me. Most of all I hated the way he hissed in satisfaction when my cock began to fill.

"Good, Bray-dee," he whispered somewhere close to my ear.

I didn't even have the strength to turn my head away. I could only hang there, my chin lolling. I stared down my scrawny, pale body as Kai-Ren pressed up behind me, his gloved hands sliding over my hip bones, over my abdomen, and down to my cock.

I knew I should be afraid, but whatever Kai-Ren had injected into me—a drug? venom?—deadened the part of my mind that should have been screaming. Kai-Ren's gloved fingertips stroked my cock, and I moaned.

No no no no no.

Except yes. Yes.

Kai-Ren moved his hands away from my cock, back to my ass.

The drug had left me too numb to struggle, but my fear found me again. Tears streamed down my face.

"Don't. Please don't. He said you wouldn't. Cam said."

Kai-Ren hissed, and maybe the sound was supposed to be soothing.

Outside, I heard a muffled noise. A dull, rapid knocking, and then a muted shout: "Brady! Brady!"

"Cam?" My mind shouted back at him even if my body could only raise a weak whimper in response.

Kai-Ren hissed again. This time the noise sounded annoyed.

I lifted my head as the door slid open, and Cam came toward me.

"Don't hurt him," he said, his voice strained. His gaze caught mine. It reflected my own fear. "Please, master, don't."

Kai-Ren scraped a gloved claw down my spine, and I shuddered. "This fear will leave him when our connection is stronger. When he understands."

"It won't," Cam said. "We're different."

He stood in front of me and put his arms around me. A useless gesture of protection and comfort, but I closed my eyes and pretended it would make a difference.

Kai-Ren ran his hand over my head. I leaned into Cam. My breath hitched.

"He must listen!" Kai-Ren hissed.

Cam shifted, kicking at the anchor point beside my left ankle. The cord whirred as it retracted. I didn't know if I should move. Not when Kai-Ren was still breathing down my back, still tracing my spine, still hissing in disapproval whenever I made a sound.

Cam kicked at the other anchor point and then reached up. His fingers curled around my left wrist, unfastening the cuff. My shoulder ached as my arm dropped. I didn't have the energy to lift it.

"Listen," he said.

"I will," I whispered through my tears, fighting the drug. "I will. Jesus, I will!"

"No," Cam said, holding me tight. "Not you, Brady."

Cam held me with one arm as he unfastened my other arm. I sagged forward into his embrace, and very gently he lowered us both to the floor. I squeezed my eyes shut and wondered if Kai-Ren was going to kill us for this.

"Do you see her?" Cam asked. "Do you feel it?"

Kai-Ren growled, but in that second we all saw her: a skinny little girl made as brown as a nut by the sun, standing in the kitchen with a towel around her shoulders while I brushed the tangles out of her wet hair.

"Can I sleep in your bed, Brady?"

"What for?"

Her gray eyes were large. *"I'm scared of the dark."*

"What if I'm scared of the dark as well?"

Lucy wrinkled her nose. *"I won't be scared if I'm with you, and then I can stop you being scared, okay?"*

"Okay."

Lucy was my other heartbeat before Cam.

She was still my universe.

"He doesn't belong here," Cam whispered. "He never will. You must feel that."

"He is for you, Cam-ren," Kai-Ren said, his sibilant voice coming from above us. "He is what you wanted."

Cam curled his fingers through mine. "Not like this."

I opened my eyes and looked over Cam's shoulder at Kai-Ren. I wondered if I imagined something in the yellow eyes that was almost thoughtful. Almost human. Then his eyes flashed, and it was gone.

He curled his thin upper lip and showed pointed teeth. "This is a gift."

"No," Cam said.

"Think carefully, Cam-ren. Have your way, and nobody wins."

"No," Cam agreed, "but maybe nobody dies."

The silence drew out. If anything passed between them, I didn't hear it over my whimpers.

Then Cam loosened his grip on me.

Kai-Ren narrowed his eyes. "On your feet, little thing."

"Cam," I whispered.

"It's okay," Cam said. He helped me to my feet. "He'll send you back, Brady, okay?"

I couldn't tell if it was a lie or not.

I couldn't tell if I was crying for Lucy, for me, or for Cam.

When Cam helped me back into what might have been the same pod that we'd shared dreams in, I couldn't stop shaking. Not for the pod this time, or for Kai-Ren standing close by, or even for the big black. This was all shock.

"It's okay," Cam said.

For the guy who was my patient, he'd been saying that to me

a lot since we first cut him out of his pod. Shit, I'd never been in charge, had I?

He ran one hand over my buzz cut. His other hand cupped my face. His green eyes were wide, drinking in everything he could in our last moments together. My eyes were just as wide.

"It will break the connection," he said. "This time, it will. If you open your eyes, don't be scared, okay?"

I remembered what he'd seen. I remembered how he'd stared into the black and it had revealed itself to him color by burning color. I remembered the thrill of spinning slowly in the infinite. Chasing starlight and catching it.

"Don't be scared," he repeated. "Every minute, you're closer to Lucy. You tell them, Brady. You tell them any fucking lie to get a transfer planetside, okay? Tell them you saw weapons, cities, anything."

I tried to grin. "You don't need to teach a reffo to lie, Cam."

"Yeah." His eyes shone with tears. "And maybe you can see my parents. Tell them a lie as well, okay?"

"I will," I said, my chest tightening. That's what you do, right, for the guys who don't come home?

"Make it a good one," he said.

The pod began to fill with fluid.

"I'm sorry," I said. My breath hitched in my throat. It caught on a strangled sob that hurt when I swallowed it down. "I'm sorry I couldn't choose you."

Cam showed me a shaky smile. "No, you're not."

I thought of Lucy. "No, I'm not."

"And you shouldn't be." Cam leaned down and brushed his lips against mine before I even realized it was a kiss. A last kiss. It was over before I knew. "I'll miss you."

"It's more than that," I said. My heart skipped a beat. "We gonna say it?"

"Yeah." For a second his hair curtained his face; then he met my gaze again. "I love you, Brady."

"Love you, Cam."

It made no fucking difference at all, but at least we got to say it once.

FUCK THE UNIVERSE.

Fuck eternity and creation and a million colors boiling together in the black.

What the hell use was that to me?

My heart broke either way.

FOR THE SECOND time in as many days—was it only days?—I came awake when hands pressed against the skin of the pod. This time the face peering down at me was human. Our hands touched against the skin, and I fixed my gaze on that craggy old face as awareness crept slowly over me.

The skin melted, the fluid drained away, and I sucked in a lungful of cold, recycled air in the med bay of Defender Three.

"Brady," Doc said, sliding one hand in under my jaw to find my pulse while the other one cradled my cheek. "Brady. Jesus fucking Christ. Brady."

Doc was talking at me. Behind him, Commander Leonski and Lieutenant Commander Chanter were staring at me. I couldn't see behind them, but people were talking.

And I was lying there naked.

Noise, lights, cold, naked, but the only thing I heard was my own heartbeat: solitary. There was no synchronicity. Not even an echo in the emptiness. And the only voice in my head was my own.

Jesus.

Alone.

I blinked at the lights in the ceiling.

"Cam?" I liked the sting of silence, so I asked it again. *"Cam?"*

I shivered. Yeah, could rip that scab off a million times or more before it wouldn't bleed anymore. Bleeding was the least I could do for him.

"You feel that?" I'd asked Cam once.

"Hurts."

Always did, always would.

I slid my hand up my naked ribs and held it over my heart. Once, Cam's had beat in time with it. Once, Lucy's had. It would again. I had to believe that.

Doc's hand closed over mine.

"Brady," he gasped. "What the hell happened to you?"

I blinked, and the lights in the ceiling burst like coronas. I raised my shaking hands to my eyes to wipe some of the slimy Faceless fluid away.

"Wade bashed me," I said, even though he probably didn't mean that. He probably meant what happened with Kai-Ren. "You listening, Doc? Wade and his asshole buddies bashed me, but it was that fucker Branski's idea to put me in the UV chamber. Could've killed me, Doc."

"Brady," Doc said again. His hairy eyebrows did a complicated dance. "Jesus Christ, Brady, I thought they did."

"Fuck miracles," I whispered. "Fuck the universe."

"Jesus," Doc said and pulled himself together. "Let's get you out of here and cleaned up."

"Yeah."

It took two of them to help me out of the pod: Doc and

Captain Loh. When they finally had me standing, Doc leaned me against Captain Loh and checked me for breaks.

"Let's get you into a shower," Doc said at last.

A wall of gray uniforms parted, and that was when I saw it. For a second I thought I'd got turned around somehow, or that my vision was more fucked-up than I thought, but it was real: a black, oily thing that looked like a giant bug lying on its back with its legs clasping a sac. An intact sac.

"What the hell is that?" I asked, my voice breaking.

Doc frowned at me. "That's the other pod."

The other...

The cold universe crumbled to pieces around me. I couldn't breathe, but it didn't stop me from moving.

Funny. The pods had scared the living shit out of me when I first saw one, black, insect-like. Right then I couldn't wait to get to this one, to get up on my toes and stare into the milky fluid at the body underneath. Couldn't wait to press my hands against the slimy sac and watch it melt away.

"Cam!"

The first time I'd seen him, he had an air bubble caught in his eyelashes. He had one this time as well, shining like a tear on his face.

I put my hands on the sac. Cam raised his. His eyes were closed, he was still in the weird place the pod took him—maybe the spiraling universe, maybe some memory of his, or maybe just the scrubby paddock in Kopa that I'd shown him—but the same old electricity sparked through us when we touched. His lips curved into a smile even before the skin of the pod dissolved, even before the fluid began to drain away, even before he opened his eyes.

When he did, it was like the dawn.

"Hey, Brady," he rasped, shivering as his flesh was exposed to the air.

My short, sharp bark of surprise wasn't exactly a laugh. I didn't know what the hell it was. I reached into the pod and gripped his hand. Our slimy fingers slid together.

"Am I dreaming?"

No answer. That was okay. It gave me a chance to translate the question from my brain to my mouth into something that was less pathetic.

"What the fuck happened?"

Cam's grip tightened on mine. His eyes were wide. "He listened. He *listened.*"

Then, not caring that he was naked, slimy, and surrounded by officers, Cam started to laugh. A second later I joined in. I didn't even care if every officer in the med bay thought we were crazy.

Fuck 'em.

CHAPTER TWENTY-TWO

IN KOPA TOWNSHIP, the factories and the smelter spewed smoke into the flawless blue sky.

The sun beat down on my back as I walked up the hill. I'd made this walk a thousand times before, but it felt different now. It felt like I was a stranger. My feet remembered the way, but it was like my eyes were seeing it all for the first time.

Red dust covered my boots. It was hotter than I remembered. Sweat stuck my shirt to my back and slipped down my spine.

And then we were at my house. The fibro walls, the sagging roof, and the scrubby little garden where nothing except weeds had grown for years. Rubbish littered the cracked concrete path, and I was suddenly ashamed. It was a fucking hovel.

"Is this your place?" Cam asked me, putting a hand on my shoulder.

I fought not to shake it off. I didn't want his...was it *sympathy?* I didn't want Cam to look down on me, seeing that I was shit. Didn't want him to feel sorry for me. And I didn't want half the fucking population of Kopa to guess that I was a fag.

This shit was a lot easier when Cam was in my head, listening, understanding, and never judging.

Also, I really had to work on that terminology stuff.

"Yeah," I said. I squatted down in the dirt partly to get a look at the house, and partly to put some distance between us. Last time I was here I had a girlfriend. It just goes to show, I guess.

Fuck. I don't know what it goes to show.

Last time I was here I had a father as well, and there might have been holes in the fibro walls and more rust than tin on the roof, but it was still a house. My dad had worked hard to keep that roof over us. It was more than a lot of people had.

The sagging washing line extended from the side of the house. It was hung with clothes that belonged to strangers. Houses didn't stay empty for long in Kopa.

I stood. "Denise is on the other side of the hill."

Cam nodded.

Cam might have had one of the most famous faces on the planet, but with his scruffy long hair and civvies nobody recognized him as the same guy from the posters or the TV. I got more looks that him. People in Kopa knew me.

Cockatoos screamed in the distance, and a stab of panic caught me in the guts. This was just how the Faceless pod had projected Kopa for me. So vivid, so alive. What if I was still in that fucking pod? What if Kai-Ren had never let me go?

Cam might not have been in my head anymore, but it was never that complicated in there. He saw the look on my face and smiled. "Déjà vu, right?"

"Don't flash your five-dollar education around here, LT," I said. "You'll get your head kicked in."

"Don't call me LT," Cam returned. "We're on leave."

On leave because otherwise we'd be AWOL. The first time I'd walked out of provisional HQ in the middle of my repatriation course, they thought I was suffering from PTSD. The second, third, and fourth times they put me in the stockade. The stockade at provisional HQ was a hell of a lot nicer than the brig on Defender Three, and I wasn't in as much trouble as I should have been. It helps when you've got a medical certificate in your pocket saying you're crazy.

Also, you get a lot of leeway when you're one of only two guys in the universe who have seen a Faceless in the flesh and lived to tell the tale. So far, I hadn't been formally charged, and nobody had told Cam to cut his hair.

"You look like a criminal," Cam had said when he visited me in the stockade.

"You look like a fucking hippie."

"You like my hair," he reminded me. *"Get used to it."*

I leaned on the bars. *"And you like my attitude. Get used to this."*

So we were even, I guess.

Eventually the brass realized that it would be a hell of a lot easier to just let me go to Kopa. They sent Cam with me to make sure I came back. That made me laugh like nothing had since forever. I didn't want to *stay* in Kopa. Who the fuck would want to stay in Kopa? They must really have thought us reffos were stupid.

What they made of Cam and me, they didn't say.

They knew, though. Shit, we shared quarters. Bunk beds, which weren't exactly ideal, but I guess that was as far as the brass was willing to go. I didn't even know what they disapproved of most: his hair and my attitude, that he was an officer and I was enlisted, or that thanks to the Faceless we'd been in each other's heads. And other places.

I smirked at that and shoved my hands in my pockets.

Cam caught my gaze and grinned. He didn't need to be in my head to know I was thinking something dirty.

"Come on," I said, and we headed up the hill.

The air smelled of salt and smoke and red dust. The day was humid. We kicked up dust as we walked.

Cam was wide-eyed in Kopa. Maybe it was the barefoot kids and the holes in the walls, or the bottles smashed on the streets. Maybe it was because he really saw me for who I was: a feral, ignorant reffo. I'd seen photographs: the house I'd just shown him was nothing like the one he'd grown up in, and neither were the six or seven apartments we'd looked at online.

"The four bedroom will give us a spare room, but I really like the open living area in the three. What do you think?"

I'd thought that he was talking a foreign language.

I worried that we really had nothing in common, and that Kopa would show him that beyond a doubt.

We crested the hill. A gaggle of kids played in the scrubby grass beside the road.

"Jesus," Cam said, his voice laced with wonder. "It's *her*. It's Lucy."

My heart skipped a beat when I saw her: a skinny little girl in a faded green dress and bare feet. Her hair was plaited and tied with a ribbon.

"It's her," Cam said again.

And then I realized that I was wrong, that Kopa was as much a part of Cam's memory now as it was mine. That every mixed-up, fucked-up piece of my life that had ever stuck in my memory, my subconscious, or my dreams was a part of his life now as well. He'd given me wet dreams about Chris and nightmares about the Faceless. And I'd given him Lucy.

So maybe this would be okay. Maybe, for once, everything didn't have to go to shit.

Lucy walked toward us slowly, chewing her bottom lip.

I wanted to reach out and grab her, to never let her go, but shit, it had been three years. It was almost half her lifetime. I was just some stranger.

"Hi," I said.

"Hello."

The sound of her voice after so long made something inside me crumble. It was my anger, I think. My anger, all wrapped up in my fear. The loss left me shaking. "Do you remember me, Lucy?"

She nodded shyly and reached into the pocket of her dress. She withdrew a crumpled piece of cardboard and showed it to me. It was a photograph. Me, sixteen years old, with big, scared eyes and a buzz cut.

"You're my brother," she said. "You're Brady."

"Yeah," I said. "I'm Brady, and this is Cam."

Lucy's face was solemn as she transferred her gaze to Cam. "You're on the posters," she said.

I remembered the one from the storeroom where we drank on Defender Three: *Join the Military and Save the Earth.* Bullshit, I'd thought, but it turned out they'd got it right when they'd used Cam's face for the posters. He'd saved the Earth.

"Am I prettier in real life?" Cam asked her with a grin.

Lucy's smile reminded me of Dad's.

I held out my hand to her, and she took it.

Three years of misery melted away. It was hard to breathe and fucking impossible to speak. That was okay. I had no words anyway.

"Look after your sister," my dad always told me.

I did. I will. I promise.

My knees hit the dirt. I held Lucy as she burrowed into my chest. Home. This was home.

I looked up at Cam, smiling, crying, I don't fucking know.

I'd never thought past this. I didn't really care about apartment hunting or career planning or discussing whatever it was that Cam and I had, or any other damn thing, because a part of me had never believed this would happen. I hadn't dared dream that one day I would be back in Kopa, with my arms around my little sister. Just for once not waiting for everything to go to shit. Just for once expecting the best instead of the worst.

I didn't have much experience with optimism.

I rose to my feet, still holding Lucy. She was heavy, but I didn't care. I'd never put her down, probably. Not for a while anyway.

"What happens now?" I asked Cam, my voice breaking.

Cam smiled at me like he knew exactly what I meant. Maybe he did. He reached out and put his arms around me, sandwiching Lucy, and fuck what anyone thought.

Yeah, fuck you, Kopa. I'm coming out, and then I'm getting out. See you all in hell.

I guess I didn't lose all my anger like I thought.

Cam drew a deep breath before he released us. His smile was brilliant. "I don't know what happens now, Brady. Wanna figure it out together?"

I couldn't stop my own smile from spreading across my face.

"Yeah," I said, holding Lucy tight. "That sounds like a plan."

AFTERWORD

Thank you so much for reading. I hope that you enjoyed it. I would very much appreciate it if you could take a few moments to leave a review on Amazon or Goodreads, or on your social media platform of choice.

AN EXCERPT FROM DARKER SPACE:

The military was never going to let Cam go. Me neither, probably, except I wasn't a valuable asset to intel so much as I was a dead end. I'd spent my captivity by the Faceless curled up in the fetal position, whimpering and panicking, in a dark room on Kai-Ren's ship. So yeah, a dead end. But I didn't care if I spent the rest of my life in fatigues and boots that didn't fit right as long as I had the sun at my back. As long as I got to keep Cam and Lucy, I didn't care how many ways the military had its claws in us, or how many floors I had to scrub.

Once upon a time, back on Defender Three, I'd been a trainee medic. Here, planetside, there were enough real doctors and nurses and medics that they didn't need to scrape the bottom of the barrel for guys like me, so I was an orderly at the base hospital. I didn't mind. It meant a lot of hours leaning on a mop, but there were worse jobs. And just like on Defender Three, I got to finish off the meals the patients couldn't.

This one kid, Mike Marcello, had gotten hurt in a training exercise. He copped a face full of explosives, and now he could really only eat pudding and whatever had gone through a blender first. But he always asked for biscuits with his meals, and then gave them to me because I played cards with him in the afternoon and didn't freak out about his face. So I guess I still had the bedside manner Doc had praised me for back when I was still a trainee medic, or at least I had a thing where I liked food more than I hated looking at the way Marcello's jaw hung slack from his face with titanium staples and wires.

His good eye lit up when I walked in to visit him, and he gave me what was probably a smile but looked more like the grimace of a death's head. "Ay, Arret."

Hey, Garret.

His speech was pretty fucked up too.

"Hey, Marcello." I pulled my cards out of my pocket. "What's up?"

Because of the way he talked, he didn't get many visitors. Most of his mates, the guys he'd been in training with, were orbiting the planet on Defenders now anyway, which at least saved him from having to find out the hard way they were assholes.

But I don't know. Maybe they would have visited him.

His parents lived in Murray Bay. The military was going to ship him back there as soon as they gave him a jaw he could chew with and some more reconstructive surgery so that when he closed what was left of his mouth, there was enough skin to give him a cheek.

"Yor ate."

Late? Every day it took a little while to attune my ear to the way Marcello spoke.

"Fuck off." I pulled up a chair and dealt the cards. "You got any idea how these assholes are riding me?"

Marcello rolled his eyes, and I told him all about Lucy's birthday party. Marcello was from a refugee township too. He didn't know about Pass the Parcel either. We played cards for an hour before some nurse came looking for me to clean up a patch of vomit in the hall.

"See you, Marcello."

"Ee you."

I cleaned up the vomit and headed down to the basement to get a fresh mop and a cigarette.

My boss at the hospital was a dickhead of a lance corporal called Lingard. He didn't like me much, and the feeling was absolutely mutual. He was a pinch-faced, petty-minded fucker who thought I was the one with the attitude problem, when what really got his goat, although he didn't have the balls to admit it, was that I was twenty years younger than him, twice as smart, and had actually seen some service in the black that didn't involve pushing a mop.

"Think you're better than me, Garrett?" he'd asked once, squaring up to me.

My smirk told him I knew I was.

I mean, what could he do to me, really? Make me clean up twice as much vomit?

The rest of the orderlies were okay. We didn't talk much and usually only saw one another at the beginning and the end of every shift when we stowed our gear in the basement. Or maybe they talked to one another but not to me; I don't know. Even though what had happened out in the black wasn't public knowledge, this was the military, and gossip traveled fast. Everyone knew I was one of only two guys who'd been taken and then returned by the Faceless.

I was a horror story, probably.

Just like Marcello.

When I got to the basement, a few of the other guys were there too, hanging around.

"Hey." Jones nodded at me as I passed him.

"Hey."

He followed me into the locker room. "You hear anything about the Shitboxes?"

"Nope." I opened my locker to grab my cigarettes. "What Shitboxes?"

"Three of them in the last week. Landing at night." Jones tapped the side of his nose. "I've got a buddy in the motor pool. Says he got sent out each time to collect brass from the runway."

Shitboxes were shuttles. They were mostly used to ferry men and supplies between Defenders, but they could break atmo as well. Well, hit it like a fucking brick wall first. If Shitboxes were landing, they were coming in from the black, not from planetside.

I slammed my locker door shut. "Why the hell would I know anything about it?"

Jones scowled at me and showed me his palms. "I was just asking!"

"Yeah, just asking because if something weird's going on, it's gotta have something to do with me, right?" I pulled a cigarette out of the pack. "Fuck you."

He rolled his eyes. "Whatever, asshole."

"Yeah. What-the-fuck-ever." I hadn't even guessed before Jones had started talking that I was wound up tight enough to be itching for a fight. Jones didn't give me the satisfaction, though. Just shook his head and walked away.

I don't know.

Maybe he wasn't making anything of it except conversation, but I'd only look like a dick if I asked, so I didn't say anything. Just let him walk away.

"Garrett!" Lingard shuffled into the locker room. He looked to be in a foul mood. Fouler than usual, which, considering he'd been born an asshole of the highest order, was really saying something.

"Where the fuck are the syringes? The med director is all

over me because there are no fucking syringes, and they ordered them three weeks ago!"

I leaned on my locker and watched his face turn red. I was fairly certain that nobody, not even the med director, would be all over Lingard without a hazmat suit and at least ten shots of vodka behind him. He was ugly as sin on the outside and twice as ugly on the inside. He was married too. I once heard one of the guys say his wife must've lost a bet.

"Get over to logistics and find out what the fuck happened to those syringes!"

"Right now?"

"No, for fucking Christmas, what do you reckon?"

I shoved my cigarettes in my pocket, threw a sloppy salute in Lingard's direction, and bit down a grin. Logistics? Lingard never would have sent me if he'd known he was doing me a favor.

I stopped at the med director's office on the way, to get a copy of the work order for the syringes. I'd been in the military long enough to know that they wouldn't believe you had ten fingers and ten toes if you didn't have the paperwork to prove it. The clerk on duty was a decent guy and didn't give me any shit over it. Just made a copy of the order, which I folded up and shoved in my pocket.

A legitimate excuse to visit logistics. I hadn't had one of those in a while. And hopefully, if I was argumentative enough, I'd get referred up the line until I was shown into the office of a particularly hot lieutenant, where I'd immediately forget what I'd been so belligerent about a few minutes before. Pretty sure I'd be open to all sorts of interdepartmental negotiations.

I headed out across the base.

Back when I'd been a recruit and done my basic training here, I'd known where my barracks and the mess hall were, and not much else. But I'd only been here for a couple of weeks before getting loaded onto a Shitbox and sent into the black. Now

I knew the base a lot better. I knew the names of the buildings. I knew which shortcuts to use to avoid running into officers. And I knew that slipping some cash to the enlisted guys who worked at the Q-Store meant you'd get boots that didn't cripple you.

Logistics was in the secondary administration building toward the center of the base. It was crawling with officers. Cam always laughed when I started ranting about how much quicker everything would get done in the military if only the poor bastards at the bottom of the food chain didn't have to stop every second and salute some guy with stripes.

There was a queue at the front office at logistics. I was third in line. I stared at the clock on the wall, sighed loudly, and took the work order out of my pocket to read it. The guy in front of me had grease-stained hands. Mechanic, probably, or motor pool. The guy in front of him was talking with the scrawny clerk behind the counter and, by the sounds of it, getting nowhere.

I folded the work order into a plane. I thought about sending it sailing over the clerk's head, then unfolded it instead.

I watched the stammering second hand of the clock for a while.

"Lucky I'm not here for a medical emergency or anything," I announced.

The guy in front of me huffed and shuffled his boots on the floor.

The clerk and the guy at the counter ignored me.

"Seriously," I said. "I was being sarcastic. This is actually an emergency. The hospital's syringes never got delivered."

That got the clerk's attention. "See the line? You're in it."

"Yeah, I see the line. And I'm betting syringes are a hell of a lot more important than whatever you're dealing with right now." I caught the mechanic's gaze. "Logistics. Couldn't organize a fuck in a brothel, right?"

He grinned.

The clerk stalked away.

That's right. Go and get some backup from an officer. Hopefully my officer.

The guy he'd been talking to turned around to glare at me. He was only a crewman like me, but he didn't belong on base according to the patches on his uniform: *Def 1*, along with the wings that marked him as Shitbox crew. He had the pallor of a guy who'd been living in the black for a while.

I remembered what Jones had said about all the traffic coming in from the black. I guess it hadn't been bullshit.

The guy shook his head at me, then turned back as the clerk reappeared.

"Are you Garrett?" the clerk asked.

"Guilty as charged."

"Lieutenant Rushton says he'll see you."

I grinned and walked behind the counter. Waved my work order at the clerk.

Cam's office was the third one down the corridor on the left. He was waiting for me in the corridor, leaning against the wall. "Wallace said there was a crewman from the hospital here complaining about syringes."

"And you knew it was me?"

"He might have said an insubordinate, loudmouthed little fucker from the hospital." Cam shrugged. "You fit the description."

You can buy Darker Space on Amazon: Darker Space

ABOUT LISA HENRY

Lisa likes to tell stories, mostly with hot guys and happily ever afters.

Lisa lives in tropical North Queensland, Australia. She doesn't know why, because she hates the heat, but she suspects she's too lazy to move. She spends half her time slaving away as a government minion, and the other half plotting her escape.

She attended university at sixteen, not because she was a child prodigy or anything, but because of a mix-up between international school systems early in life. She studied History and English, neither of them very thoroughly.

Lisa has been published since 2012, and was a LAMBDA finalist for her quirky, awkward coming-of-age romance *Adulting 101*, and a Rainbow Awards finalist for 2019's *Anhaga*.

You can join Lisa's Facebook reader group at Lisa Henry's Hangout, and find her website at lisahenryonline.com.

ALSO BY LISA HENRY

The Parable of the Mustard Seed

Naked Ambition

Dauntless

Anhaga

Two Man Station (Emergency Services #1)

Lights and Sirens (Emergency Services #2)

The California Dashwoods

Adulting 101

Sweetwater

He Is Worthy

The Island

Tribute

One Perfect Night

Fallout, with M. Caspian

Dark Space (Dark Space #1)

Darker Space (Dark Space #2)

Starlight (Dark Space #3)

With Tia Fielding

Family Recipe

Recipe for Two

A Desperate Man

With Sarah Honey

Red Heir

Elf Defence

Socially Orcward

Writing as Cari Waites

Stealing Innocents

ALSO BY J.A. ROCK AND LISA HENRY

When All the World Sleeps

Another Man's Treasure

Fall on Your Knees

The Preacher's Son

Mark Cooper versus America (Prescott College #1)

Brandon Mills versus the V-Card (Prescott College #2)

The Good Boy (The Boy #1)

The Boy Who Belonged (The Boy #2)

The Playing the Fool Series

The Two Gentlemen of Altona

The Merchant of Death

Tempest

Made in the USA
Middletown, DE
16 September 2023

38495742R00161